LOVING

Henry Green was the pen name of Henry Vincent Yorke. Born in 1905 near Tewkesbury in Gloucestershire, he was educated at Eton and Oxford and went on to become managing director of an engineering business, writing novels in his spare time. His first novel, *Blindness* (1926) was written whilst he was still at school and published whilst he was at Oxford. He married in 1929 and had one son, and during the Second World War served in the London Fire Brigade. Between 1926 and 1952 he wrote nine novels, *Blindness, Living, Party Going, Caught, Loving, Back, Concluding, Nothing* and *Doting*, and a memoir, *Pack My Bag*. Henry Green died in 1973.

D1396429

ALSO BY HENRY GREEN

Henry Green

LOVING

With an introduction by
Sebastian Faulks

VINTAGE

Published by Vintage 2000

4 6 8 10 9 7 5 3

First published in Great Britain by The Hogarth Press 1945

Vintage
Random House, 20 Vauxhall Bridge Road, London SW1V 2SA

Random House Australia (Pty) Limited
20 Alfred Street, Milsons Point, Sydney
New South Wales 2061, Australia

Random House New Zealand Limited
18 Poland Road, Glenfield,
Auckland 10, New Zealand

Random House (Pty) Limited
Endulini, 5A Jubilee Road, Parktown 2193, South Africa

The Random House Group Limited Reg. No. 954009
www.randomhouse.co.uk

A CIP catalogue record for this book is available from the British Library

ISBN 0099285096

Papers used by Random House are natural,
recyclable products made from wood grown in
sustainable forests. The manufacturing processes
conform to the environmental regulations of the
country of origin

Typeset in 10½/12 Sabon by
MATS, Southend-on-Sea, Essex

Printed and bound by CPI Antony Rowe, Eastbourne

Introduction

IF YOU ARE SOMEONE who enjoys reading novels, the claim that Henry Green has on your attention is a simple one: reading him is not like reading any other novelist. Every worthwhile writer has a distinct tone of voice, and no worthwhile reader would confuse a page of – to pick two of Henry Green's contemporaries – Graham Greene with a page of Evelyn Waugh. The way each deals with religion, inner drama, external action, emotion, character, dialogue and so on does vary, and every page bears the personal imprint of the author; yet I would suggest that the pack of cards that each is playing with, and the range of effect open to them, is similar. More importantly, the range of reader's responses, of shared intimacy, satirical laughter, moments of moral judgement, curiosity and so forth, is therefore also a variation on a set number of possibilities.

With Henry Green, however, the reaction of the reader – both in the head and the heart – is different. Green produces new sensations – readerly experiences you have not felt before and will not feel again with any other novelist. Take the first sentence of *Loving*. 'Once upon a day an old butler called Eldon lay dying in his room attended by the head housemaid, Miss Agatha Burch . . .'

At once we hear a distinct music, solemn and lyrical on the one hand, mundane and comic on the other. It is the characteristic sound of Henry Green's fiction, and nowhere in his work are the elements held in more tantalising balance than in this humane and beautiful novel. 'Once upon a day' announces that the book is to be wistful, not quite serious, a kind of fairy story dealing with events that might or might not have actually happened. Green has taken a worn-out phrase, 'once upon a time', and turned it, so that it keeps its familiar, weary cadence, but is subtly renewed. This will be one of the tasks of the book: to imbue the workaday with a sense of beauty, without disguising its rough texture. The next clause, 'an old butler called Eldon lay dying' mixes straightforward narrative information of a slightly comic timbre (old butlers, after all, are the subjects of postcards and farces, not tragedies) with a biblical cadence at the end, 'lay dying'. The first name of the butler is withheld, and the secreting and release of narrative information at odd times is one of the ways in which Green, throughout the book, destabilises the reader in order the better to mystify and enchant. Compare the full details of 'the head housemaid Miss Agatha Burch', where marital status and Christian name are included. Of the first sentence that leaves only the linking words 'in his room attended by', yet even these are significant. It is Eldon's own room in a castle where ownership of space is important and disputed (Miss Burch later complains that she had no more than a cupboard to call her own), and even the word 'attended' has a resonance. It is formal, as though Miss Burch were the chief mourner in waiting, but in a book called *Loving* we are free to ask why a mature spinster is sitting in a man's bedroom: we next come across Miss Burch, after Eldon's death, uncontrollably weeping.

By the time the reader reaches the fourth paragraph, he is aware that Green is not playing by the normal syntactical rules (the two sentences of the third paragraph, for instance, would normally be one.) Then we read 'Came a man's laugh', where the dropping of the word 'There' has the effect of making the laugh more immediate, more shocking. But is this allowed? It is not really conventional grammar at all, and the reader is likely to be thrown, even alienated by the unfamiliarity; but there is a purpose to it all, as Green is set to draw you into his web. He will play with you, inviting you to grow close to his characters, then pushing them away from you again; then, when you are lost in his obliquity, he will hit you hard with Anglo-Saxon rhythms and dramatically clear statements of feeling.

Loving is set during the Second World War in a castle in Ireland, occupied by an English widow, Mrs Tennant, her daughter-in-law Violet ('Mrs Jack') and their numerous servants. Its subject is the life of the big house and the developing affections between the characters. These are determined by the usual things – by outside events (in this case, the worry about the War, about a possible German invasion of Ireland, and the IRA), by lust and, very much, by money. In addition, the characters in the book are activated by their response to beauty, whether in one another, in the huge, shrouded rooms of the castle, or outside, in the feathers of the peacocks or the antics of the mating doves.

Kinalty Castle is a place of unheard footsteps and sudden shrieks. The soft carpeting makes the characters unaware of the approach of others, so they are frequently letting out exclamations of fright, surprise, or mirth: 'Came a man's laugh . . .' And if it is not Edith, the underhousemaid, screaming at the sight of a mouse caught in a clockwork mechanism, it is the shriek of the ubiquitous peacocks that cuts through the moist Irish air. In some ways, this stately home is comparable to the settings of Evelyn Waugh and Anthony Powell, yet Green does not bring to Kinalty the snobbish awe that Powell and Waugh can seldom keep from their descriptions of the aristocracy and its large homes. Perhaps Green has the natural ease of one personally used to such surroundings; perhaps it is just that he is more interested in the lives of the servants.

For if there were to be a film of *Loving* (and I think on balance one very much hopes that there would not be), the names above the title on the poster would be those of the actors playing Charley Raunce, the head footman who becomes butler after Eldon's death, and Edith, the under-housemaid, with whom he is in love. Close behind would come Kate Armstrong, the second underhousemaid, Edith's almost but not quite inseparable companion, and the formidable Miss Agatha Burch. There are some enticing character-parts in Bert, Raunce's 'yellow pantry boy' (it is, typically, not until late in the book that we discover that the adjective refers to his hair, not to his lack of courage; on the contrary he wants to go to England to be an air-gunner in the RAF), in Mrs Welch, the alcoholic cook, and in Paddy O'Conor, the bucolic Irish lampman.

Henry Green's greatest achievement as a novelist, in my view, was in the way that he redrew the triangular relationship between writer, reader and character. The result, at its considerable best, is that the reader is able to enjoy a closeness, an intimacy, with the characters unmatched in the work of any English novelist. The way in which he manages this is – in large measure – grammatical. You are invited into a confidence, then find that you have stubbed your toe on some deliberately awkward phrase. A common technique is to refer to a character as 'this man', even when it is clear who the person is. For instance, in an early scene, Mrs Welch is referred to as 'this woman' in the same sentence that we have been given her name, so Green could easily have said 'she'; in the same scene, Edith and Kate (at this stage in the story, a unit) are referred to as 'these two girls'. The result is suddenly to distance them and to make us look at them again: it is an alienation effect that has the paradoxical result of bringing us closer to the characters. By sticking his nose into our story at these moments, the author sets us in alliance with the characters against him; he gives us the glorious sense that we actually enjoy a closer relationship with them than he does.

He cannot refer to Edith and Kate, after all, as 'these two girls' when he has just given us a scene of erotic beauty between the two of them in their attic bedroom, when one of them, half-naked, strokes and massages the other. Having allowed us this intimacy, how dare he now try to distance them from us? We will not accept it, and from now on presume to understand Edith and Kate better than he does. But just as he sometimes pushes us away with his superfluous 'this woman' or 'these girls', at other times Green is mysterious about who is saying or doing what to whom. For instance, in the scene in the maids' bedroom, it is for a moment unclear whether it is Edith or Kate who is half-naked; you have to read it two or three times to be sure, and this is presumably what Green wants you to do.

And it is important that we know, in the end, that it is Edith who is undressed, because then the scene has a quality of innocence, whereas if it were Kate, it would be more crude. When the two girls come across Paddy O'Conor asleep in the straw next to his peacocks, Kate wants to strip him off and rub him down like a horse, but to Edith even the idiot lampman is a romantic figure. Kate has a 'doll's face and tow hair'; her eyes are little, sharp, and, frequently, 'gimlet'; she is generally described in terms of the artificial, whereas Edith is given to us in the vocabulary of nature. Her dark eyes, 'fathoms deep', catch the light 'like plums dipped in cold water'; when she blushes, which the superior delicacy of her nature causes her to do frequently, these eyes sparkle as though frosted; when she is naked to the waist, her skin shines 'like the flower of white lilac under leaves'; when we first see her, she has a peacock's feather above her 'dark-folded hair'. Mostly we register Edith's beauty through the stupefying effect it has on others: on Charley Raunce, in particular, on his pantry boy Albert, and on Kate, who is wounded by the loss of Edith's affections to Raunce. Even the gentry, who hardly notice anything, have recognised Edith's qualities: Violet Tennant sighs, 'I wish I had that girl's skin', and her mother-in-law concedes, 'Yes she's a lovely child isn't she?' This is a subtle if fairly well-known procedure in manipulating a reader's erotic response; few things repel more quickly than the airport novelist's desperate assertion that a character is 'drop-dead gorgeous', 'fabulously attractive' and so forth. Green himself appears besotted by Edith, yet hardly ever departs from his oblique and subtle presentation of her; only once, perhaps, do we see the prestidigitator's hand falter, when Edith confronts the absurdly lisping insurance investigator, Matthewson, and Green cannot hold himself back from the direct: 'She looked for a second full at him seriously with her raving beauty'. In the context, however, the direct phrase does work for him; the moment is sufficiently pompous, the idea of her beauty so comically discordant beside a loss adjuster in full flow.

We can forgive Green for loving Edith; the delicacy of her nature has been so beautifully given, in her consolation of old Miss Burch, in the modesty of her blushes, in the sensitivity that causes her to shriek then faint at the sight of a trapped mouse (though her faintness is also caused by the hysteria of her suppressed desire for Raunce) and in the natural and loving way that she plays with Mrs Tennant's grand-daughters, Miss Moira and Miss Evelyn. Indeed, the game of blindman's buff between Edith and the children in an abandoned room of the old castle is one of the great lyrical scenes of the novel. Edith plays with us as she plays with Raunce, always slithering out of his arms, away from his eager lips; and it must be said that for an 18-year-old girl (she is three months older than Albert the pantry boy, who is revealed late in the book to be 18) she plays her 39-year-old suitor with fabulous skill. When she finally kisses him full on, he is astounded by the passion and candour of her sensuality, of what lies in wait for him after their planned marriage. Edith's previous evasiveness is vindicated by the sincerity of her passion for Raunce, news of which crashes on us in her unheralded confession to Kate that she loves him so much that she would open the veins of her right arm for him. It must have pained Green to recall to her and to us that even Edith was a poor working girl, and, like all the servants in Kinalty Castle, not above swindling the employers, or at least suggesting relatively harmless ways of doing so. ' "Edie," Kate said in an admiring voice, "you've changed." ' But only because underhousemaids need to provide for their married homes, and not so much that we cannot all go on loving her.

Raunce loves Edith; big Albert the pantry boy loves Edith; Edith loves Raunce; Mrs Jack loves Captain Davenport; Miss Burch loves dead Mr Eldon; Kate half loves Paddy and half loves Edith; Miss Moira loves little Albert, Mrs Welch's nephew. To the background sound of billing doves, Kinalty is an enchanted forest of comical affections; it is reminiscent of the Forest of Arden or the Wood near Athens, in the sense of fairy tale concealing a profound appreciation of the changing nature of emotional realities and in its author's fond but dispassionate eye. Shakespeare had two characters called Jacques in *As You Like It*; Green has two Alberts in *Loving*, and perhaps this is less a coincidence than a tipping of the cap.

The reader new to Green's work will also notice that, unlike most novelists he renders speech more or less as it is actually spoken, with its inconsequential loops, stumbles and repetitions. Reading Henry Green's dialogue makes one aware of how artificial is the speech of characters in every other 'realistic' novelist. The result is again an increased intimacy with the characters; they seem defenceless before us; we eavesdrop on the incoherent noises that mimic as best they can the movement of their hearts. Once more we are in alliance with them, not with the author; we feel protective of them, as though we fear that Green will give too much of them away, will betray their secrets and confidences. This effect is not simply achieved. It seems that Green gives their speech raw and unedited, but one can be sure that these rough sounds arc as worked over as an exchange in Noël Coward or Harold Pinter. The risk of such a manoeuvre, which many other writers have considered and abandoned, is that the result will be tedious, like listening to strangers on a bus. Much of Green's craft has gone into creating this illusion of spontaneity which nevertheless preserves an artful momentum. The choric scene towards the end in which the servants laugh helplessly at the insurance assessor is an example of something that could have gone wrong, as one after another they produce their phonetic lisping imitations. Yet although it is not actually funny, nor is it tiresome; there is a sensation of warmth and release that a less exhaustive reproduction of their speech might not have created.

There are many other sensations and surprises in store for the new Green reader. I particularly like the narrative jump-cuts, as when the maids are watching their masters walking in the garden and suddenly we are with the dialogue of the latter, as though they have been wearing microphones throughout and it has been only a matter of waiting for the camera to zoom. This is startling, though not exactly a new technique; it recalls the famous leap in the Ballad of Sir Patrick Spens: 'The king has written a braid letter, / And signed it wi' his hand; / And send it to Sir Patrick Spens, / Was walking on the sand.'

Another new readerly sensation is that of controlled

confusion, particuarly at the beginning of the book, when Green releases the information in staccato bursts, making it difficult to follow exactly what is happening. His passionate concern is for the actual world of the characters, not for the comfort of the reader, who feels he is eavesdropping or spying through a cloudy window pane. This technique mimics the way in whch we come to know people in life, with mishearings, misconceptions and only occasional jolts of clear insight; in the book it makes us care much more for these partly obscured people, and to feel more inquisitive and tender towards them. When Green then suddenly illuminates Edith in the full glare of lyrical description, or gives her hammering declaration of her love for Raunce in unequivocal speech, the clarity is the more devastating for the shade that has surrounded it.

For all the unique sensations of a Henry Green novel, there is a small price to pay. Sometimes the effects are won at the price of narrative momentum. The oblique passages require more concentration than people are used to giving to a novel and benefit from the occasional rereading of a page or paragraph, though the rewards comfortably repay the effort. In *Loving* there seems to me a slight loss of tension in the last quarter, where the story dwells perhaps excessively on Mrs Tennant's lost ring, even though the outcome of the Raunce-Edith affair is still tantalisingly open. It might have been better to move one of the great lyrical passages from the earlier part of the book and relocate it later on: Kate and Edith dancing beneath the broken light of the chandelier in the deserted ballroom, 'the two girls, minute in purple, dancing, multiplied to eternity in those trembling pears of glass'; the lampman asleep in the straw, beneath a cobweb in the sun, when 'it might have been almost that O'Conor's dreams were held by the gold binding his head beneath a vaulted roof on which the floor of cobbles reflected an old king's molten treasure from the bog'; the picnic at the beach, when Raunce's 'Albert laid himself under a hedge all over which red fuchsia bells swung without a note in the wind the sure travelling sea brought with its low heavy swell . . . [and he] could watch the light blue heave between their donkey Peter's legs, and his ears were crowded with the thunder of the ocean.' These are passages with few equals and, as far as I have read, no superiors in the English novel of the last century; but even when you want to surrender to the beauty of the writing, moved by the generous democracy that makes Green apportion such moments to the most lowly characters, it is worth still keeping your eyes open or you may miss the fact that the image of bells without tongues, used of the fuchsia flowers above Albert's head, is also used of Edith's dark curls, as she shakes them loose; so for Albert there is no escape from the torment of her beauty: as the under-housemaid is first realised in the terms of the natural world, here the compliment is repaid, as Nature imitates Edith.

Loving does not have the narrative satisfaction of *Back*, with its unforgettable conclusion; nor does its language – daring, footsure and innovative as it is – have the revolutionary ardour of that in Green's industrial novel *Living*, where English grammar seems to be melted down, forged and reshaped into some hard, new clanking thing from the Birmingham foundry in which the novel is set. Yet *Loving* has a balance and a sweetness of nature all its own; it is a complete and deeply satisfying novel. At the centre of *Loving* lies a paradox, and it is this: how can something so obviously literary, so self-advertisingly artificial in its procedures yet give to the reader the exquisite sensation that what he is doing is something less like reading than living; or even, in the book's exalted moments, of which there are many, like loving?

Sebastian Faulks

ONCE UPON A day an old butler called Eldon lay dying in his room attended by the head housemaid, Miss Agatha Burch. From time to time the other servants separately or in chorus gave expression to proper sentiments and then went on with what they had been doing.

One name he uttered over and over, 'Ellen.'

The pointed windows of Mr Eldon's room were naked glass with no blinds or curtains. For this was in Eire where there is no blackout.

Came a man's laugh. Miss Burch jerked, then the voice broke out again. Charley Raunce, head footman, was talking outside to Bert his yellow pantry boy. She recognized the voice but could not catch what was said.

'. . . on with what I was on with,' he spoke, 'you should clean your teeth before ever you have anything to do with a woman. That's a matter of personal hygiene. Because I take an interest in you for which you should be thankful. I'm sayin' you want to take it easy my lad, or you'll be the death of yourself.'

The lad looked sick.

'A spot of john barley corn is what you are in need of,' Raunce went on, but the boy was not having any.

'Not in there,' he said in answer, quavering, 'I couldn't.'

'How's that? You know where he keeps the decanter don't you? Surely you must do.'

'Not out of that room I couldn't.'

'Go ahead, don't let a little thing worry your guts,' Raunce said. He was a pale individual, paler now. 'The old man's on with his Ellen, 'e won't take notice.'

1

'But there's Miss Burch.'

'Is that so? Then why didn't you say in the first place? That's different. Now you get stuck into my knives and forks. I'll handle her.'

Raunce hesitated, then went in. The boy looked to listen as for a shriek. The door having been left ajar he could hear the way Raunce put it to her.

'This is my afternoon on in case they take it into their heads to punish the bell,' he told her. 'If you like I'll sit by him for a spell while you go get a breath of air.'

'Very good then,' she replied, 'I might.'

'That's the idea Miss Burch, you take yourself out for a stroll. It'll fetch your mind off.'

'I shan't be far. Not out of sight just round by the back. You'd call me, now, if he came in for a bad spell?'

Charley reassured her. She came away. Bert stood motionless his right hand stiff with wet knives. That door hung wide once more. Then, almost before Miss Burch was far enough to miss it, was a noise of the drawer being closed. Raunce came back, a cut-glass decanter warm with whisky in his hands. The door stayed gaping open.

'Go ahead, listen,' he said to Bert, 'it's meat and drink at your age, I know, an old man dying but this stuff is more than grub or wine to me. That's what. Let's get us behind the old door.'

To do so had been ritual in Mr Eldon's day. There was cover between this other door, opened back, and a wall of the pantry. Here they poured Mrs T.'s whisky. 'Ellen,' came the voice again, 'Ellen.'

At a rustle Raunce stuck his head out while Bert, farther in because he was smallest, could do no more than peek the other way along a back passage, his eyes on a level with one of the door hinges. Bert saw no one. But Charley eyed Edith, one of two under-housemaids.

She stood averted watching that first door which stayed swung back into Mr Eldon's room. Not until he had said, 'hello there,' did she turn. Only then could he see that she had stuck a peacock's feather above her lovely head, in her dark-folded hair. 'What have you?' he asked pushing the decanter

2

out to the front edge so much as to say, 'look what I've found.'

In both hands she held a gauntlet glove by the wrist. He could tell that it was packed full of white unbroken eggs.

'Why you gave me a jump,' she said, not startled.

'Look what I've got us,' he answered, glancing at the decanter he held out. Then he turned his attention back where perhaps she expected, onto the feather in her hair.

'You take that off before they can set eyes on you,' he went on, 'and what's this? Eggs? What for?' he asked. Bert poked his head out under the decanter, putting on a kind of male child's grin for girls. With no change in expression, without warning, she began to blush. The slow tide frosted her dark eyes, endowed them with facets. 'You won't tell,' she pleaded and Charley was about to give back that it depended when a bell rang. The indicator board gave a chock. 'Oh all right,' Raunce said, coming out to see which room had rung. Bert followed sheepish.

Charley put two wet glasses into a wooden tub in the sink, shut that decanter away in a pantry drawer. 'Ellen,' the old man called faintly. This drew Edith's eyes back towards the butler's room. 'Now lad,' Raunce said to Bert, 'I'm relying on you mind to see Mrs Welch won't come out of her kitchen to knock the whisky off.' He did not get a laugh. Both younger ones must have been listening for Mr Eldon. The bell rang a second time. 'O.K.,' Raunce said, 'I'm coming. And let me have that glove back,' he went on. 'I'll have to slap it on a salver to take in some time.'

'Yes Mr Raunce,' she replied.

'Mister is it now,' he said, grinning as he put on his jacket. When he was gone she turned to Bert. She was short with him. She was no more than three months older, yet by the tone of voice she might have been his mother's sister.

'Well he'll be Mr Raunce when it's over,' she said.

'Will Mr Eldon die?' Bert asked, then swallowed.

'Why surely,' says she giving a shocked giggle, then passing a hand along her cheek.

Meantime Charley entered as Mrs Tennant yawned. She said to him,

3

'Oh yes I rang didn't I, Arthur,' she said and he was called by that name as every footman from the first had been called, whose name had really been Arthur, all the Toms, Harrys, Percys, Victors one after the other, all called Arthur. 'Have you seen a gardening glove of mine? One of a pair I brought back from London?'

'No Madam.'

'Ask if any of the other servants have come across it will you? Such a nuisance.'

'Yes Madam.'

'And, oh tell me, how is Eldon?'

'Much about the same I believe Madam.'

'Dear dear. Yes thank you Arthur. That will be all. Listen though. I expect Doctor Connolly will be here directly.'

He went out, shutting the mahogany door without a sound. After twenty trained paces he closed a green baize door behind him. As it clicked he called out,

'Now me lad she wants that glove and don't forget.'

'What glove?'

'The old gardening glove Edith went birds'-nesting with,' Raunce replied. 'Holy Moses look at the clock,' he went on, 'ten to three and me not on me bed. Come on look slippy.' He whipped out the decanter while Bert provided those tumblers that had not yet been dried. 'God rest his soul,' Raunce added in a different tone of voice then carried on,

'Wet glasses? Where was you brought up? No we'll have two dry ones thank you,' he cried. 'Get crackin' now. Behind the old door.' Upon this came yet another double pitiful appeal to Ellen. 'And there's another thing, Mrs T. she still calls me Arthur. But it will be Mr Raunce to you d'you hear?'

''E ain't dead yet.'

'Nor he ain't far to go before he will be. Oh dear. Yes and that reminds me. Did you ever notice where the old man kept that black book of his and the red one?'

'What d'you mean? I never touched 'em.'

'Don't be daft. I never said you did did I? But he wouldn't trouble to watch himself in front of you. Times out of mind you must have seen.'

'Not me I never.'

4

'We shan't make anything out of you, that's one thing certain,' Raunce stated. 'There's occasions I despair altogether.' He went on, 'You mean to stand and tell me you've never so much as set eyes on 'em, not even to tell where they was kept.'

'What for Mr Raunce?'

'Well you can't help seeing when a thing's before your nose, though I'm getting so's I could believe any mortal idiotic stroke of yours, so help me.'

'I never.'

'So you never eh? You never what?' Raunce asked. 'Don't talk so sloppy. What I'm asking is can you call to mind his studying in a black or a red thrupenny notebook?'

'Study what?' Bert said, bolder by his tot now the glass he held was empty.

'All right. You've never seen those books then. That's all I wanted. But I ask you look at the clock. I'm going to get the old head down, it's me siesta. And don't forget to give us a call sharp on four thirty. You can't be trusted yet to lay the tea. Listen though. If that front door rings it will likely be the doctor. He's expected. Show him straight in,' Raunce said, pointing with his thumb into the door agape. He made off.

'What about Miss Burch?' the boy called.

'Shall I call her?' he shouted, desperate.

Raunce must have heard, but he gave no answer. Left alone young Albert began to shake.

In the morning room two days later Raunce stood before Mrs Tennant and showed part of his back to Violet her daughter-in-law.

'Might I speak to you for a moment Madam?'

'Yes Arthur what is it?'

'I'm sure I would not want to cause any inconvenience but I desire to give in my notice.'

She could not see Violet because he was in the way. So she glared at the last button but one of his waistcoat, on a level with her daughter-in-law's head behind him. He had been standing with arms loose at his sides and now a hand came uncertainly to find if he was done up and having found dropped back.

5

'What Arthur?' she asked. She seemed exasperated. 'Just when I'm like this when this has happened to Eldon?'

'The place won't be the same without him Madam.'

'Surely that's not a reason. Well never mind. I daresay not but I simply can't run to another butler.'

'No Madam.'

'Things are not what they used to be you know. It's the war. And then there's taxation and everything. You must understand that.'

'I'm sure I have always tried to give every satisfaction Madam,' he replied.

At this she picked up a newspaper. She put it down again. She got to her feet. She walked over to one of six tall french windows with gothic arches. 'Violet,' she said, 'I can't imagine what Michael thinks he is about with the grass court darling. Even from where I am I can see plantains like the tops of palm trees.'

Her daughter-in-law's silence seemed to imply that all effort was to butt one's head against wire netting. Charley stood firm. Mrs T. turned. With her back to the light he could not see her mouth and nose.

'Very well then,' she announced, 'I suppose we shall have to call you Raunce.'

'Thank you Madam.'

'Think it over will you?' She was smiling. 'Mind I've said nothing about more wages.' She dropped her eyes and in so doing she deepened her forehead on which once each month a hundred miles away in Dublin her white hair was washed in blue and waved and curled. She moved over to another table. She pushed the ashtray with one long lacquered oyster nail across the black slab of polished marble supported by a dolphin layered in gold. Then she added as though confidentially,

'I feel we should all hang together in these detestable times.'

'Yes Madam.'

'We're really in enemy country here you know. We simply must keep things up. With my boy away at the war. Just go and think it over.'

'Yes Madam.'

'We know we can rely on you you know Arthur.'

'Thank you Madam.'

'Then don't let me hear any more of this nonsense. Oh and I can't find one of my gloves I use for gardening. I can't find it anywhere.'

'I will make enquiries. Very good Madam.'

He shut the great door after. He almost swung his arms, he might have been said to step out for the thirty yards he had to go along that soft passage to the green baize door. Then he stopped. In one of the malachite vases, filled with daffodils, which stood on tall pedestals of gold naked male children without wings, he had seen a withered trumpet. He cut off the head with a pair of nail clippers. He carried this head away in cupped hand from above thick pile carpet in black and white squares through onto linoleum which was bordered with a purple key pattern on white until, when he had shut that green door to open his kingdom, he punted the daffodil ahead like a rugger ball. It fell limp on the oiled parquet a yard beyond his pointed shoes.

He was kicking this flower into his pantry not more than thirty inches at a time when Miss Burch with no warning opened and came out of Mr Eldon's death chamber. She was snuffling. He picked it up off the floor quick. He said friendly,

'The stink of flowers always makes my eyes run.'

'And when may daffodils have had a perfume,' she asked, tart through tears.

'I seem to recollect they had a smell once,' he said.

'You're referring to musk, oh dear,' she answered making off, tearful. But apparently he could not leave it alone.

'Then what about hay fever?' he almost shouted. 'That never comes with hay, or does it? There was a lady once at a place where I worked,' and then he stopped. Miss Burch had moved out of earshot. 'Well if you won't pay heed I can't force you,' he said out loud. He shut Mr Eldon's door, then stood with his back to it. He spoke to Bert.

'What time's the interment?' he asked. 'And how long to go before dinner?' not waiting for answers. 'See here my lad I've got something that needs must be attended to you know where.' He jangled keys in his pocket. Then instead of entering Mr Eldon's room he walked away to dispose of the daffodil in a bucket. He coughed. He came back again. 'All right,' he said, 'give us a whistle if one of 'em shows up.'

He slipped inside like an eel into its drainpipe. He closed the door so that Bert could not see. Within all was immeasurable stillness with the mass of daffodils on the bed. He stood face averted then hurried smooth and his quietest to the roll-top desk. He held his breath. He had the top left-hand drawer open. He breathed again. And then Bert whistled.

Raunce snatched at those red and black notebooks. He had them. He put them away in a hip pocket. They fitted. 'Close that drawer,' he said aloud. He did this. He fairly scrambled out again. He shut the door after, leaving all immeasurably still within. He stood with his back to it, taking out a handkerchief, and looked about.

He saw Edith. She was just inside the pantry where Bert watched him open mouthed. Raunce eyed her very sharp. He seemed to appraise the dark eyes she sported which were warm and yet caught the light like plums dipped in cold water. He stayed absolutely quiet. At last she said quite calm,

'Would the dinner bell have gone yet?'

'My dinner,' he cried obviously putting on an act, 'holy smoke is it as late as that, and this lad of mine not taken up the nursery tray yet. Get going,' he said to Bert, 'look sharp.' The boy rushed out. 'God forgive me,' he remarked, 'but there's times I want to liquidate 'im. Come to father beautiful,' he said.

'Not me,' she replied amused.

'Well if you don't want I'm not one to insist. But did nobody never tell you about yourself?'

'Aren't you just awful,' she said apparently delighted.

'That's as may be,' he answered, 'but it's you we're speaking of. With those eyes you ought to be in pictures.'

'Oh yeah?'

'Come on,' he said, 'if we're going to be lucky with our dinner we'd best be going for it.'

'No, you don't,' she said slipping before him. And they came out through this pantry into the long high stone passage with a vaulted ceiling which led to the kitchen and their servants' hall.

'Now steady,' he said, as he caught up with her. 'What will Miss Burch say if she finds us chasing one after the other?' When they were walking side by side he asked.

'What made you come through my way to dinner?'

'Why you do need to know a lot,' she said.

'I know all I can my girl and that's never done me harm. I got other things to think to besides love and kisses, did you know?'

'No I didn't, not from the way you go on I didn't.'

'The trouble with you girls is you take everything so solemn. Now all I was asking was why you looked in on us while you came down to dinner?'

'Thinkin' I came to see you I suppose,' she said. She turned to look at him. What she saw made her giggle mouth open and almost soundless. Then she slapped a hand across her teeth and ran on ahead. He took no notice. With a swirl of the coloured skirt of her uniform she turned a corner in front along this high endless corridor. The tap of her shoes faded. He walked on. He appeared to be thinking. He went so soft he might have been a ghost without a head. But as he made his way he repeated to himself, over and over,

'This time I'll take his old chair. I must.'

He arrived to find the household seated at table waiting, except for Mrs Welch and her two girls who ate in the kitchen and for Bert who was late. There was his place laid for Raunce next Miss Burch. Kate and Edith were drawn up ready. They sat with hands folded on laps before their knives, spoons and forks. At the head, empty, was the large chair from which Mr Eldon had been accustomed to preside. At the last and apart sat Paddy the lampman. For this huge house, which was almost entirely shut up, had no electric light.

Charley went straight over to a red mahogany sideboard that was decorated with a swan at either end to support the top on each long curved neck. In the centre three ferns were niggardly growing in gold Worcester vases. He took out a knife, a spoon and a fork. He sat down in Mr Eldon's chair, the one with arms. Seated, he laid his own place. They all stared at him.

'What are we waiting for?' he said into the silence. He took

9

out a handkerchief again. Then he blew his nose as though nervous.

'Would you be in a draught?' Miss Burch enquired at last.

'Why no thank you,' he replied. The silence was pregnant.

'I thought perhaps you might be,' she said and sniffed.

At that he turned to see whether he had forgotten to close the door. It was shut all right. The way he looked made Kate choke.

'I heard no one venture a pleasantry,' Miss Burch announced at this girl.

'I thought I caught Paddy crack one of his jokes,' Raunce added with a sort of violence. A grin spread over this man's face as it always did when his name was mentioned. He was uncouth, in shirtsleeves, barely coming up over the table he was so short. With a thick dark neck and face he had a thatch of hair which also sprouted grey from the nostrils. His eyes were light blue as was one of Charley's, for Raunce had different coloured eyes, one dark one light which was arresting.

The girls looked down to their laps.

'Or maybe she swallowed the wrong way although there's nothing on the table and it's all growing cold in the kitchen,' Raunce continued. He got no reply.

'Well what are we waiting on?' he asked.

'Why for your precious lad to fetch in our joint,' Miss Burch replied.

'I shouldn't wonder if the nursery hasn't detained him,' was Charley's answer.

'Then Kate had better bring it,' Miss Burch said. And they sat without a word while she was gone. Twice Agatha made as though to speak, seated as he was for the first time in Mr Eldon's place, but she did not seem able to bring it to words. Her eyes, which before now had been dull, each sported a ripple of light from tears. Until, after Kate had returned laden Raunce cast a calculated look at Miss Burch as he stood to carve, saying,

'Nor I won't go. Not even if it is to be Church of England I don't aim to watch them lower that coffin in the soil.'

At this Miss Burch pushed the plate away from in front of

her to sit with closed eyes. He paused. Then as he handed a portion to Edith he went on,

'I don't reckon on that as the last I shall see of the man. It's nothing but superstition all that part.'

'And the wicked shall flourish even as a green bay tree,' Miss Burch announced in a loud voice as though something had her by the throat. Once more there was a pause. Then Raunce began again as he served Paddy. Because he had taken a roast potato into his mouth with the carving fork he spoke uneasy.

'Why will Mrs Welch have it that she must carve for the kitchen? Don't call her cook she don't like the name. There's not much I can do the way this joint's been started.'

The girls were busy with their food. O'Conor was noisy with the portion before him. Raunce settled down to his plate. Agatha still sat back.

'And how many months would it be since you went out?' she asked like vinegar.

'Let me think now. The last occasion must have been when I had to see Paddy here to the Park Gates that time he was "dronk" at Christmas.'

This man grinned although his mouth was watering in volume so that he had to swallow constantly.

'Careful now,' said Raunce.

Kate and Edith stopped eating to watch the Irishman open eyed. This man was their sport and to one of them he was even more than that. In spite of Miss Burch he looked so ludicrous that they had suddenly to choke back tremors of giggling.

'It was nearly my lot,' Raunce added.

'It couldn't hurt no one to show respect to the dead,' Miss Burch tremulously said. Charley answered in downright tones,

'Begging your pardon Miss Burch my feelings are my own and I daresay there's' no one here but yourself misses him more than me. Only this morning I went to Mrs T., asked leave and told her,' but he did not at once continue. The silence in which he was received seemed to daunt him. With a clumsy manner he turned it off, saying,

'Yes, I remember when I came for my first interview she said I can't call you Charles, no she says "I'll call you Arthur. All the first footmen have been called Arthur ever since Arthur Weavell, a real jewel that man was," she said.'

He looked at Miss Burch to find that she had flushed.

'And now I make no doubt you are counting on her addressing you as Raunce,' Miss Burch said in real anger. 'With Mr Eldon not yet in the ground. But I'll tell you one thing,' she continued, her voice rising, 'you'll never get a Mr out of me not ever, even if there is a war on.'

'What's the war got to do with it?' he asked, and he winked at Kate. 'Never mind let it go. Anyway I know now don't I.'

'No,' she said, having the last word, 'men like you never will appreciate or realize.'

Next morning Raunce chose to enter Mrs Jack's bedroom when Agatha Burch was at work on the Aubusson carpet.

He carried a large tray on which he had arranged three stacks of fresh blotting paper coloured pink, white and yellow, two saucers of Worcester china in which were knibs of bronze and gold plated, two bottles of red and blue ink with clean syringes to fill the inkwells, and piles of new stationery which matched those three shades of blotting paper.

He laid this down on a writing table. When he saw her face which was as it sometimes looked on her bad days so called, pale or blotchy as a shrimp before boiling, he cleared his throat. He watched her close but she did not regard him. He cleared his throat again. He spoke.

'Just the very person,' he said warmly.

'Oh yes,' was her answer.

'I had a bit of a shock this morning,' he went on, looking out of the window onto a glorious day, 'I moved down into the butler's apartment yesterday as will be known to you because one of your girls got the room ready.'

'I don't know how you had the heart,' she said.

'That's all right Miss Burch, everyone has their feelings, but I'm sure Mrs T. would not wish the strongroom left unguarded of a night time.'

'I hope everything was to your fancy,' she remarked.

'I slept very well thank you, mustn't grumble at all. Sheets nicely aired, a good night's sleep considerin'. But I had a bit of a shock when my tea was fetched me.'

'Tea! I never knew you took it first thing.'

'Oh yes I must have me cup of tea, and I'm not alone in that I believe. I couldn't start the day without.'

'And was it all right?' she asked, so cheerfully she might have thought she had the advantage of him. 'Had it been made with boiling water?'

'Yes,' he said weak, 'it was a good cup of tea.'

'Then they'll have warmed the pot. I'm glad, I am really. Because I'll tell you something,' and her voice rose. 'D'you know I can't get one for meself at that hour?'

'You can't? Is that so? There's a lot wrong there if you'll pardon me with all the girls you've got to serve you. I should say that wants to be looked into.'

'They've got their work to do same as I have,' she said in a voice charged with meaning.

'Yes I had a bit of a shock first thing,' he went on, ignoring this. 'It was nasty to tell the truth. That lad of mine Albert brought my tea.'

'You don't say. Why I didn't know he was up so prompt.'

'I'll guarantee you this,' Raunce said, his voice beginning to grate a trifle, 'he's up before anyone in the Castle.'

'I won't argue,' she announced.

'No but if you know any different you'll oblige by contradicting.'

'I never argue, I'm not that way,' she said.

'Nor me,' he answered, 'I never was one to contradict this or that. No, all I had in mind was the lad. It's his first place and he's a good obliging boy.'

'I'm not saying he's not.'

'Then you don't deny it,' Raunce said on a rising tone.

'Deny what?' she replied. 'I'm denying nobody.'

'That's O.K. Miss Burch. It was only to make certain I understood like any man has a right. I may have misinterpreted. For if you must know it upset me to see that lad of mine Albert carry me my tea.'

13

'That was what he always used to do surely.'

'Yes, in Mr Eldon's day that's the way it used to be every morning,' Raunce admitted. Then he went on,

'But one of the girls always brought the old man's.'

'And now I suppose you won't be satisfied unless one of my girls brings you yours,' Miss Burch said with surprising bitterness. 'And I don't doubt she must be Kate,' she added.

'I can't seem to follow you,' he said.

'You can't? I'll ask you this then. How's the work to get done of a morning?'

'Well same as it always has I presume.'

'Now then,' she said taking up this last remark. She drew a great breath and was about to loose it probably in a storm of angry sentences when Mrs T. entered.

The passage carpet was so thick you never could hear anyone coming.

'Oh Raunce,' she said using his new title for the second time, 'I've just come from nanny. Such a nuisance. I don't really know what we can do. Of course the children must come first but I'm sure everyone is doing their best. We shall simply all have to put our heads together.' At this point Miss Burch left. Her back was stiff. She seemed indignant. Mrs T. watched her go with no change in expression. Then turned back to Charley. 'Raunce,' she said, 'surely you aren't proposing to put that pink blotting paper in the Gold Bedroom.'

'This is the only shade they could send us Madam.'

She walked away and tried the mantelpiece with her finger which she then examined as though it was going to smell. He cleared his throat. Having established there was no dust he rearranged the peacock's feathers that for years had stood in a famille rose vase which was as always on a woollen scarlet mat in the centre.

'You write to London for the blotting paper of course?'

'Yes Madam but this is all Mr Eldon could get. I believe he was going to speak about it.'

'No, he never did,' she said, 'and naturally it would be hopeless trying to buy anything in this wretched country. But tell me why if there are several pastel blues can they do only one shade of pink?'

'I believe it's the war Madam.'

She laughed and faced him. 'Oh yes the shops will be using that as an excuse for everything soon. Mind I'm not blaming anyone,' she said, 'but it's going to be hopeless. Now Raunce I'm so very worried about these nursery meals.'

'Yes Madam.'

She began to smile, as though pleading with him. 'I want your help. Everyone is being so very awkward. Nanny has complained that the food is quite cold by the time it gets to the nursery and Mrs Welch tells me it leaves the kitchen piping hot so what am I to believe?'

They looked long at each other. At last he smiled.

'I'm sure Albert carries the meals up soon as ever they are served,' he said. 'But if it would be of any assistance Madam I'll take them up myself for the next few days.'

'Oh thank you Raunce, yes that is good of you. Now I promised Michael I would go along, why was it he wanted me? Yes well that will be all.' She started off to the head gardener. She did not get far. Miss Burch stopped her in the Long Passage.

'Could I speak to you for a moment Madam?'

'Yes Agatha?'

Before going on Miss Burch waited until Raunce, who was leaving Mrs Jack's room, should be out of earshot.

'It's Kate Madam. I wouldn't bother you Madam only it does seem not right to me that a slip of a girl can take him his tea first thing while he lies in bed there.'

'Whose tea good heavens?'

'Arthur Madam.'

'We must call him Raunce now Agatha. It does sound absurd I know. What's more I don't like that name.' Her voice had taken a teasing note. 'I think we shall have to change it don't you?'

'And he would not go to the funeral. He even boasts about it Madam.'

'Well we wouldn't have wanted him there would we?' she said. Miss Burch seemed pleased. 'And now he's moved down to Eldon's room and wants his morning tea brought him?' Mrs Tennant went on. 'Yes well thanks very much for telling me. I suppose one of the girls used to carry Eldon his cup first thing?'

'Yes Madam but that was different.'

'I know Agatha but I fancy that's the difficulty you see.'

'Very good Madam,' Miss Burch said grim.

'Oh yes and I forgot, where is the man,' and she called for Raunce. There was no reply. 'He must have gone.' She rang the bell. 'I meant to tell you both,' she continued, 'it's about Mrs Welch. Her nephew is coming over to-morrow. Not for long mind, just a few weeks. He's old enough to look after himself. She'll do everything for the little chap.'

Miss Burch did not look delighted but she said, 'Yes Madam.'

'He's a dear boy I believe and it will be nice for the children to have someone to play with. His name is Albert. Why what a coincidence. Yes Albert what is it?'

'You rang, Madam.'

'Oh it's of no consequence it was Raunce I wanted. That's all thank you. There's nothing else I think. I will see Raunce some other time. I've simply got to rush out now to Michael.'

The morning was almost over and that afternoon, as Raunce was in his new armchair putting his feet up to study those two notebooks Edith, upstairs in the attic she shared with Kate and half undressed, was filling into a jam jar those eggs she had been carrying in Mrs Tennant's glove and which she intended to preserve with waterglass.

'You're surely not ever goin' to put that dirtiness on your face and neck sometime Edie?'

'I am that. It's good.'

'But not peacocks. Edie for land's sake.'

'Peacocks is no use. They only screech.'

'I can't make you out at all.'

Edith explained. 'Their eggs've got to be lifted when there's not a soul to witness, you understand, an' they must be peacocks. I wouldn't know for why. But you just ask anyone. They are the valuablest birds, the rarest.'

'And what if you come out in the spots like they have stuck on their tails?'

Edie turned at this to face Kate and put a hand along her

cheek. She was naked to the waist. In that light from the window overgrown with ivy her detached skin shone like the flower of white lilac under leaves.

'Oh dear,' she said.

'And who's it for?' Kate went on. 'Patrick?' and in one movement she jumped on her bed, lay back. But at the mention of a name and as though they had entered on a conspiracy Edith blocked even more light from that window by climbing on the sill. The sky drew a line of white round her mass of dark hair falling to shoulders which paled to blue lilac. She laughed in her throat.

As they settled down Kate said:

'So Mrs Welch is to have her sister's little boy to visit. Albert his name is.' Edith made no reply. 'That'll be more for us that will,' Kate added.

'He'll do his own work. He's old enough,' Edith said. 'And it'll be a change for the children,' she went on referring to Mrs Jack's girls. 'They don't get much out of forever playing on their own the sweet lambs.'

'I wish I was back 'ome the age they are Edie.'

'Hard work never done a girl any harm.'

'But doesn't Miss Burch keep us two girls at it dear. Oh my poor feet.'

'Take your stockings off Katie and I'll rub 'em for you.'

'Not in that old egg you won't.'

Edith jumped down off the sill. She took up a towel which she laid under Kate's feet. She turned back to the washbasin to wet her hands in cold water. Then leaning over Kate who had closed her eyes she began to stroke and knead the hot feet. Her hair fell forward. She was smiling as she ministered, all her bare skin above Kate's body stretched white as spring again.

'Clean your teeth before you have to do with a woman,' Edith said, 'what talk is that?'

'Have you gone out of your mind then?' Kate asked, murmuring. 'But whoever said?'

'Mr Raunce.'

'So it's Mr to you? I shan't ever. I couldn't, not after he's been Charley all this time. Oh honey is that easing my arches.'

17

'It's only right now he's got the position,' Edith said. 'I wish I had your ankles dear I do.'

'But why the teeth?' Kate asked.

'I expect it's smoking or something.'

'Does Patrick?'

'Oh he's got a lovely lot,' Edith said. 'But I can't say as I shall see him even this evening. Talk of half days off in this rotten old country, why, there's nothing for a girl when your time is your own.'

'You're telling me,' said Kate.

Then Edith sat down on the side of the bed, and shook the hair back from off her face.

'Here we are,' she went on, 'the two of us on a Thursday and still inside, with nothing to move for. And the Germans across the water, that might invade any minute. Oh I shall have to journey back home. Why I'm browned off absolutely.'

Kate took her up. 'I don't think there's much in this talk about the Jerries. And if they did come over that's not saying they'd offer any impoliteness, they're ordinary working folk same as us. But speak of never going out why Charley Raunce hasn't shoved his head into the air these three years it must be.'

'Wrong side of the window is his name for it. He should've grown up with us as children. Kate, my mother had every window open rain or shine and so they stayed all day.'

'He writes to his,' Kate said, 'not like you you bad girl. When did she get word from you last?'

'There's times I say that's the one thing keeps me here. I daresn't go back when I've kept silent such ages, while she's on every week writing for news.'

'Why, listen to those birds,' Kate said.

Edith looked out. A great distance beneath she saw Mrs Tennant and her daughter-in-law starting for a walk. The dogs raced about on the terrace yapping which made the six peacocks present scream The two women set off negligent and well dressed behind their bounding pets to get an appetite for tea.

'Was it the beginning or the end of June Jack wrote that he expected to get leave?'

'Why I told you,' Mrs Jack answered sweet and low. 'Any time after the third week in May he said.'

'I'm so glad for you both. It's been such a long time. I expect you'll go to London of course.'

'Simply look at the daffodils,' her daughter-in-law exclaimed 'There's masses of new ones out you know. Oh isn't it lovely. Yes it's a hopeless time of the year here isn't it? I mean there's no shooting or fishing yet. He'd get very restless poor dear.'

'D'you know what I thought last night?' said Mrs Tennant. 'As I got into bed? I shall probably be down at Merlow all the time and you won't see anything of me but I half made up my mind I would come over with you.'

'How lovely,' her daughter-in-law replied clear as a bell. 'Oh but then we must have an evening all together. Jack would be terribly disappointed.'

'Darling you've seen so little of each other with this war coming directly after the wedding. I do feel for your generation you know. Of course I'd love it. Still I don't mean to butt in. I mean the leave is precious, you must have all of him.'

There fell a silence.

'Really,' she added, 'I'm not sure what I'm saying,' and dared to look full at her son's wife. This young woman was poised with an object, it may have been the dry white bone of a bird that she was about to throw. She flung it a short distance. The dog faced in the wrong direction, ears cocked, whining, while attendant peacocks keenly dashed forward a few paces.

'Oh Badger,' she said and wiped her fingers on a frilled handkerchief, 'you are so dumb.'

'We could do a play together,' Mrs Tennant proposed.

'How lovely. The only thing is the children. I imagine it's all right leaving them. I mean nothing can happen can it?'

'I'd thought of that. I don't think so. We did before.'

'I know. Then that will be lovely.'

'When d'you think he'll let you know dear?'

Mrs Jack showed irritation. 'No Badger no,' she said. On being spoken to the dog made as if to leap up at her. 'Down damn you,' she said. 'Oh you know how it is,' she went on, 'the usual, three days notice at the most. On top of everything you've got to be looking your best as though you'd been in and out of the London shops all winter.'

'You won't have to worry your head over that,' Mrs Tennant archly told her. 'Oh by the way did I ever mention about Mrs Welch's nephew coming over to stay?'

'How old is he?'

'Just the right age Violet, nine next March. I thought it would be nice for the children that's why I bought his ticket. His father's the chauffeur to old Lord Cheltenham.'

'My dear have you broken it yet to nanny?'

'No darling to tell you the truth I didn't dare.'

'It is a bit of a facer isn't it?'

'You see I couldn't very well refuse,' Mrs Tennant said, 'and it will be so good for the children.'

'What's he like?'

'Oh Mrs Welch is a most superior woman. I'm sure he'll be perfect. I wouldn't mind if there were any possible children down in the village. But even Michael's eldest boy at the Lodge Gates is dressed as a girl.'

'Do they really still believe the boys get carried off by fairies?'

'Well if they do they could expect fairies to see through the skirts. But couldn't you say the little chap's been ill?' she asked her daughter-in-law.

'Then she'd think she'll have to nurse him,' Mrs Jack objected.

'But couldn't you promise her that Mrs Welch won't let him out of sight Violet?'

'It is so difficult isn't it? And it's just what Evelyn and Moira have been wanting. Anyway bother nanny.' The two women smiled at one another, grew mischievous. 'I'll tell you what,' Mrs Jack went on, 'why don't we say it's Mrs Welch's illegitimate? Then she'll be so thrilled she'll look after him like one of her own.'

Mrs Tennant tee hee'd.

'Oh Violet you are naughty,' she said.

'Well I don't know why not. After all the worry they bring

it would be a score to give them something to really chatter about.'

'And then we should have to find another cook and another nanny,' Mrs Tennant objected. 'It's quite bad enough having them die on one. Besides, Nanny Swift will think it out for herself. I shouldn't be a bit surprised if she didn't start throwing dark hints before the child has been here ten days.'

'D'you think it's true then?'

'My dear what do we know about the servants? Agatha took the trouble only this morning to let out some frightful double meanings in connection with Kate and Arthur. I must remember to call him Raunce.'

'Kate? I'd've thought it would be Edith. I wish I had that girl's skin.'

'Yes she's a lovely child isn't she? D'you know Violet I don't think I care what they do so long as they stay.'

'You poor dear,' Mrs Jack said. 'Why look,' she went on, 'there it is already.' And there it was close, on a low hill, surrounded by cypresses amongst which grew a palm tree, the marble pillars lying beside jagged cement topped walls against a blue sky with blue clouds. 'D'you think we have to go right up this time?' she asked.

'I don't think we need to-day, do you?' her mother-in-law replied. Calling to the dogs they turned for home. They began a talk about underclothes.

But Kate and Edith were not to get out of the Castle without difficulty. As they came down their passage ready dressed for the afternoon they were halted by a broken noise of sobbing.

'Why listen,' Kate said, 'it must be the old girl herself. Now what do you say to that?'

'You go on dear,' Edith answered, 'don't wait for me.'

'Ah now come on Edie, half the day's gone already, you don't want to bother.'

'Why the poor soul,' Edith said and went in, shutting the door after.

Miss Burch lay on her bed wrapped in a huge blue crocheted shawl. She had taken off her wig and wore a lace mob cap which hung askew. With hands inside that shawl and face sideways on the pillow over a patch of wet Miss Burch seemed given over to despair and sobbed and shook and hiccuped.

Edith took off her beret, sat on the bedside shaking her hair free.

'Oh Burchie Burchie,' she said, 'why whatever's the matter?'

She got no other answer than a wail. Then Miss Burch rolled over face to the wall. The cap twisted off her head. Edith gently put it back and because her shiny skull was sideways on that pillow she could only place the cap so that it sat at right angles to Miss Burch's pinched nose, as someone lying in the open puts their hat to protect their face and terrible eyes.

'Now then,' Edith tried again, 'what's this?' She spoke soft.

'Oh I can't bear it,' Miss Burch cried out, 'I can't bear it.'

'Can't bear what dear?' But the sobbing started redoubled.

'Now Burchie don't take on so, you shouldn't,' Edith went on, searching over this cocoon with her hand for Miss Burch's where it lay wrapped warm to her side, 'listen to me dear, it can't be so bad. You let me bring you a nice cup of tea.'

'I can't bear it,' Miss Burch replied a trifle calmer.

'It wouldn't take me more than a minute to run down. No one would ever know, the kettle was nicely on the boil in the hall when I just left it. You see now if that mightn't do you good.'

'Nothing'll ever be the same,' was all Miss Burch said.

'Now don't talk so wild Burchie. You just go easy and let me fetch you a good cup of tea.'

'You're a good child.'

'Of course I am. There dear. Rest yourself.'

Miss Burch began to sniff, to show signs of coming round.

'It wouldn't take but a minute to nip down,' Edith went on but Miss Burch interrupted.

'No don't leave me, Edith,' she said.

'Then what is it now?' the girl asked, 'what's happened to upset you like you are?'

Then it came out much interrupted and in a confused flow after she had adjusted her cap. What Miss Burch felt so she said was that nothing would ever be the same, that after thirty-five years in service she could not look forward to being in a respectable house again where your work was respected and in which you could do your best. Yet with the same breath she told Edith that Kate and her were lucky to be in a place like this. She went on that there were not many girls in their position able to learn the trade as she was able to teach it, to pass on all she had acquired about the cleaning and ordering of a house, particularly when over at home they were all being sent in the army to be leapt on so she honestly believed by drunken soldiers in darkness. She said they were never to leave the Castle, that they didn't know their luck. But at the same time, with another burst of sobs, she repeated that nothing would ever be the same, that it was to throw away a life time's labour for her to go on here. She made no mention of Mr Eldon. In the end a cup of tea had finally quietened Miss Burch so that the two girls were at last able to set off down the back way which joined the main drive not far from Michael's Lodge Gate, cut in the ruined wall which shut this demesne from tumble-down country outside.

Another morning, as he had been warned that Captain Davenport and Mrs Tancy were coming over to luncheon, Charley went to his room, got out the red and black notebooks, consulted the index and looked these people up. He read:

'Davenport Captain Irish Rifles ret'd salmon trout Master Dermot first term. Wife passed away flu' 1937. Digs after the old kings in his bog.' Then there was a long list of amounts with a date set against each. These possibly were tips. But Raunce noticed that Mr Eldon had touched the Captain for larger and larger amounts. At the last which was for a fiver Charley whistled. He said out loud, 'Now I wonder.'

Then he turned to the woman's page. 'Mrs Tancy her old Morris,' he found set down and the word Morris had been crossed out. Mr Eldon had added above, 'her old pony male eleven years.' There came another long list of dates with unvaryingly small payments, not one larger than a shilling, the last in August.

Mr Eldon had always seen to opening the door himself so that when the Captain rang it was the first time that Raunce had received him.

'Well now if it isn't Arthur,' this man said hearty and also it appeared with distaste. He put up the cycle for himself. 'And what news of Eldon?'

After Raunce told him and he had expressed regret he stood there awkward so to speak. Charley took his chance.

'And how are the salmon trout running sir?' he asked.

'Salmon trout? No fishin' yet. Close season.'

'And Master Dermot sir?' Raunce enquired without a flicker.

'Very fit thank you very fit. He's in the eleven. I'll find me own way thank you Arthur.'

'Not a sausage, not a solitary sausage,' Raunce muttered at his back referring to the fact that he had not been tipped.

He waited for Mrs Tancy behind the closed door, presumably so as to have nothing to do with Michael who stood outside to take over this lady's pony and trap.

'I'm late,' she said when she did come. 'I'm late aren't I?' she said to them both. 'Could you?' she asked Michael handing him the reins. 'Oh Punch there now!'

For the cob with lifted tail was evacuating onto the gravelled drive. One hundred donkey cart loads of washed gravel from Michael's brother's pit had been ordered at Michael's suggestion to freshen the rutted drive where this turned inward across the ha-ha. Gravel sold by Michael's brother Patrick and carted by Danny his mother's other son who had thought to stop at the seventy-ninth load the donkey being tired after it was understood that Mrs Tennant would be charged for the full hundred.

Michael ran forward to catch Punch's droppings before these could fall on the gravel which he had raked over that very morning.

'Asy,' he said as though in pain, 'asy.'

'The dear man he should not have bothered,' Mrs Tancy remarked in a momentary brogue.

With a pyramid steaming on his hands Michael glared about at the daffodil sprouted lawn. Then he shambled off till he could scatter what he carried on the nearest border. Meantime Charley looking his disgust, stood at the pony's hazy violet eyes. After a moment of withdrawal Punch began to nose about his pocket.

'The cob is looking well Madam,' he brought out.

'Isn't he, isn't he?' she said. 'Well thank you Arthur.' she said slipping a British threepenny bit into his hand and sailed past with not so much as a thank you for Michael.

When there were guests to lunch the servants had theirs afterwards. So it was not until ten past two that Raunce sat down in Mr Eldon's chair. He carved savagely like a head-hunter. They ate what he gave them in haste, silent for a time. Then Charley thought to ask,

'That Captain Davenport? Now where would I have heard he seeks after treasure in a bog?'

He got no answer.

'Do they dig for it,' he went on, 'or pry long sticks into the ground or what?' he mused aloud.

'Are you thinking you'll have a go?' Kate said.

'Now there was no cause to be pert my girl,' he said. 'Why goodness gracious me,' he remarked to Edith, 'whatever are you blushing for?'

She looked as though she was going to choke. If he had only known she was stricken by embarrassment. She knew very well that the last time the lady had been over to view the excavations Mrs Jack returned without her drawers. And it was with not a single word. They had vanished, there was not a trace. To turn it perhaps, she said to the lampman,

'What d'you know Paddy?'

'Why here we are sitting and we never thought of him,' Kate said. 'Come on now. You'd know Clancarty.'

He made no answer. But he laughed once, bent over his dish.

'Clancarty Paddy,' Kate tried again, 'Mr Raunce is asking you?' Charley watched Edith. He said under his breath, 'it's funny the way she blushes but then she's only a kid.'

'Are they makin' a search?' Kate went on and she fixed her small eyes unwavering on Edith. The lampman made no reply. He seldom did.

Edith while she blushed hot was picturing that wet afternoon Mrs Jack had last been over to Clancarty. While Mrs T. and her daughter-in-law were on with their dinner Edith had been in the younger woman's room busily clearing up. She hung the thin coat and skirt of tweed which held the scent used, she put the folded web of shirt and stockings into drawers of rosewood. She laid the outdoor crocodile skin shoes ready to take down to Paddy. She tidied the towels then went to prepare that bed, boat-shaped black and gold with a gold oar at the foot. She moved softly gently as someone in devotion and handled the pink silk sheets like veils. The curtains were drawn. Then all that she had to do was done. Those oil lamps were lit. But she stuck a finger in her mouth, looked about as if she missed something. Then she searched, and faster. She had gone through everything that was put away faster and faster. When she was sure those drawers Mrs Jack had worn to go out were astray her great dark eyes had been hot to glowing.

'I'll wager they had everything of gold,' Raunce said, still on about the excavations.

'And wore silk on their legs,' said Edith, short of breath.

'Don't talk so silly,' Miss Burch took her up. 'They never put silk next to themselves in those days my girl. It wasn't discovered.'

'Did they have silk knickers then Paddy,' Kate asked giggling.

'I never heard such a thing,' Miss Burch replied. 'You'll oblige me by dropping the subject. Isn't it bad enough to have dinner late as it is,' she said. 'You just leave the poor man alone. You let him be.'

Bert spoke. 'The nursery never had much of theirs,' he said. 'I must've took back the better part of what I carried up.'

'Oh dear,' cried Raunce in the high falsetto he put on whenever he referred to Nanny Swift.

'You should have seen 'er,' Bert added.

Both girls giggled softly while Charley still in falsetto asked whose face, holy smoke.

'Now that's quite enough of that,' Miss Burch said firm. There was a pause. 'I knew Mrs Welch had been upset,' she went on, 'and now I perceive why, not that I'm trying to excuse those potatoes she just gave us,' she said. All of them listened. She seemed almost to be in good humour. 'They were never cooked,' she added, 'and I do believe that's why they put salt on spuds,' looking at Paddy, 'but I'll say this, those precious peacocks of yours would have spurned 'em.'

Right to the last meal Mr Eldon had taken in this room it had been his part to speak, to wind up as it were, almost to leave the impress of a bishop on his flock. This may have been what led Charley to echo in a serious tone,

'Miss Swift is a difficult woman whilst she's up in her nursery. But she can be nice as you please outside.'

'That's right,' Miss Burch said, 'and as I've often found, take someone out of their position in life and you find a different person altogether, yes.'

The two girls looked at one another. a waste of giggling behind their eyes again.

'But our potatoes this afternoon were not fit for the table,' Raunce said to Miss Burch.

'Thank you Mr Raunce,' she replied. In this way for the first time she seemed to recognize his place.

'Well look sharp my lad,' he said to Bert. He appeared to ooze authority. 'Holy Moses see what time it is.'

He hastened out like a man who does not know how long his new found luck will hold. Also he had to make his first entry in the red notebook, to record the first tip. He put the date under Mrs Tancy's name, and then '3d'. 'Wonder what happened in that six months gap,' he murmured to himself about Mr Eldon's last date, 'she's been over to lunch many a time since and he'll have had the old dropsy out of her. He was losing grip not entering it, that's what,' he added aloud. Then he laid the books aside.

He first addressed an envelope. 'To Mrs William Raunce,' he wrote in pencil, '396 May Road Peterboro' Yorks' and immediately afterwards traced this with a pen. Next he began on the letter, again in pencil.

'*Dear Mother*,' he wrote without hesitating, '*I hope you are well. I am. Mr Eldon's funeral was last Tuesday. The floral tributes were grand. He will be sadly missed. At present I am doing his work and mine. I am not getting any extra money which I have spoken of to Mrs Tennant. This war will make a big difference in every home.*

'*Mother I am very worried for you with the terrible bombing. Have you got a Anderson shelter yet? I ought to be over there with you Mother not here. But perhaps he will keep to London with his bombing. What will become of the old town.*

'*We are all in God's hands Mother dear. I am very perplexed with what is best to do whether to come over or stay. If I went away from here to be with you there would be the Labour Exchange and then the Army. They have not got to my age yet because I will be forty next June you remember. But I'm thinking they shall Mother and sooner than we look to. We must all hope for the best.*

'*With love Mother to my sister Bell. I do hope she looks after you all right tell her. Your loving son, Charley.*'

Then he inked it in. As he licked the envelope flap after putting in the Money Order he squinted a bit wild, and this was shocking with his two different-coloured eyes. Lastly he laid his head down on his arms, went straight off to sleep.

There was often no real work went on in the Castle of an afternoon. Generally speaking this time was set aside so that Edith could sew or darn for Mrs Jack whom she looked after, and for Kate to see to the linen. But this afternoon as there had been guests they lent Bert a hand to clear away, then helped Mrs Welch's two girls Jane and Mary whose job it was to wash up everything except the tea things. The four of them chattered in Mrs Welch's scullery while this woman, seated in an armchair behind the closed door of her kitchen, stared grimly at her own black notebook.

'How is she?' Edith asked jerking her head and in a whisper.

'She's all right,' Mary whispered back, 'though we wondered a bit in the morning didn't we dear?' she said to Jane.

'I'll say we wondered.'

'But it was O.K. at the finish,' Mary went on. 'All's well

that ends well as they say. There was practically nothing came back from the luncheon nor the nursery and you people do seem to've enjoyed your dinners.'

'Just old Aggie Burch as didn't like 'er spuds,' Kate said, 'but you don't want to take notice. I know I don't.'

'Doesn't this sink make your back ache,' Edith remarked. 'But there,' she said, 'I expect her nephew on his way over is bringing a big change in Mrs Welch. I shouldn't be surprised if she didn't have him on account of the bombing. Isn't it dreadful?'

'The war's on now all right,' Kate said, 'and do these rotten Irish care? They make me sick.'

'What's the Irish got to do with it?' Jane asked. 'They're out aren't they? If they mean to stay out who's to blame 'em?'

'If it wasn't for the children the little angels I wouldn't ever remain. I couldn't really,' Edith announced. 'Look I'm going to dry, my back's broke. I could worship the ground they walks on. They're real little ladies. And how Mrs Jack dresses them. They've got everything so nice. I cherish those kids.'

'Well they're goin' to have a boy to keep 'em company now,' Kate said with malice. 'Very nice too and so they should,' she added.

'But what will Miss Swift say to that?' asked Edith.

'Oh that's O.K.,' Mary said, 'Miss Swift she come down to have a chat and Jane and me gets out of the light thinking there will be ructions but not a sound come past that closed door not one. We stayed here to see too didn't we love?' she said to Jane. 'Then in the end they both came through proper buddies, Mrs Welch seein' 'er out as pleasant as you please and her saying "well I hope the air will do him good. It's like this with children Mrs Welch," she says. "One and all they're better for a change," she says. I was that surprised.'

'There now I'm very glad,' said Edith, 'I am, honest.'

'Now you girls hurry with that washing up,' said the dreadful voice, 'oh, I see you've some help. There's quite a change come over this house I must admit. And don't you start a'wagging of those light tongues. But would you two young ladies like a glass of milk?'

It was Mrs Welch. It was almost unheard of that she should offer refreshment. Kate and Edith could only giggle.

'Mary,' she went on, 'you run and fetch that pitcher from the larder. What I've said over and over is at the age you are you girls don't get sufficient milk. My sister writes it's short enough at home.'

'Might it be your sister's little boy who is coming to visit, Mrs Welch?'

'That's so Edith and his name is Albert, same as that Raunce's sick lad. One name less for Mrs T. to remember. And if he had been christened Arthur we wouldn't understand what to think would we? All the men in this place having to be of the same name, whoever heard of such stuff and nonsense.'

They laughed. Then when Edith and Kate had had their milk these two girls judged it best to be gone.

'You can't be sure of her, love,' Edith said as they made their way up the back stairs. 'We did leave a bit for them yet but I'm positive she meant us to go really, calling us young ladies did you hear? You know what she is.'

'That's O.K. Edie an' if there were a few plates over it's not our work anyway. I got those sheets from the Gold Bedroom to mend. I wish the people they have to stay would cut their toenails or lie quiet one or the other.'

'Hush dear they'll hear,' Edith said and then went on: 'But have you ever seen such a change in anyone? Why she made herself quite pleasant.'

'Well what if she did the old nanny goat . . .'

'Hush love.'

'With that great beard she's got . . .'

'Oh Kate you are dreadful you are really. But do be careful, anyone could hear.'

'It's Miss Burch's afternoon out isn't it? Besides who would there be to come our way worse luck.' They had arrived at the door of their room. Kate flung it open. 'There,' she cried, 'look at the great boy you've got waiting inside.'

'What you don't mean Bert wouldn't presume,' said Edith going in. 'Why Kate you are silly there's no one. No,' she went on sitting down on her bed to take off shoes and stockings, 'it's her nephew coming over has softened 'er, that's what it is, love.'

Kate got down by Edith on her bed.

'What would you have said Edie if Bert had been in 'ere?'

'Why I'd've sent him packin'.'

'Would you Edie? Even if I hadn't been along?'

'How d'you mean? Kate, I never heard you speak so.'

Both girls giggled. The sky was overcast so that the light was dark as though under water. The afternoon was warm. It was the first afternoon to be warm since autumn. Though they could not see them the peacocks below were beginning to parade.

'And if it had've been Charley Edie?'

Edith gave a screech then slapped a hand over her mouth. A peacock screamed beneath but they were so used to this they paid no notice.

'Kate Armstrong what d'you mean?'

'What I say stupid. Suppose you was come alone up here,' and her voice went rising, 'and found 'im waitin' on yer bed,' she ended, with a shriek of bed.

Both gave way at this, collapsed back across the eiderdown giggling. Edith pulled herself together first. 'No,' she said, 'for land's sake have a mind to the quilting. Come on,' she added, 'we might as well be comfy' and they both got underneath, lay at ease with pillowed heads.

'Suppose it was Charley,' Kate said again.

'Why I daresn't even look at the man with his queer eyes. Each time I have sight of 'em I can't stop laughing,' Edith said. 'And the strange thing is I didn't ever properly take it in that they was a different colour till the other day. Not after two years and five months here, not till just the other day,' she added.

'You watch out Edie that's a sign.'

'A sign? A sign of what, I'd like to know?' she asked.

'Ah now you're asking,' Kate said. 'I wonder is she married or was she ever d'you reckon?'

'No dear she's only called Mrs like all cooks if you're referrin' to Mrs Welch. Whatever made you say?'

'Why nothing. But I wish he was goin' to be older that's all.'

31

'Kate I'm getting too hot.'

'Take off some of your clothes then silly. Come on with you I'll help.'

'Quiet. There's Mrs Jack's stockings I've got to go over.'

'If you lie on your buttons I can't undo 'em at the back can I?' Kate said. Then she tickled Edith to make her shift.

'Mercy stop it,' Edith screamed. 'Whatever are you doin'?'

'You said you was too warm. And struggling like you are will only make you warmer. There.'

'Kate Armstrong I thought I asked you. It tickles. Why you aren't pulling the dress off my back surely? Whatever are you at?'

But she made it easier for Kate by moving her body here and there as was required.

'It's only your old uniform,' Kate said and soon Edith was lying almost naked.

'I'll stroke you dear if you like,' Kate said. 'Shut your eyes now.'

'I ought to be going over those silk stockings.'

'If you don't take good care I'll run over you like you was an old pair Edie and darn you in all sorts of places you wouldn't think.'

They giggled in shrieks again at this then quietened down. Kate began to stroke up and down the inside of Edith's arm from the hollow of her elbow to the wrist. Edith lay still with closed eyes. The room was dark as long weed in the lake.

'What if it had been Charley?' Kate asked.

'Why d'you want to go on at me about him?'

'But supposin' it was Edie?'

'Well how would you have acted?' said Edith.

'Me? He would never've had to ask me twice. Not the way I am these days.'

'Oh Kate you are dreadful.' But Edith's voice was low. Kate's stroking was beginning to make her drowse.

Then there was a real outcry from the peacocks. Kate slipped out of bed to look. She saw Mrs Jack walking down the drive far beneath with Captain Davenport who was pushing his bike.

'What is it?' Edith asked.

32

'Just those two again.' Then Edith got up to look. The girls blocked their window, made night in the room.

'What two?' Edith said her back to the darkness. And answered herself. 'Oh Mrs Jack and the Captain. But won't the children be disappointed. I know they was counting on their mother taking them out the little loves.'

'Well they can count on summat else then and so can she very likely,' Kate said.

'Now Kate you've no call to say such a thing.' Edith's voice was truly indignant. They could not hear their masters.

'It's not fair. You could get one of these,' Davenport was saying.

'Now Dermot,' she replied, 'you've no right to be beastly.'

'But a bike's the only way to get about these days,' he said.

'Darling I've already told you,' she said.

'She couldn't surely object to your having a bike Violet after all.'

'Oh I can't go on like this behind her back,' she announced from an expressionless face but with tears coming into her blue, blue eyes that matched the curtains in her room, 'no I can't Dermot any longer.' She stopped. She stamped the ground, 'Oh darling,' she said, 'I do wish I could get you out of my system.'

'Now you're upset,' he began. 'By the way,' he went on, 'what's the matter with that footman you've got here? He asked me how the salmon trout were runnin'. I thought everyone in Old Ireland knew it was close season.'

'Dermot you don't mean he suspects anything?'

'Suspect anything? My dear girl I only mentioned it to change the conversation. Good Lord I only meant he seemed a funny sort.'

'And why d'you say you wanted to change the conversation?' she asked.

'Now you're all upset.'

'You don't understand,' she wailed.

'All I meant was I'd rather have him than Eldon,' the Captain said with bitterness. But it seemed that she was not thinking of the servants.

*

Charley now studied the black and red notebooks each afternoon. In the black he found Mr Eldon had written down peculiarities of those who were invited to Kinalty Castle with a note of the tips received on mentioning those peculiarities. But he did not as a rule spend long over this. There were not many people came to the Castle in wartime.

In the red Charley found Mr Eldon had kept a record of everything he drew under the petty cash account, which was presented monthly to Mrs Tennant. At one end was a copy of each account on which he had been paid. Against every item was an index number. At the other end of this red notebook the leaves were numbered and at least one whole sheet was given over entirely to copious notes on the item in question. Thus with a charge for sashcord of 7s 6d in March 1938 which reappeared in September of that year in an amount of 6s 8d and did not recur until July 1939 at 8s 9d, Raunce turned up the page on sashcord to find that hardly a yard had been bought or used in these last three years and that Mr Eldon was reminding himself to charge for more but had not lived to do it.

Once he had got the hang of things and had well studied the amount of corn bought for the peacocks at certain periods, Charley turned to that part which dealt only with the Cellar. By keeping open a Cellar Diary which had also to be shown each month to Mrs Tennant and by comparing the two, he was able to refer from one to the other. Thus much that would otherwise have been obscure became plain.

For instance it was Mrs Tennant's custom to have on tap a cask of whisky, which had to be replenished at regular intervals by means of ten-gallon jars shipped from Scotland. Not only had Mr Eldon never credited her with the empties, that was straightforward enough, but he had left whole pages of calculations on the probable loss of the volatile spirit arising from evaporation in a confined space from which the outside atmosphere was excluded. He had gone into it thoroughly, had probably been prepared for almost any query. Charley appeared to find it suggestive because he whistled. There was also an encouraging note of recent date to say that no questions had been asked for years.

After the whisky had been blended in cask for a period at a calculable loss it was Mrs Tennant's custom to have her butler bottle it. Mr Eldon had charged her for new bottles every time. There was even a note of his about a rise in the cost of corks which he had not been able to use over again.

What this forenoon halted Charley in the study while on his weekly round rewinding clocks was a reminder in the red notebook to charge 10s 6d for a new spring to the weathervane. This was fixed on top of the tower and turned with a wind in the usual way. Where it differed from similar appliances was that Mr Tennant had had it connected to a pointer which was set to swing over a large map of the country round about elaborately painted over the mantelpiece. Raunce did not know yet how the thing worked. He stood and pondered and asked himself aloud where he could say he was going to fix the replacements if she asked him.

This map was peculiar. For instance Kinalty Church was represented by a miniature painting of its tower and steeple while the Castle, which was set right in the centre, was a fair sized caricature in exaggerated Gothic. There were no names against places.

As Charley stood there it so happened that the pointer was fixed unwavering E.S.E. with the arrow tip exactly on Clancarty, Clancarty which was indicated by two nude figures male and female recumbent in gold crowns. For the artist had been told the place was a home of the old kings.

Mrs Jack came in looking for a letter from Dermot. The carpets were so deep Raunce did not hear her. He was staring. She noticed he seemed obsessed by the weathervane and turned to find what in particular held him.

When she saw and thought she knew she drew breath with a hiss.

'Raunce,' she said and he had never heard her speak so sharp, 'what is it?'

He faced about, holding himself quite still.

'Why Madam I never heard you. The thing seems to have got stuck Madam.'

'Stuck? What d'you mean stuck?'

'It does not seem to be revolving Madam, and I'm sure the wind is not in that quarter.'

She reacted at once. She strode up to that arrow and gave it a wild tug presumably to drag the pointer away from those now disgusting people lying there in a position which, only before she had known Dermot, she had once or twice laughed at to her husband. The arrow snapped off in her hand. The vane up top might have been held in a stiff breeze or something could have jammed it.

Charley knew nothing as yet about Clancarty. 'It's the spring Madam,' he said cheerful as he took that broken piece from her. 'You noticed the arm did not have any give Madam?'

'Oh get on with your work,' she said appearing to lose control and half ran out. Shaking his head, grumbling to himself, Raunce made his way upstairs.

He made his way smooth down the Long Passage until he found one of the girls. It was Edith opposite Mrs Jack's chamber, doing out this lady's bathroom.

'Hello ducks,' he whispered.

'What brings you here?' she asked as soft

'Who d'you think?' he answered.

'Get on with you,' she said.

'Look it's like this,' he began. 'This weathervane now. Where's the old works? I mean behind a little door or suchlike there must be a spring to do with some clockwork. At least that's what I'm led to understand.'

She looked disappointed.

'Behind a little door there's clockwork? Whatever's that?' she enquired.

'Don't ask me but Mr Eldon's left a book of directions which makes mention. Here,' he said, 'give us a kiss.' She said no as though she had been waiting to say this. She backed away against sweet primrose tiles. 'No,' she repeated quite loud and decided.

'Whatever's the matter with you these days?' he asked.

'I'm fed up I shouldn't wonder.'

'No need to take it out on me is there? What's up?'

'It's the war most likely,' she said pouting. 'I shall have to get me out of this old place.'

'You don't want to talk like that my girl. Why we're on a good thing here all of us. Trust Uncle Charley, he's seen some. There's a war on, the other side. You don't want none of it do you? And there's the grub question. You got to consider that. About this weathervane now. I'll have to find the other one of you then, that's the only thing left for me to do.' He leered at her. 'Where is she?' he demanded.

Edith looked sideways as though embarrassed but she told him.

'Next door in Mrs Tennant's bathroom,' she said.

He whipped out and along that passage. He looked in the next open door. Against deep blue tiles Kate with her doll's face and tow hair was rearranging a scarlet bathrobe on the chromium towel horse. Edith had followed. But where he went in she stayed by the door, through which she watched as though reluctant.

He slipped up behind Kate, put his palms over her eyes.

'Guess baby,' he said, still whispering.

She gave a great screech beneath her breath, so discreetly she hardly made a sound.

'Why Charley you did give me a start.'

'I don't know,' he said, 'but I can't seem to bring it off these days. See here,' he went on, hands still over her eyes, 'where's there a kind of box in the wall with clockwork inside to do with that weathervane?'

She stood quiet, seemed almost to press her face into his palms. But she let out a giggle at the question.

'Oh my,' she said, 'what next?'

'Come on,' he said murmuring yet, 'give us a kiss,' as he turned her. And while he heartily kissed Kate's mouth her right eye winked at Edith under one of his outstanding ears.

Charley straightened himself at last, passed a forefinger over his lips. At once Edith said as though she could hear somebody. 'It's this way Mr Raunce.'

He came smoothly out, automatic. She led him along. Neither looked back. Soon she stopped at a panel with a button. She opened it. He put his head forward to peer. He saw two shafts which met to be joined by three gear wheels

37

interlocked. And caught between those teeth, held by the leg was a live mouse.

At this Edith let a shriek with the full force of her lungs. A silence of horror fell.

Then even over the rustle of Kate hurrying up a paper-thin scream came as if in answer from between the wheels. And as Raunce looked for the person Edith said she had heard and except for Kate not a soul appeared, not one, Edith fainted slap into his arms.

After a moment Miss Burch came bustling towards them. 'What's this?' she asked, 'and what trick have you played on that poor girl now? Let go of her this instant goodness gracious whoever heard,' she said to Raunce and taking Edith, stretched her rather rough on the floor.

That same afternoon after dinner Miss Burch paid a call on Mrs Welch, slipping from the servants' hall out through the vast scullery straight into her kitchen.

'Come right in,' Mrs Welch welcomed from where she was seated concentrating over the opened notebook. 'Jane,' she called, 'Miss Burch will have a cup of tea.'

'Why thanking you,' Miss Burch said, 'and is this Albert?'

'Yes this is Albert,' Mrs Welch replied. 'Get up when you're spoken of,' she added and the boy stood. He had been crying. 'Come to think of it,' she went on, 'run out now and don't get in the way of my girls at their work nor into any more trouble my word.'

'Trouble,' Miss Burch remarked once they were alone as she stirred with a teaspoon, 'trouble. This morning's just been one long worry an' what it's going to come to I don't know.' There was no reply. Miss Burch watched steam from off her tea.

'I don't know I'm sure,' she continued eventually, 'but it's him or me that's the long and short of the whole matter. We can't go on like it and that's a fact,' she said.

'A large big bird like that,' Mrs Welch insisted, 'and with a powerful wallop in each wing. Why 'e might've got killed the little terror.'

'Killed?' Miss Burch asked, giving way. 'I hope he's not gone and had an accident on his very first day at the Castle?'

'Children is all little 'Itlers these days,' Mrs Welch answered. 'D'you know what 'e done. Up and throttled one of them peacocks with 'is bare hands not 'alf an hour after he got in. Yes that's what,' she said.

'Oh dear,' Miss Burch said, 'one of the peacocks?'

'I got'm covered up in the larder,' Mrs Welch went on. 'I'll choose my time to bury'm away at dusk. He might've been killed easy. I 'adn't turned my back not above two minutes to get on with their luncheon when I heard a kind of squawking. I ran to that window and there 'e was with one in 'is two fists. Oh I screamed out but 'e 'ad it about finished the little storm trooper. There wasn't nothing left to do but 'ide the dead body away from that mad Irish Conor.'

'Yes he's taken up with the things that man,' Miss Burch agreed.

'As to that I've only to pluck it,' Mrs Welch said, 'and 'e won't never distinguish the bird from a chicken they're that ignorant the savages. Mrs Tennant can't miss just the one out of above two hundred. But I won't deny it give me a start.'

'There you are,' Miss Burch said, 'but listen to this. I was upstairs in the Long Gallery this morning to get on with my work when I heard a screech, why I thought one of the girls had come by some terrible accident, or had their necks broke with one of the sashcords going which are a proper deathtrap along the Passage out of the Gallery. Well what d'you think? I'll give you three guesses.'

'You heard me 'oller out very likely,' Mrs Welch replied, watching the door yet that Albert had shut behind him.

'It was Edith, and that Raunce had been after her,' Miss Burch said, 'that man who makes this place a deathly menace.'

'Excuse me a moment,' Mrs Welch remarked and got up. She moved painful across the kitchen dragging her feet. Opening the door between she looked into her scullery. Albert was seated over a cup of tea while Mary and Jane went on with their work.

'You stay there quiet,' she said to him. 'You've been trouble enough this morning my oath,' she said, 'without your plotting something fresh.' Her voice was thick with love. She shut the door.

'Oh these long spaces,' she exclaimed as she came back.

'This place won't ever be the same, not since Mr Eldon left us,' Miss Burch began again. 'I said it over his open grave and I don't care who hears me this minute. With Raunce let loose without check about the house there's no saying what we'll come to. And there's the trouble of his morning tea. He will insist on one of my girls fetching it. They won't even tell me which one of them it is but I keep watch. She's Edith though I told Mrs Tennant different by being mistaken at the time. What I say is who's to answer for it when he gets up to his games with her in the bedroom. Tormenting a girl till she faints will be child's play Mrs Welch.'

'It's the food,' Mrs Welch answered, 'though I do speak as shouldn't seein' as I occupy meself with the kitchen. They're starving over there my sister says in her letter she sent. If it wasn't for that I'd go tomorrer, I would straight. He's that thin.'

'Nothing'll be like it was,' Miss Burch repeated. 'I said so at the time.'

Mrs Welch had the last word. 'Not but what Albert makes a difference being a refugee like the Belgians we had in the last war,' she said. 'Yes 'e'll be a tie,' she ended, 'and he'll take feedin'.'

But not more than half an hour after Miss Burch had left there fell another blow. Mrs Welch went into the larder for a last look before going to her room. While fixing a cheese cloth in front to hide the plucked peacock she chanced to regard the great jar where she kept her waterglass. With arms upraised in the gesture of a woman hanging out smalls she watched that jar with pursed lips. She called Albert.

'Ever set eyes on that before?' she asked.

'No'm I ain't,' he replied in the manner of Raunce's lad.

'Ever been in this larder in your puff?'

'No'm.'

'You wouldn't tell me an untruth would yer?'

'Oh no'm.'

'Because what I 'ave to say to you is this: it's 'ighly dangerous that stuff is. A sup of that and it would be your lot d'you hear me?'

'Yes'm.'

'So you never seen it before?'

'No'm.'

'And you've not even been in this place? Is that right?'

'Yes'm.'

'All right then and I don't want to hear any more. But if you so much as breathes a word of what 'as just passed I'll tan the 'ide clean off your back you little poulterer you h'understand?'

'Yes'm.' He turned, ran out.

Then high shrieking giggles came faint with distance from without. Mrs Welch moved over to perforated iron which formed a wall of the larder, advanced one eye to a hole and grimly watched.

The back premises of this grey Castle were on a vast scale. What she saw afar was Kate and Edith with their backs to her in purple uniforms and caps the colour of a priest's cassock. They seemed to be waiting outside O'Conor's lamp room. This was two tall Gothic windows and a pointed iron-studded door in a long wall of other similar doors and windows topped by battlements above which was set back another wall with a greater number of windows which in its turn was terraced into the last storey that was almost all blind Gothic windows under a steep roof of slate. Mrs Welch after seeming to linger over the great shaft of golden sun which lighted these girls through parted cloud let a great gust of sigh and turned away saying,

'Well if Aggie Burch can't hold 'em in leash it's none of my business, the pair of two-legged mice, the thieves,' she added.

But as Edith reached for O'Conor's latch Kate screamed at her,

'And what if there's a mouse?' Then Edie, hands to the side over a swelling heart, gave back, 'Oh love you can't say that to me,' and leant against the door post. 'That you can't say love,' she said, dizzy once more all of a sudden.

'Aw come on I only meant it for a game.'

'Oh Kate.'

'You're soft that's what it is dear.'

'Not after what come to pass this very morning you didn't ought.'

'Why see who's brought 'erself to have a peek at him,' Kate said of a moulting peacock which head sideways was gazing up with one black white-rimmed eye. 'Get off,' she cried, 'I don't like none of you.'

'Quiet dear. It's likely his favourite.'

'Why what d'you know,' said Kate, 'she's not taken up with us at all at all, it's the buzzard above she's fixed on, would you believe.'

'A buzzard?'

'And if I said I didn't care.'

'No Kate you mustn't, don't strike her I said. You can't tell what might happen if he came to learn.'

'Oh Paddy,' Kate said, 'I'll bet he's well away after that dinner he ate. He'll never stir. But I shan't if you wouldn't rather.'

'She's his special I know,' Edith went on. 'I can't distinguish one from the other but there's something tells me. And who's to say if he is asleep in the dark?'

'You go on in to oblige me then,' Kate said.

'Not me I shan't. I couldn't.'

'Well I will at that.'

'Nor you won't either,' Edith said. 'You've made me frighted.'

'I will then,' Kate answered, raising the heavy latch. 'But love I'll never cause a sound even the smallest,' she said low. Edith plastered her mouth over with the palm of a hand.

'No,' she said muffled, 'no,' as O'Conor's life was opened, as Kate let the sun in and Edith bent to look.

What they saw was a saddleroom which dated back to the time when there had been guests out hunting from Kinalty. It was a place from which light was almost excluded now by cobwebs across its two windows and into which, with the door ajar, the shafted sun lay in a lengthened arch of blazing sovereigns. Over a corn bin on which he had packed last autumn's ferns lay Paddy snoring between these windows, a web strung from one lock of hair back onto the sill above and which rose and fell as he breathed. Caught in the reflection of spring sunlight this cobweb looked to be made of gold as did those others which by working long minutes spiders had drawn from spar to spar of the fern bedding on which his head rested. It might have been almost that O'Conor's dreams were held by hairs of gold binding his head beneath a vaulted roof on which the floor of cobbles reflected an old king's molten treasure from the bog.

'He won't wake now, only for tea,' Kate said. 'Because after he's had his he feeds the birds.'

'Oh Kate isn't he a sight and all.'

'Well come on we can't stand looking. What's next?'

'If I make a crown out of them ferns in the corner,' Edith said, 'will you fetch something he can hold?'

'You aim to make him a bishop? Well if I 'ad my way I'd strip those rags off to give that pelt of his a good rub over.'

'Don't talk so. You couldn't.'

'Who's doing all the talking?' O'Conor gave a loud snore. Both girls began to giggle.

'Oh do be quiet dear,' Edith said picking a handful of ferns and starting to twist them. Then they were arrested by movement in the sunset of that sidewall which reflected glare from the floor in its glass.

For most of one side of this room was taken up by a vast glass-fronted cupboard in which had once been kept the bits, the halters and bridles, and the martingales. At some time O'Conor had cut away wooden partitioning at the back to make a window into the next chamber, given over nowadays to his peacocks. This was where these birds sheltered in winter, nested in spring, and where they died of natural causes at the end. As though stuffed in a dusty case they showed themselves from time to time as one after another across the heavy days they came up to look at him. Now, through a veil of light reflected over this plate glass from beneath, Edith could dimly see, not hear, a number of peacocks driven into view by some disturbance on their side and hardly to be recognized in this sovereign light. For their eyes had changed to rubies, their plumage to orange as they bowed and scraped at each other against the equal danger. Then again they were gone with a beat of wings and in their room stood Charley Raunce, the skin of his pale face altered by refraction to red morocco leather.

The girls stood transfixed as if by arrows between the Irishman dead motionless asleep and the other intent and quiet behind a division. Then dropping everything they turned, they also fled.

Miss Swift was deaf and could not always hear her charges' words as along with Evelyn and Moira and Mrs Welch's Albert she came that afternoon to the dovecote round by the back. She groaned while she settled herself in the shady seat and the doves rose in a white cloud on softly clapping wings.

'What's troublin' 'er?' Albert asked.

'It's only nanny's rheumatism,' Miss Moira quoted.

'Why come to that I got an uncle 'as 'is joints boiled Tuesdays and Thursdays over at St Luke's down the old Bow Road.'

'Now shall poor old nanny tell you a story of the two white doves that didn't agree?'

Moira nudged Evelyn and pointed. A pair of these birds on a ledge were bowing beak to beak. The two girls copied them, nodding deeply one to the other as they sat on either side of Miss Swift. This woman rubbed a knee with both hands without looking at it. She had closed her eyes.

'Once upon a time there were six little doves lived in a nest,' she began and Raunce came out of an unused door in that Castle wall. The rusted hinges creaked. The two girls waved but Mrs Welch's Albert beyond Evelyn might almost have been said to cringe. Raunce put a finger to his lips. He was on his way back from the round he had made of the peacocks' corn bins and during which he startled Kate and Edith. Then Miss Evelyn and Miss Moira each put a finger to their mouths as they went on bowing to each other. Raunce made off. Miss Swift continued,

'Because they were so poor and hungry and cold in their thin feathers out there in the rain.' She opened her eyes. 'Children,' she said, 'stop those silly tricks' and the girls obeyed. 'But the sun came out to warm them,' she intoned.

'Jesus,' Albert muttered, 'look at that.'

This dovecote was a careful reproduction of the leaning tower of Pisa on a small scale. It had balconies to each tier of windows. Now that the birds had settled again they seemed to have taken up their affairs at the point where they had been interrupted. So that all these balconies were crowded with doves and a heavy murmur of cooing throbbed the air though at one spot there seemed to be trouble.

'You're very very wicked boy,' said Evelyn to Albert looking where she thought he looked. What she saw was one dove driving another along a ledge backwards. Each time it reached the end the driven one took flight and fluttered then settled back on that same ledge once more only to be driven back the other way to clatter into air again. This was being repeated tirelessly when from another balcony something fell.

'That's ripe that is,' Albert said.

'I didn't see,' Evelyn cried. 'I didn't really. What came about?'

'And then there was a time,' the nanny said from behind closed eyes and the wall of deafness, 'oh my dears your old nanny hardly knows how to tell you but the naughty unloyal dove I told of.'

'It was a baby one,' Albert said.

'A baby dove. Oh do let me see.'

'I daresn't stir,' he said.

'Where did she fall then?' Evelyn asked.

'Quiet children,' Miss Swift said having opened her eyes, 'or I shan't finish the story you asked after, restless chicks,' she said. 'And then there came a time,' she went on, shutting her eyes again, hands folded.

'What? Where?' Moira whispered.

'It was a baby one,' Albert said, 'and nude. That big bastard pushed it.'

'The big what?' Evelyn asked. 'Oh but I mean oughtn't we to rescue the poor?'

'Where did she drop then?' Moira wanted to be told. But a rustle made them turn about on either side of Miss Swift who sat facing that dovecote shuteyed and deaf. They saw Kate and Edith in long purple uniforms bow swaying towards them in soft sunlight through the white budding branches, fingers over lips. Even little Albert copied the gesture back this time. All five began soundlessly giggling in the face of beauty.

'Did you see Mr Raunce?' Kate asked at last.

''E went that way,' Albert answered while the two girl children sat with forefingers still on their mouths.

'What did 'e come out of?' Kate asked.

'That door,' Albert said.

'And then they were in great peril every mortal one,' Miss Swift continued.

'And oh Edith,' Miss Evelyn announced, 'we've been watching the doves they are so funny.'

'I shouldn't pay attention if I was you dear.'

'Why shouldn't I pay attention?'

'Not if I was you I shouldn't.'

'Why shouldn't I?' Miss Evelyn asked.

'Because they're very rum them birds,' Kate said also whispering.

'Why are they rum?' Miss Moira asked.

'I'll say they're rum,' Albert announced. 'One of the old 'uns shoved a young bird and 'e fell down right on 'is nut.'

'Well I never,' Kate remarked to Edith. They watched that dovecote over the children's heads.

'Sssh,' said Edith watching rapt. The children turned. There were so many doves they hardly knew which way to look.

'And then there came a time when this wicked tempting bird came to her father to ask her hand,' Miss Swift said, passing a dry tongue over dry lips, shuteyed.

'It don't seem right not out in the open,' Kate mentioned casual.

'And again over there too and there,' said Edith.

'Where?' cried Miss Evelyn too loud though not sharp enough as she thought to interrupt Miss Swift. The nanny just put a hand on her arm while she droned.

'Oh what are they doing then?' Miss Moira cried.

'They're kissing love,' Kate answered low.

'Hush dear,' said Edith.

'But where Kate I don't see. Oh look at those two oh look she's got her head right down his beak, she's going to strangle him,' and Moira's voice rose. 'Nanny nanny stop it quick.'

'Good gracious child what's this?'

But the children had got up and as they rose every dove was

apart once more and on the wing, filling the air with sighing.

'Why now Edith and Kate whatever do you think you're about?'

'We've just finished our dinner,' Kate replied.

'Wandering all over the grounds where anyone might see. Who's ever heard?' the nanny said. 'Sit down children and you Albert. If you're going to stay with us you'll do as you're told.'

'Yes'm.'

'Well we're accustomed to let our dinner settle,' Kate said. 'And I make no doubt you use that to get away of an afternoon and let the work look after itself. You'll have Miss Burch after you.'

'Come away, dear,' Edith said to Kate.

'Doves kissing indeed,' Miss Swift called surprisingly after their backs, 'stuff and nonsense. That's the mother feeding her little one dears. If you sit quiet enough you'll see for yourselves,' she said to the children. 'And now where was I?'

'You were at that bit where the kind old father says he can marry her 'cause he's getting too old to know better.'

'Well now that's right,' Miss Swift began once more and the doves, spiralling down in the funnel made by trees which were coming out all over in a yellow green through chestnut sheaths the colour of a horse's coat, settled one after another each outside the door to his quarters and after strutting once or twice went on quarrelling, murdering and making love again. 'So then not knowing any better he let him have her hand,' the nanny said.

Breathless the children watched this leaning tower. Very soon one white dove was crouching with opened beak before another with stuck-out chest. Not long after that they were at it once more and the fat bird, grown thin now, had his head deep down the other's neck which was swallowing in frantic gulps that shook its crescent body. Elsewhere another bird trundled an egg to the edge. Yet another chased a fifth to a corner until it fluttered over behind where these two began again. In pairs they advanced and retreated. Then one more small mass fell without a thud, pink.

'There y'are,' said Albert.

'Where? I didn't see. Oh I've missed again,' Evelyn said. 'Did you?' to Moira.

'You're none of you listening you naughty children,' the nanny said. 'Here's poor nanny wasting her breath and you don't pay attention. We'd better get on with our walk if you ask me.'

'Why nanny?'

'Are you coming?'

'Yes'm.'

'But why nanny?'

'Because nanny says so. Come on now. We'll go down by the fish 'atchery,' and she made off, holding Evelyn by the hand. She dragged on her right leg.

'Tell you what,' Albert said to Moira as they loitered to follow, 'I'll bite 'is little 'ead off'n.'

'You'll what?'

'Like they did in the local where I was evacuated.'

'What's the local?'

'In the pub down in the country. There was a man there bit the 'eads off of mice for a pint. The lady I was evacuated with said so.'

'You shan't you wicked boy I'll call nanny.'

'I'll show yer,' he said darting sideways towards the base of that tower. 'You wait till I find'm,' he said and she burst out wailing. Miss Swift came back, mopped the child's face. The others watched as though disinterested. She did not ask Albert. 'I'll tell Mrs Welch about you' was all she told him.

Later that same afternoon Raunce was in the pantry lending his lad a hand with the tea things. That is to say while his Albert washed the cups and saucers, the spoons and plates, Raunce held up a heavy silver tray like a cymbal to polish it. 'Ha' he went at the expanse of mirror metal, 'ha,' then he rubbed his breath away as he whistled through his teeth in time to the short strokes in the way a man will when grooming a horse, and squinting terribly the while.

Suddenly he spoke. Bert grew quiet at his voice. Raunce said, 'I could have laughed right in her face,' and stopped.

'When was that?' Albert enquired.

'Yes so I could and with you sitting there still as a mouse.'

48

The boy looked speechless at him.

'Oh get on with your work,' Raunce quoted from another context. There was another lull while Albert redoubled his effort and the butler watched. 'It's not as if we had all night,' Raunce went on, 'which is to say I have not,' he said speaking genteely and he let a short guffaw, 'lucky Charley they call me, begorrah,' he added.

'Yes Mr Raunce,' mumbled Albert.

'It won't wash your acting the innocent my lad. The moment she come in that door between the scullery and where we was sitting over our tea I could tell you felt the draught.'

'I didn't feel nothing.'

'When Mrs Welch reported present on the steps there was something caused my eyes to settle on that cheese face of yours, something told me. And when she started about that waterglass of 'ers which is missing I says to myself Charley you don't have to look far, it's plain as my face in the mirror. What induced you to take the stuff?'

'I never.'

'Come on tell uncle.'

'I never took nothing.'

'You've no call to feel uneasy my lad. I've not made out I was any different from what I am now have I?'

'Mr Raunce I haven't so much as seen it.'

'Well, if you won't, then I will. I'll tell you. It's because you overheard me say what my old mother had written that they was on the very brink of starvation over in London with the bombing. You must've idea'd you'd go get hold of some to send 'em a few eggs in.'

'Gawd's truth I did not Mr Raunce.'

'Don't stand there like a stuck pig my lad. Get down to it for the love of Moses. We aren't finished with the day's work by a long chalk. But you got your parents in London yet?' he went on. 'Haven't you?'

There was no reply except for the slop of sink water.

'Well haven't you?'

'Yes Mr Raunce.'

'All right then why make a mystery? You thought you might send 'em along an egg or two.'

'I tell you I never.'

'I'm not saying you did, all I'm telling you is you thought you might. There's times I despair of you my lad,' Raunce said. 'We'll not possibly make anything out of you that's one item dead certain. And another thing now. Once you can shine a bit of good silver up like this here you'll have learned a start of the trade that's took me many a long year to master. And I'm still learning.'

'I couldn't even name what that glass is for,' the boy uttered deep in his sink.

'D'you want me to fetch you one?' Raunce shouted at once. 'Would you provoke me to strike you? No? Then don't attempt impudence again. There's the National Service Officer waiting the other side for growing lads such as you soon as you're of age.'

'Yessir,' the boy said as though galvanized.

'And don't call me sir,' Raunce said calmer, 'give a Mr when you address me that's all I ask. Well if you won't tell you won't. You may be right at that. See nothing know nothing as they say in the Army.'

Albert tried a furtive smile.

'I don't say I blame you,' Raunce went on after pondering a moment. He was picking his teeth with a needle he had taken from underneath the lapel of his coat. 'But one thing we will get straight here and now,' he said. 'Keep all of it to yourself if you wish. And clean your teeth of course before you have anything to do with a woman. Yet if I 'ave any more of that side from you there's one thing you can bet your life. A word to Mrs T. from me, just one little word and it's the Army for you my lad, old king and country and all the rest d'you understand.'

'Yes Mr Raunce.'

'Where'd those two girls of Miss Burch go working after tea did you happen to notice?'

'Over in the empty place.'

'Yes but what part?'

'I couldn't tell. I never 'eard. On my oath I don't bloody know.'

'O.K. O.K. what's all the excitement?' Raunce said. 'If you

don't know you don't,' he said. 'That's all there is to it. But I got a message to give one or both of 'em see? Lucky Charley they call me. I chanced upon one of their little games this dinnertime. And if that bell was to go just you answer it. If they should want to know where I am say I'm down in the cellar d'you understand. All right? But I shan't be more'n a minute,' he said as he glided softly out softly whistling. The boy trembled.

As has been explained most of this great house was closed. It was for Kate and Edith once or twice each week to open various dust-sheeted rooms to let the air in. When Raunce after making his way up the Grand Staircase, going through the Long Gallery and past the Chapel came to a great sombre pair of doors which divided one part of this Castle from the other, he passed once he had opened these into yet another world. And in spite of his training they made a booming sound as he shut them behind him.

He stood to listen through a white-wrapped dimness. For what he heard was music. In a moment he knew he heard a waltz.

'What are they up to now?' he asked half under his breath. 'What's Edith after?' he repeated. He was grave all of a sudden.

He started on his way, then almost at once stopped by a large bowl which sat naked on a window ledge and which had a sheet of cardboard laid over. He picked this up, set it aside, then dipped his fingers in the rustle of potpourri which lay within. Walking on again he sniffed once at his fingers he had dabbled in the dry bones of roses and to do this was a habit with him the few times he was over in this part.

He went forward, still intently listening. To his left was a range of high windows muted by white blinds. On his right he passed objects sheeted in white and to which he had never raised the cloths. For this house that had yet to be burned down, and in particular that greater part of it which remained closed, was a shadowless castle of treasures. But he was following music. Also he went like the most silent cat after two white mice, and to tell them as well that what had been missing was now found to have been stolen by a rat.

The music came louder and louder as he progressed until at the white and gold ballroom doors it fairly thundered. He paused to look over his shoulder with his hand on a leaping salmon trout in gilt before pressing this lever to go in. There was no one. Nevertheless he spoke back the way he had come. 'They'll break it,' he said aloud as though in explanation, presumably referring to the gramophone which was one of the first luxury clockwork models. 'And in a war,' he added as he turned back to these portals, 'it would still fetch good money,' talking to himself against the thrust of music. 'The little bitches I'll show 'em,' he said and suddenly opened.

They were wheeling wheeling in each other's arms heedless at the far end where they had drawn up one of the white blinds. Above from a rather low ceiling five great chandeliers swept one after the other almost to the waxed parquet floor reflecting in their hundred thousand drops the single sparkle of distant day, again and again red velvet panelled walls, and two girls, minute in purple, dancing multiplied to eternity in these trembling pears of glass.

'You're daft,' he called out. They stopped with their arms about each other. Then as he walked up they disengaged to rearrange their hair and still the waltz thundered. He switched it off. The needle grated.

The girls said nothing. They stood with arms up rolling their curls and watched. He went over to the window, twitched down that blind. He came back. He spoke at last.

'Oh all right,' he said, 'I only happened to be passing. O.K.? Yes I know it's none of my business. Go on play it once more if you like.'

'Not now,' Kate said.

'It was only that one of them might hear you,' he explained.

'It's over now,' Edith answered him.

'And that reminds me,' he went on seeming to forget he had just given another reason for his presence. 'What I came to tell you girls was I found out about the waterglass. It's my lad has been and had some. Only a trifle, not enough to notice. He took what he did more out of curiosity than anything.'

'Albert?' Edith exclaimed.

'Fortunate 'e didn't try a taste,' Raunce continued. 'He's that sort. He'd never think twice if it came over him to see what the effects might be. He's a crank that's why. I know I've tried along of that lad but there's some you can't do anything with.'

Kate laughed. 'So it was Albert, Albert after all,' she said.

'I came special to mention the matter,' Raunce added and he had not left Edith with his eyes. 'Ever since Mrs Welch barged in like that at teatime I thought well you never know maybe these girls will take what she said wrong, think it was addressed to them.'

'That cap didn't fit, we never took no notice,' Kate announced.

'It's Edith here,' Raunce said, 'with her talk of she must get home and being dissatisfied.'

'Well thank you very much,' Edith replied as though astounded.

'Don't mention,' he said. 'And I must be off. Busy Charley that's me,' he wound up with what seemed an empty return to his old manner as he abruptly turned away. He went straight out not saying another word.

'Well would you believe that?' Edith murmured half giggling. But Kate was looking at her like she might have been a stranger and she stopped.

'All right come on,' Kate said vicious, 'we're not goin' to stay here all night are we? I reckon we've done what we can. Enough's enough,' she said and they set about leaving this end of the great room as they had found it. And then made their way back to the part that was inhabited, their day's work done.

It may have been a few days later that Miss Burch came in late for her elevenses. She looked worried. As she sat down she said,

'She's mislaid her big sapphire cluster.'

There was no need to ask whose ring that was. Ever since the French maid went back to her own country Miss Burch had been in charge of Mrs Tennant's things. But Mrs T. was always finding what she had just lost, while she seldom bothered to announce that whatever it might be was no longer missing. Charley seriously said, and at the same time imitated Mrs Welch's nephew,

'Maybe she put'm down and forgot to pick'm up.'

Except for Miss Burch they none of them bothered. It could be assumed if she did not in good time come across the ring that she would get another of equal value out of the Company and better because it was fresh.

'Which reminds me,' Charley asked his lad, 'did you remember to take her back that glove? Now don't give me the old answer, don't say which glove?'

'It's in the pantry Mr Raunce,' Albert said.

'What is?'

'The gardening glove.'

'You'll excuse me it's not. I ought to know seeing that's my own pantry. Where is it then?'

'I put 'er glove in the cupboard,' Albert said, 'on the bottom shelf. I seen it only this morning.'

'Oh well if you've hidden the thing,' Raunce replied and they fell back on silence.

Edith looked up to find Kate watching her. She blushed.

'Land's sakes there she goes colouring again,' Raunce announced hearty. 'She should go and give one of them blood transfusions they are asking volunteers for, she's got too much,' he commented out of one side of his mouth to Miss Burch next him.

'Don't be disgusting,' was all this woman said.

But he had obviously recollected. Eggs must have made him think of waterglass. 'Wait a minute,' he cried. Kate watched. 'I've just remembered summat,' he went on. He paused, and his eyes were on Edith while her blushes flooded once more. 'I do believe I done you a real injustice,' he said to Albert perhaps. But he did not seem able to take his eyes off the girl while she looked at him melting as though at his mercy.

'We shall have to make them open up the drains for us that's all,' Miss Burch stated, still on about the ring.

'Oh forget it,' Charley said to Edith, probably meaning this remark for Albert. He lowered his eyes and an odd sort of bewilderment showed in his face. But Miss Burch must have understood that he was answering her for she objected,

'I can't forget,' and she spoke resigned. 'I'm sure I've

looked every place and it was a beautiful ring, an antique,' she added.

At this moment Mrs Welch had an idea away in the kitchen. Leaving her black notebook she shuffled swift into the scullery where little Albert was at table over a cup of cocoa while the two girls prepared vegetables in one of six sinks.

'There's none of you girls go talking to the tradesmen?' she asked in a menacing voice and gave no warning.

'Oh no m'm.'

'There's not one of you so much as passes the time of day with that butcher?'

'No m'm truly.'

'Because remember what I said. Don't have nothing to do with them Irish or you'll likely bring our own blood on us. By reason of the I.R.A. And never forget.'

'Yes m'm.'

'And where do they carry the victuals when they call?' Mrs Welch went on to ask.

'They leave 'em in the outside larder like you said.'

'Now when d'you fetch what they've left?'

'When they're gone,' the girls answered.

'That's right. Also I'll take up with those merchants what they've delivered short, what they owe me, on the blower, understand. Nor you 'aven't spoken with one of them?'

'No m'm.'

'And 'ow d'you know when they've been?'

'They ring the little bell as they're leavin'.'

'That's right. Then it can't be one of the tradesmen after all,' she said going back into the kitchen and there cried out loud to herself, 'Oh my waterglass.'

What she had lost still seemed uppermost on Mrs Welch's mind when after dinner that same day Miss Burch dropped in to have a word.

'I've been and measured'n again,' she greeted Agatha, 'and there's above a quart gone without trace. Mary bring Miss Burch a cup of tea.'

'I do miss Mr Eldon, I do miss that man,' Miss Burch said. 'No matter who couldn't happen to lay their hands on something he always imagined where to find it. He startled you that way.'

'Not what is short out of my jar he never could.'

'No matter where it was Mrs Tennant dropped whatever it might be,' Agatha went on regardless, 'he was on 'and to restore it. He knew where things had lodged before they were rightly out of your fingers. There you are Mrs Welch it's a gift.'

'It's a gift right enough the way some is born sticky fingered.'

'Now I wouldn't say anyone had taken that ring, no I'd never go so far as that. I don't believe there's a soul in this Castle would do such a thing.'

'I've 'ad the matter over with my girls,' Mrs Welch said, 'right into things I've been, and I've given Albert a talkin' to my word. If 'e'd known the slightest bit I'd've had it out of 'im you can lay your oath on that.'

'It's a mystery.'

'A dark mystery's right,' Mrs Welch echoed. 'A ring will roll I grant, but don't tell me above a quart of waterglass will fly out of what it's in without a drop spilled on the floor, the diabolical stroke,' she added.

'I knew a woman once went down to Brighton for the Whitsun,' Miss Burch began, 'and her ring slipped in the sand. The next day she went back with her little nipper's wooden shovel, dug away where she'd been seated, and there it was after the tide had been over even.'

'You'll 'ave to get the plumbin' opened up that's all.'

'Just what I said with the cup of cocoa this morning,' Miss Burch replied. 'Of course I've got my girls searching this minute but they would never see the Crown jewels laying right before them they're so occupied looking over their shoulders for that Raunce.'

'I won't 'ave 'im in my kitchen.'

'Oh you're fortunate, you've a place you can call your own. Though he's improved the last few days, I will allow that. We may make something of him yet.'

''Ave they so much as glanced at those drains in the last twelve-month?' Mrs Welch enquired.

'They should be done out,' Miss Burch said. 'But the proper time will be when they both go over for Mr Jack's leave which will be any time now or so I'm led to believe.'

'I was goin' to speak to 'er myself on it,' Mrs Welch announced. 'It ain't 'ealthy in these old buildings that has a cesspool dug before sewers come to be invented. Not with children about that is.'

'And where would the little chap be this afternoon?'

'My Albert? Oh I sent 'im up to Miss Swift to get 'is run out.'

'That's right,' Miss Burch said. 'It's not right for them to be all day inside. Like Raunce is for instance.'

'Gawd 'elp us with the man when they do go over the other side for Mr Jack.' As she spoke Mrs Welch started to look wild again.

'You think so?' Miss Burch asked seeming at once to dread.

'It's not thinking, I'm certain sure. Well there's just the one thing for it,' Mrs Welch cried suddenly frantic, 'every mortal object must be under lock and key. There maun't be a drawer can be opened or a door they shall get in by. And as for my pots and pans I'll get me a padlock and chains and stake 'em down to me dresser,' she almost shouted pointing to the vast array of burnished copper and aluminium. 'And if I can't get a chain will go through them 'oles in the 'andles so 'elp me God I'll send to Berlin if I shouldn't find what'll suit in this poor law island.'

'To Berlin?' Miss Burch asked with a gasp.

'That's right,' Mrs Welch answered and seemed gratified. 'We're in a nootral country aren't we?'

'Bless me but I can't stay sitting here,' Miss Burch said getting up, 'I must do a bit more I suppose. I'm obliged to you for the cup of tea I was parched,' she added.

'You're welcome,' Mrs Welch replied as she reopened her black notebook.

Agatha walked stiffly through the back premises towards Mrs Tennant's bedroom which was being given a thorough turnout by her girls. She had made the loss of this ring an excuse to favour the room with a proper doing. But unusual sounds of activity in the pantry made her choose to go through this on the way upstairs. She found Raunce hard at it with silver out over green baize cloths across every table he could lay hands on and even into his bedroom. Saucers filled with a violet coloured polish, old toothbrushes, shammy leather and the long white soft-haired brushes were laid out for use among sauceboats, salvers, rose bowls and the silver candlesticks of all shapes and sizes. She passed Raunce and his lad in a silence which seemed to grant gracious approval.

'The old cow,' Charley remarked once she was out of earshot

'You've said it,' the boy replied.

'You know Bert I sometimes marvel women can go sour like that. When you think of them young, soft and tender it doesn't 'ardly seem possible now the way they turn so that you would never hold a crab apple up to them they're so acid.'

'That's right,' the boy said as he worked.

'And what Mr Eldon could see in her is a mystery but then he was deep,' Raunce commented with admiration in his voice. 'He was deep if ever there was one.' At any pause in what he was saying he whistled between his teeth like a groom while he rubbed and polished. He was apparently in fine fettle.

'What day is it?' he asked.

'Why Saturday,' the boy answered.

'Holy smoke if we was to creep upstairs tomorrow after dinner and find those two slaves of hers laid out on their little beds where they'll be of a Sunday afternoon. What would you do eh?'

Albert stopped work and stared. He seemed astonished.

'After cleaning your teeth of course,' Charley added.

'Why what d'you mean?' Albert asked.

'What would you say to Kate? A lovely blonde? Now then take your hands out of those pockets and get on with the work or we'll be here all night. Have you ever had anything to do with a woman?'

The habitual look of obstinacy appeared on Albert's face. He did not answer.

'There's no call to be bashful,' Raunce said. 'Everyone's got to make a start one time or another. Have you or have you not? You won't answer. I don't blame you neither. Broadminded Charley that's what I'm known as. But one thing you can get into that thick skull of yours. You lay off Edith, understand. You can muck about with Kate all you please but Edith's close season, get me?'

'Yes Mr Raunce, whatever you say.'

'What d'you mean whatever I say? You be careful my lad else you'll be getting me upset in another minute. Strike me blind I don't for the life of me know why I'm talking to you. But I lie awake at night moithering about that lass. Have you ever lain awake at night?'

'No Mr Raunce.'

'Don't. It's not worth it. Tell me something. D'you shave?'

The boy's left hand went to his chin.

'Not yet I don't.'

'Then put it out of mind, she wouldn't think of you. Kate might now. She's different. What say we go to their room to-morrow eh?'

'You wouldn't dare.'

'I wouldn't dare! Who d'you take me for? Let me tell you there was many an occasion I went up to Mamselle's boudoir to give her a long bongjour before she went back to France.'

'That's different,' the boy said and said under his breath, 'oh Christ help me.'

'What d'you mean that's different? They're all made the same aren't they an' that means they're built different from you and me doesn't it? What are you gettin' at talking so soft?'

'Then why ask me then?'

'Because you're sweet on 'er, that's why,' Raunce said in a sort of shout. 'Holy Moses I don't know why I allow myself to get put out,' he went on calmer. 'But there's a certain way you have of looking down that dam delicate snotty nose you sniff with that gets my goat. Gets my goat see?' he added in rising tones.

'Yes Mr Raunce.'

'That's all right then. Don't pay attention to uncle, at least not on every occasion. No you're going the wrong way about it with that toast rack,' he said as helpful as you please. 'Hand over and I'll show you.' And he proceeded to demonstrate.

Meantime Mrs Tennant and her daughter-in-law were making their way as usual to the ruined temple.

'Violet,' she said, 'Mrs Manton, poor Mother's old friend, has asked me to stay with her at Belchester on my way over.'

'Yes dear.'

'I thought I might. It would be a change.'

'Yes dear.'

'When did you say Jack was definitely getting his leave? The twenty-first isn't it? Well if I crossed over on the eighteenth that would give me three days with Hermione at Belchester before coming up to London. You wouldn't mind just forty-eight hours down here alone?'

Every part of the young woman's body except her Adam's apple was crying out the one word Dermot. She could not trust herself to speak.

'Because if you did,' Mrs Tennant went on in a doubtful voice, 'I could visit Hermione after Jack had gone back to his unit. Because I expect you will be staying on in London for a few days.'

'Don't you bother about little me,' Mrs Jack brought out at last. 'I shall be all right.'

'Are you sure? Really I feel I would rather get away from this place for a bit. The servants are being so truly beastly. And then there was my lovely cluster ring Jack's Aunt Emily gave me. D'you know I haven't had a word of sympathy yet from one of them about it.'

'Darling it is a shame,' Mrs Jack said. 'Badger come here. Come here when I tell you.'

'I know it's an absurd thing to expect,' Mrs Tennant went on looking up into the sky, 'but Eldon with all his faults always had a word of comfort when there was a disaster. Oh isn't it really too dreadful? Violet dear what d'you think?'

'I think it'll turn up. I know they haven't found anything in your bedroom but it can't simply have disappeared.'

'That's why I think if I went away somehow the luck might change,' Mrs Tennant said. 'I know there's a voice tells me the minute I turn my back they'll find my ring.'

'But Raunce is a bit of a wet rag isn't he?' her daughter-in-law remarked.

'Wet blanket you mean,' Mrs Tennant said. 'Oh well what can you expect with servants nowadays.' She spoke much more cheerfully. 'Then that's settled,' she went on, 'I'll go over a day or two ahead and we'll all meet in London to try and give the dear boy a good time. But talking of Raunce,' she went on and Mrs Jack could have had no suspicion of what was coming, 'he brought me his book this morning. You know I hardly ever look at it but well this was the first time he'd presented the thing himself and I don't know why, I suppose it's the war, but four pounds seven and six for a new arm to the map in the study why I could hardly believe my eyes. Why darling whatever's the matter?' Because Mrs Jack was leaning helpless against a tree with her face averted.

'Nothing,' she murmured weak voiced.

Mrs Tennant asked herself under her breath if the child was going to have another baby, and counted up the months from when the darling had seen her husband last.

'Sit down. No it's damp. Lean on my arm,' she said, and then her lips shaped March April May.

'I shall be all right in a minute.'

'I should never have dragged you out like this you poor child,' Mrs Tennant said. 'You should have said you didn't feel quite the thing.'

'What did he say?' Mrs Jack enquired as though in spite of herself.

'What did who say? Here sit here. At least it's dry.'

'That man Raunce,' the younger woman answered.

'My dear really I shall always repeat what you've just asked as the most wonderful example of self possession that's ever come my way. I must say your generation's too extraordinary. Here you are you poor child nearly in a faint and yet you remember I was talking about the compass arm over the map in the study. Lean back against me now. And keep your head down.'

Her daughter-in-law made a great effort.

'Well you wouldn't want me to go on about my silly old tummy, would you?' she asked in stronger tones.

'Why my darling,' Mrs Tennant exclaimed in what was almost a fruity voice, obviously visualizing a third grandchild. 'Why darling . . .'

'No, it isn't that,' Mrs Jack said and the searing rage, which that very moment swept over her as she realized, showed in how loudly she spoke. 'I expect it's something I had for lunch,' she added subsiding, guilty.

'I'll speak to Mrs Welch.'

'Oh no don't, please don't,' her daughter-in-law implored. Mrs Tennant said no more but she had made up her mind. The pots and pans were not being kept clean. That was all, or was it?

Raunce also became the subject in Mrs Tennant's bedroom. Miss Burch had not stayed long. When they were alone, turning the place upside down, Edith tried without success to get Kate to talk. They took the covers off all the armchairs, removed every rug and stripped the bed but to each comment Edith made such as 'well it's not here,' or 'I can't see it love can you?' Kate made answer with a silence that might have begun to work on Edith. For at last this girl said,

'D'you think I did ought to have told Mr Raunce about that waterglass?'

'Ah you're a deep one you are,' Kate immediately replied.

'I'm not and I don't know what you're after,' Edith protested beating a monogrammed pillow edged with lace between the palms of her two hands. But Kate made no reply and Edith apparently did not want to leave the matter for she tried again.

'When all's said and done love it's not as if Albert was suspected. That's just Mr Raunce's way,' she said.

'What makes you give him a Mr?' Kate asked.

'Why he's got the position now surely?'

'But he's no different to what he was,' Kate objected.

'According to one way of takin' it he's not,' Edith said, 'but whichever way we regard him he sees himself the butler.'

'O.K. if that's how you look at it.'

'Now Kate what's come over you? You wouldn't wish to spite him surely?'

'Listen,' Kate said, 'it don't matter to me what he thinks we think. All he'll be to me is Charley same as he always has been.'

'All right,' said Edith, 'I'll call him Charley and drop the mister.'

'And blush right in 'is face?'

'Kate Armstrong I'm surprised.'

'You can be surprised all right. I should worry. No I'm disappointed in you Edie, I am that.'

They stood on either side of the bed looking at each other.

'Then you do think I should never have kept silent. What you say is I should have talked up at the first go off when Mrs Welch came in at teatime?' Edith spoke as though she had been running but Kate only smiled. Kate said,

'I wouldn't play the innocent if I was you, not with me. It don't come off and that's a fact.'

'Then what you're gettin' at, without you're having what it takes to tell, what you're tryin' to say is you think I'm after 'im when he's something to you? Is that right?'

'Christ 'e's nothing to me. Charley Raunce? I'd sooner be dead.'

'I'll bet you'd sooner be dead.'

'What d'you insinuate by that Edie? I don't have to tell you you can go so far and no farther where I'm concerned thank you.'

'All right then I'll learn you something,' Edith said and she panted and panted. 'I love Charley Raunce I love 'im I love 'im so there. I could open the veins of my right arm for that man,' she said, turned her back on Kate, walked out and left her.

'You needn't have told me. I knew, don't worry,' Kate said to the now empty room, but with a sort of satisfaction as it seemed in pain.

On the 18th Mrs Tennant left for England and Belchester. That same evening Captain Davenport dined at the Castle alone with Mrs Jack who had instructed Raunce that he need not wait up to see the Captain out.

There was nothing unusual in this to draw comment, and

next morning Edith was rubbing her face, yawning like a child when it was time to call the lady. She gently knocked. She got no reply but then she never did. When she went in after knocking a second time the curtains which Miss Burch had already drawn back in the passage outside let sufficient light for Edith to see her way across the room. But she went soft, cautious so as not to stumble against the gold oar that stood out from the bed. Then she drew those curtains. She folded the shutters back into the wall. And Edith looked out on the morning, the soft bright morning that struck her dazzled dazzling eyes.

A movement over in the bed attracted her attention. She turned slow. She saw a quick stir beside the curls under which Mrs Jack's head lay asleep, she caught sight of someone else's hair as well, and it was retreating beneath silk sheets. A man. Her heart hammered fit to burst her veins. She gave a little gasp.

Then the dark head was altogether gone. But there were two humps of body, turf over graves under those pink bedclothes. And it was at this moment Mrs Jack jumped as if she had been pinched. Not properly awake she sat straight up. She was nude. Then no doubt remembering she said very quick, 'Oh Edith it's you it's quite all right I'll ring.' On which she must have recognized that she was naked. With a sort of cry and crossing her lovely arms over that great brilliant upper part of her on which, wayward, were two dark upraised dry wounds shaking on her, she also slid entirely underneath.

When Edith came to herself she found she was outside in the Long Passage, that bedroom door shut after her and with Miss Burch halted staring at her face. She said, all come over faint,

'I don't know how I was able to find me way out.'

'How d'you mean Edith?'

'An' if I'd been a'carryin' her early tea I'd 'a' dropped it.'

'And so you might dashing into me as you did.'

'In there,' Edith added. She seemed at her last gasp.

'In where?' Miss Burch asked grim.

For two moments Edith struggled to get breath.

'A man,' she said at last.

'God save us a man,' Miss Burch muttered, knocked and went straight through, shutting the door after. Edith leant against the table, the one that had naked cupids inlaid with precious woods on its top. She bent her head. She seemed afraid she might be sick. But when Miss Burch came out again as she did at once Edith drew herself straight to hear the verdict.

''E's puttin' 'is shirt on,' was all Miss Burch said, shocked into dropping her aitches. Then she added as though truly broken-hearted,

'Come on away my girl. Let 'im get off h'out.'

Edith made no move, stayed gazing at her.

'Come will you,' Miss Burch repeated gentle, 'this is no place for us my dear,' she said drawing a hand across her mouth.

At that Edith took to her heels and ran. She ran. She went straight up the back stairs. And along their passage into the deep room she shared with Kate. This girl was doing her hair before she went down to breakfast. She was at variance with Edith yet, which may have been why she did not turn round at first. But Edith's panting made her look.

'Why whatever . . .?' she began.

'There 'e was,' Edith broke out between gasps, 'I seen the hair of 'is 'ead, large as life, you could 'a' knocked me down with a leaf,' she said.

'The what?' cried Kate arrested.

'A man,' Edith said.

'A I.R.A. man?' Kate asked, voice rising.

'The Captain,' Edith replied calmer, put a hand to her throat and swallowed. With obviously a great leap of her mind Kate got there.

'In your young lady's bed. Oh goody,' she shouted, at which both began to giggle helpless. 'Large as life,' one said, the other repeated, then the two of them giggled again. 'In her bed,' one said, the other echoed, and both shouted with laughter. 'All night?' shrieked Kate, and it seemed she forgot she had been at odds with Edith about Charley Raunce. 'All night,' Edith screamed back. Holding their sides they crowed with laughter.

'And 've you told old Mother Burch?' Kate asked when both were quieter.

'She seen him too,' Edith answered, as she dabbed the heel of her right hand at her eyes where these had been running.

'She did?' Kate echoed.

'She went in,' Edith called out with a high yell then fell back on the eiderdown and howled she laughed so much, faintly kicking with her legs.

Kate began to gasp as if she could not get enough air to speak.

'She went in?' she asked.

'And d'you know – what she said?' Edith said choking.

'What's that?'

'When she come out,' Edith went on by fits and starts, 'oh you'll never guess – no love you could never – oh I shall die – Katie it hurts my side – d'you know what she said?' – and by this time Kate as she stood in front of her was doubled up hands on knees in such shrieks that she was dribbling – 'she said' – and Edith fought to get the words out – 'oh she said why 'e's puttin' 'is shirt on.' At this Kate collapsed, fell back. Both girls howled. Between screeches Kate managed to get out, 'Take care I'll wet myself.' Edith calmed at once.

'Hush dear someone'll hear.'

'Just puttin' 'is shirt on,' Kate quoted sobering.

'That's what she said,' Edith answered.

'Well Edie I'd've given a week's wages to be there I would really. What did you do?' And at this Edith went into a long description of each thought she had and every step she took after so gently knocking on that bedroom.

'But then who was it dear?' Kate asked at last.

'Oh I never saw his face only the top of his head like I told you where he was going thin. It was the Captain make no mistake.'

They giggled a bit more at this then Kate wanted to know if she had not asked old Aggie Burch.

'Hush Kate she'll hear,' Edith said, 'but if you'd seen her face you could never've questioned her.'

'Look I'll just sluice some cold water over me and then I'll get down to the 'all,' Kate answered. 'I wouldn't miss the look she'll be wearin' for nothing in the world, not for a 'ug from an old ugly bastard of a tinker even,' she said.

'An old ugly what? Why Kate Armstrong whatever are you saying?'

'Forget it dearie. There,' she said throwing her towel down, 'I'm off.' And Edith had to rush so as not to be left out below. But where Kate made straight to the servants' hall Edith struck right-handed for the pantry. She was in luck, Raunce was there yet. The moment she saw him she seemed overjoyed. With for her an altogether extraordinary animation she fairly danced up. He stood as though embarrassed, fumbling his nose, squinting.

'Why Charley,' she laughed, 'what d'you know?'

'Yes,' he said solemn.

'Well then isn't this a knock out?' she asked. 'An' it happened to me,' she added. 'After all these years.'

'Now steady on lass there's my lad Bert to consider.'

'Bert?' she asked. 'Why 'e's getting our breakfast or should be at this hour. Why what about him?'

'That lad ain't of an age yet,' Mr Raunce replied but he spoke as though in apology. She quietened down, stopped rocking backwards and forwards and ceased almost pushing her flushed face into his.

'Well aren't you glad?' she went on after a minute, 'for me I mean,' she mocked.

'I can't make you out at all,' he answered.

'Why there's all those stories you've had, openin' this door and seeing that when you were in a place in Dorset and lookin' through the bathroom window down in Wales an' suchlike oh I've heard you or Kate has and now it's come to me. Right a'bed they was next to one another. Stuff that in your old smelly pipe and smoke it.' She began once more to force her body on his notice, getting right up to him then away again, as though pretending to dance. Then she turned herself completely round in front of his very eyes. He seemed ill at ease.

'But how would you know it was me?' she asked suddenly stopping.

'Miss Burch,' he replied. 'It come as a big surprise. I didn't guess she'd have the sense of right and wrong to acquaint me. But I shouldn't pay attention to this mess up if I was you.'

'What d'you mean pay no attention?' she asked and she spoke angry.

'What they see fit to do is no concern of our own,' he said still watching her as if ashamed and surprisingly he yawned.

'You mean you're going to make nothing of it just because I found 'em? The Captain in Mrs Jack's bed?' She blushed, with anger perhaps. 'You're going to try and take that from me?'

'Take it from you how's that?' he asked.

'Take it away from me,' she repeated and her eyes filled beautifully with tears.

'Honey,' he said calling her this for the first time, 'you don't want to go and talk, see, or you'll likely lose your place?'

'Lose my place?' she echoed, 'I should worry in this lousy hole.'

'Without a reference,' he added, 'you mark what I say.'

'I should worry,' she repeated and for the moment looked as if she might burst out crying. He put on a grin. He looked appealing and upset.

'What they do is no concern of us,' he said again. 'And there's the National bloody Service Officer waitin' for you over on the other side.'

'Don't you swear at me of all people,' she answered. Turning on her heel she actually ran out in the direction of the servants' hall.

Breakfast that morning took place at first in utter silence. Even Kate looked down her nose. Raunce fidgeted and often glanced quickly at Edith who was hurried in everything she did. But as for Miss Burch she could not eat anything at all hardly. Her hand shook so she spilled the tea from out her cup. Only Paddy behaved as usual, concentrated on his food.

Before this meal was done Miss Burch hastened out by the scullery door. She passed through to the kitchen. But Mrs Welch sat adamant with little Albert and barely looked round to return Agatha's dark good morning. So Miss Burch went off to her room to be alone.

Meantime Charley spoke up in the hall. 'There's someone got to take the breakfast tray,' he said.

68

'Oh I couldn't,' Edith said at once, 'I'd spill it on that bed.' It was for her to answer because it was her duty each morning.

'There'll need be two trays,' Kate put in sly.

'There will not,' Raunce replied his eyes on Bert, 'the other party left the Castle first thing by pedal bicycle,' he said.

'The Captain?' Bert asked, 'I seen 'im as I was doin' the brass.' It was probably instinct made the lad continue as he did. 'What room did he occupy then?' he enquired.

'Ah you may well ask boy,' Raunce answered solemn. At that Edith broke out with, 'I'm surprised at you Mr Raunce I am really, that you should make a mystery out of nothing.' She seemed furious and Kate watched avidly. 'Listen Bert,' Edith went on, 'the Captain 'e spent the night in my lady's bed next 'er, an' she was nude I saw, only they overslept the two of them as I know from when I went to open the room in the morning. And don't you let anyone tell you different because it was me found it and called Aggie Burch so there.'

'I'll bet they overslept,' Kate announced while Raunce's lad gaped at Edith. Raunce could not let this pass.

'That's enough thank you my gel,' he said, 'I'll thank you . . .' he was going on when a great braying laugh started out of the lamp-man. It swelled. It filled the room. Raunce said, 'Look what you've done,' and in his turn began to laugh. Kate joined in. So at last did Edith. These two girls did not giggle this time, they both deeply laughed. Only Bert was left as if embarrassed, twisting a fork over and over on the table.

'Why?' Raunce threw out at the first pause and in Nanny Swift's falsetto. 'All night? And in the same bed as well? Oh dear.'

'And I hope she enjoyed it there,' Kate pronounced, become serious.

'Now Kate!' Edith said starting to blush. Raunce watched.

'I got nothing against 'er,' Kate went on. 'She's all right she is. Because it's not natural for a married woman with 'er 'usband away at the war. Not that Mr Jack ever was . . .' but at this Raunce interrupted loud.

'Now then,' he said, 'what d'you know about bein' a married woman?'

'Not that 'e ever was much to go on with,' Kate finished dogged.

'You can say what you please,' Edith replied scarlet and they could all see that she was truly angry still. 'But 'e tried to get me in a dark corner one morning just the same,' she said.

''E didn't,' Raunce broke out.

'Oh there's no call for you to fash yourself Mr Raunce, there was no harm done nor offence taken if you're so keen to learn.'

'I'm sure it's no concern of mine,' he said and seemed on tenterhooks.

'Now you mention it I wouldn't say he'd never made a grab at me,' Kate brought out in a small voice. With great calmness Raunce commented,

'You surprise me.'

'You don't like to say he'd never but you never have said he did,' Edith cried and seemed to accuse.

'O.K. dear O.K. I know you found Mrs Jack and the Captain.'

'Of course I found 'em,' Edith remarked subsiding.

'Well now who's going to take her tray?' Raunce asked. 'Tell you what, I will.'

'But that would give 'er the idea you thought the Captain was up there yet,' Edith objected.

'Go on then I'll take the old tray,' Kate offered.

'Then she'll think I'm on to what she was doing last night,' said Edith.

'Well so she must if you did discover 'em.'

'All right dear I needs must then even if I should drop it,' Edith announced as she got up from table. She stood there and looked full at Raunce.

'It's not the job for a man, not this morning,' she said to him and went out.

'What d'you make of that Paddy?' Kate enquired but Raunce told her to shut her mouth with such sudden violence that she dropped her gimlet eyes. Then he went out to get the tray ready for Edith.

So it was left to Edith to carry up that breakfast which she did as though nothing had occurred. She found the mistress sitting in bed wearing her best nightdress and bedjacket. She did not look at Edith but said at once, collected,

'I'm going over to England by the night boat. Would you tell Raunce to get on the phone and reserve a cabin if he can? And ask the Nanny if she would come along to see me now?'

'To-day Madam?'

'Yes to-night I think. Not the day after to-morrow any longer. I've changed my plans.'

'Very good Madam.'

As Edith came into the passage outside and shut the door she found Miss Burch waiting white-lipped. This woman asked almost under her breath,

'Were you all right dear?'

'I was O.K.,' Edith whispered back. And then, 'She's leavin' tonight instead.'

'With him d'you wonder?'

'Oh no,' Edith replied serious, 'it stands out a mile she can't bring herself to face me. That's why.'

'There was nothing between the Captain and you was there my girl?'

'Are you crazy?' Edith broke out loud. Hearing this from inside the room Mrs Jack cowered, put a trembling hand over her lips, and pushed the tray to one side. 'Can you beat that?' Edith asked violent.

'Hush dear,' Miss Burch whispered. 'Very well then. We'll never mention what you saw again. You see I trust you. Never, you understand me?'

'Yes Miss Burch,' Edith replied. From her tone she was calming down. But as she went off to find the nanny she said to herself over and over, 'now would you believe it?' By the time she had got to the nursery she was repeating way down her throat, 'that's how they are at their age, they go funny.' And she gave Miss Swift the message as though to an enemy.

'This very moment?' this woman asked frantic.

'That's what she said.'

'Of all the times? And in the morning too? Then you'll oblige me by watching 'em till I'm back or they'll go dropping each other out to their deaths.'

While the nanny patted her hair, wiped her face with a

handkerchief and then, after hesitating, was gone, Edith stood slack at one of the high windows and did not seem to see those bluebells already coming up between wind-stunted beeches which grew out of the Grove on to that part of the lawn till their tops were level with her eyes. Also there was a rainbow from the sun on a shower blowing in from the sea but you could safely say she took no notice. Nor paid heed to the shrieks next door of two little girls at a game.

Miss Swift had been Mrs Jack's nanny when this lady was a tiny tot so she addressed her as Miss Violet. When told of the journey which had been put forward Miss Swift did not beat about the bush. She said roundly there was one thing poor old nanny felt to the heart and that was forgetfulness. For this day was to have been her afternoon out. If Miss Violet was going who was there left to look after the children when nobody cared? Or would silly old nanny have to go to the wall?

'How could you when I'm not feeling well?' was Mrs Jack's answer, delivered in a little girl's whining voice and she added, 'Edith can look after them perfectly.'

'Then who's to pack for you? Not me with my back Miss Violet.'

'I'd never thought. But if I asked Agatha nicely?'

'You're pale Miss Violet, you want a pill,' was Miss Swift's answer.

'Want a pill?' and the young woman spoke sharp now as if to ask what was behind this.

'When you're that colour it means you're constipated. Even if you don't know I should who cared for you from the start. Right pale. You lie there. I won't be a minute.'

Mrs Jack possibly knew better than to argue. 'Tell Agatha I want her then,' was all she said.

Miss Swift came across Miss Burch at once. Agatha might almost have been said to be on guard in that Long Passage.

'She wants you in there,' Miss Swift told her barely civil.

'Me?' Miss Burch enquired, 'what for?'

'I couldn't say,' Miss Swift replied, 'I don't meddle in other's business.'

'Well I'm not going,' Miss Burch announced. 'Not again. Wild horses couldn't.'

72

'What's come over you?' Miss Swift asked coming to a halt some distance up the passage. 'First I get impertinence from one of your girls which I don't pay attention to because I know how it is at their age always worriting over men and now you cast Miss Violet in my face. What's this?'

'I don't mind what you tell her you can please yourself but I'm not going in,' and Miss Burch added under her breath, 'And I could tell you something about your lily would make you say poor me but I won't.'

'That's nice I must say,' Miss Swift in her innocence replied. 'You draw your monthly wage yet you're gettin' like your girls, you want this and that besides.'

'You can leave my girls out of your conversation thanking you Miss Swift. They have more to put up with than you'll ever learn I hope.'

'Now you're being nothing but ridiculous. Poor nanny,' Miss Swift added and her face seemed to wrinkle as though about to cast a skin.

'No thank you,' Miss Burch said inconsequent and turned her back.

The nanny appeared to take hold of herself. She started on her way once more. 'I don't know I'm sure,' she said over her shoulder, making off to the medicine cupboard. She left Miss Burch outside that bedroom door but when she was back with a glass of water and a flat box in her hands, she found Miss Burch inside saying, 'yes Madam, no Madam,' at the side of the bed after all, plainly ill at ease yet taking instructions about what and about what not to pack.

But Agatha did not seem able to keep her eyes from those other pillows on Mrs Jack's double bed. These had been well beaten and the clothes were pulled up smooth over where that man's body must have lain yet she stared on and off. It must have been she could not help herself. Until the young lady told her to go as soon as she had so to speak been reinforced by Miss Swift's return. And Agatha left with a stiff back. Once she was gone.

'Now take a sip and swallow it right down,' the nanny said as she bustled. Then added, 'It's liver that's what it is dear. They won't trouble to give themselves a walk to loosen the bowels. They get fat on your food and cups of tea and with leaning on their brooms.'

'Who do?' Mrs Jack asked. She was probably unsure of everything and everyone.

'Why those that's paid to keep the Castle fit for us to live in,' the nanny replied.

'Oh I'm tired. Your little girl's not slept well,' Mrs Jack broke out.

'Now isn't that a shame? You just lie back and let that pill do its duty. I'll tell your angels you'll be wanting them around midday. You go on as your old nanny says and you'll have clear cheeks for the young man.'

On this she left. The lady fell back as though exhausted. But her breakfast tray was bare. She must have found strength in between to eat it all.

'Well I've got to take those little draggers out this afternoon,' Edith announced at dinner the same day. 'It's not fair I tell you.'

'Hey?' Raunce asked at his most serious, 'and you who has always made a point they were your favourites?'

'How's the work goin' to be finished? I'll ask you that,' she said quoting Miss Burch.

'You're the one to talk when you're not going to do none,' Kate put in.

'There'll be all the more for me tomorrer then,' was Edith's answer. 'You're not a girl to take on another's share and there's no reason why you should.'

'Now then that's plenty,' Miss Burch appealed to both.

'But there's a thing I won't do,' Edith went on in a lower tone, obstinately. 'Mrs Welch's Albert. Now I won't take 'im with them.'

'Be quiet both of you please. Oh my poor head. I've got a sick headache,' Miss Burch explained to Charley Raunce at which Kate muttered, 'I wasn't sayin' nothin'.'

'Look,' Charley announced at Edith, 'if you choose I'll come along.'

'Well that's a real step forward,' Miss Burch said looking kindly. Then she added as though unable to help herself, 'It should do you a mort of good.'

In spite of the differences grown fast as mushrooms and their bad temper on this day of days, Kate and Edith glanced at each other, a waste of giggling beginning behind their eyes.

'A turn in the air might be just what your sick headache needs,' he offered still at his most courteous to Miss Burch.

'Me?' she asked, 'and with all the packin' still to be done? A aspirin is all I shall get of fresh air this afternoon.'

'Well Edith could see to that while you took the children out,' Kate said. Her little eyes sparkled.

'Why you could never expect Miss Burch to go trail after them children when she feels the way she does, with God knows what Mrs Welch's kid will get up to,' Raunce said. 'About half past two then,' he went on to Edith, speaking rather fast. 'I'll be in my room.'

Kate started to choke, Edith to blush. Miss Burch did not appear to notice.

'I think I'll go lie down for ten minutes,' she informed those present. And Edith got out of Kate's sight by rising to follow her to ask if she would care for a cup of tea.

Outside, at a quarter to three, they both wore raincoats and Charley had his bowler hat. As the little girls raced about behind, Charley bent down, picked up two peacock's feathers which he offered to Edith.

'Whatever should I do with those?' she asked low.

'You wore one the week of the funeral,' he replied.

'Not now,' she said. They walked on with a space between. 'What's happened to all those blessed birds anyway?' he asked in a tired voice.

'It's the rain,' she answered. 'They don't like wet.' There was a silence.

'Tell you where they'd be then,' he began again. 'Away in the stable back of Paddy's room.' She made no comment. 'Should we go in that direction?'

'Not now,' she said.

'If you liked I could find you some eggs? I know where they lay.'

She laughed. 'Oh no thanks all the same. That kind's no use,' and crossed her fingers in the raincoat pocket, against this lie perhaps.

'What kind then?' he asked.

'Oh I couldn't say,' she said.

'I get you,' he answered in a doubtful voice. Once more they both fell silent.

Meantime Kate had slipped out to the lampman's where he kept corn for his peacocks. Paddy was awake. He showed no surprise when she entered.

'I wasn't goin' to carry on when nobody else was workin',' she announced.

He sat where he was and grunted.

'Not your baby,' she said, wandering about to inspect this and that. She seemed familiar with the place. It was certainly not the first time she had been alone with him.

'What this old dump needs is a good scrub out,' she said, 'only you're too Irish to give it.'

He spoke then. He spoke in English and quite free although his accent was such you could take a file to it. But she must have understood.

'Not me,' she replied. 'What d'you take me for? You do your own chores for yourself thanks. I don't want none.'

He laughed. His mouth was fringed with great brown teeth. His light eyes shone through the grey hair over them.

'Look at you,' she said coming up slow, swinging her hips. 'Have you got no pride?'

He laughed again but sat quiet. She turned away saying, 'Where did you put it then?' She made a search amongst oddments overlaid with dust upon a thick shelf. He followed with his eyes and did not turn his head. As a result for a full minute one pupil was swivelled almost back of the nose he had on him whilst the other was nearly behind a temple but he grinned the while. Then she turned up a dog's comb of tinned iron. She blew on this to dust it.

Lifting the piece of broken mirror glass off a wall from between four nails which held it at the edges she said,

'Take a load of yourself while I do yer.'

Standing at the back of him she began to comb his head. She worked like a simple woman that rakes a beanfield and jerked his head back with each pull. As the hair on his forehead was lifted it uncovered a line of dirt, a tidemark, along where the laid beans of his hair started grey and black. He tilted the glass he held to watch.

'Heed yerself and the state you're in,' she said. 'Give over watchin' me.'

He muttered something. For once she could not have understood.

'Say that again,' she asked.

He spoke rapid for about thirty seconds after placing the bit of mirror between his knees. He turned to face her.

'Well that's your look out,' she answered when he was done. Kate's arms lay along her purple uniformed sides. He smelled of peat smoke and she of carbolic. She added in a softer voice, 'You want to find one of your Irish women as'll see to you.'

He put out a paw like to sugar cake.

'No you don't,' she cried sharp and dodged back. 'What's more if you can't sit there quiet as gold I'll get me gone. I've got my share to do back in the Castle.'

He muttered. He faced the way he had been, picked up the glass again.

'That's right,' she said, 'though lord knows this is good labour wasted,' and began on his head once more.

Then she started to talk almost as though to herself.

''E's out, out in the air for a walk Mr Charley Raunce is, the first time since nobody can remember. Ah but she's deep our Edith, deep as the lake there. "Will I take the little angels out bless their little white hearts, sweetheart come too, along for the stroll." And if you don't believe you've only to risk a peek outside. Takin' 'is death he is. Round by the doves at the back I'll lay they are Paddy, billing an' all the rest. What d'you say to that you Irishman? Or they're over by the water. But what've you been at with your glory since I done it for you last? 'Ere,' she said, 'clear the combings off for yourself,' she said handing the comb back to him, 'I never made out I'd free the strakes for you into the bargain.'

Once her hands were disengaged she put these up to reroll her curls but halted before she touched. Then she sniffed at her fingers.

'Christ.' she said, 'what we girls have to put up with.' Then she added, 'You might give us a break and wash it occasionally.'

He said something.

'You got nowhere you mean?' she replied. 'Well I don't wonder they won't let you be free with their sink I must say. You've only to look at you. But what's wrong with a clean bucket? When Charley's little Bert has a mind to 'is boiler the water's O.K.,' she said and took the comb back. This time she began about his right ear. 'I'll give you a roll just 'ere exactly like the Captain. Oh the Captain,' and she laughed.

Paddy's enormous head began to show signs of order with parts of the tangle, which might have been laid by hail, starting to stand once more wildly on its own on his black beanfield of hair after a ground frost.

'But lord,' she remarked, 'whatever would my mother say to you Tarzan?'

'Look,' she announced, 'I'm fed up. You take hold and finish,' she told him handing back that comb.

'I'm fed up with you,' Mrs Welch said to her Albert at this precise moment as she sat him down at the kitchen table. 'So she wouldn't take you eh? Expect me to believe that eh?' She watched the boy with what appeared to be disfavour.

'That's what she said'm.'

'What did she say then?'

'When she come in the nursery I was like you said. I 'ad my coat zipped up and me 'at in me pocket. "No," she said, "not you Albert my little man, you go down in the kitchen," she says an' she give me a bit of toffee out of a bag.'

'Where is it?'

'I've ate it.'

'Is it in your pocket this minute along with your hat?'

'No'm.'

'Let me see if you're tellin' lies.' And Mrs Welch clambered to her feet, leaned right over that table. She felt in his coat.

'Is this it?' she asked bringing the thing out, a toffee in a screw of paper. She gingerly lowered herself back while she held this sweet out at arm's length, resting her bare arm along the table top. He made no reply.

'You wouldn't lie to me would yer?' she asked.

'No'm.'

'Then is this what she give you?'

He kept silent.

'You see what I'm goin' to do with this,' she went on, and unwrapped the sweet. Then she spat on it and threw the toffee into a can of ashes by the range. 'Now listen,' she continued, 'if ever I catch you taking what she offers I'll tan the 'ide right off you d'you h'understand?'

'Yes'm.'

'For why? Because she's a nasty little piece that considers we're not good enough for 'er, and very likely a thief into the bargain. With her precious Miss Moira this and little Miss Evelyn that. Never again no more. Right?'

'Yes'm.'

'And what are you goin' to do with yerself this afternoon of springtime that you can't go h'out with the others? I'll tell you. You're goin' to set to work my lad.'

The boy who had been gazing at the floor suddenly stared at her sharp.

'Yes,' she said, 'that comes as a bit of a surprise d'ain't it? Never you mind. You got to start some day. You won't always be runnin' around with gentry and their stuck-up maids. Now you see that saucepan, the one which's last on the left?'

He looked reluctant at three burnished rows hanging on the dresser, on nails through the holes in their steel handles.

'That's right,' she went on, 'the last on the left. You'll take that down so help me and you'll make a start scourin'. The young leddy was took faint. Took faint,' she repeated giving a short laugh as Kate had done. 'Yes. One time she was out with Mrs Tennant. "It's the pots and pans," Mrs T. says to me after. "You'll oblige me by casting a look on them Madam," I said. "I can't help it Mrs Welch," she says, "I'm certain there was something in that sole or its sauce." Sauce indeed. But she never listened. So now you're going to make a start scourin' them saucepans. Even if you bring all the tin off and they get copper poison. Get on then.'

The boy got up slow.

'And don't you go break that thread I've 'ad put through

79

the handles,' she cried frantic all of a sudden. 'You'll find where it's tied there by the side. I'm gettin' me chains and a padlock,' she explained grim as grim.

Kate had left the comb stuck at an angle in Paddy's head. The lampman sat where he was on a corn bin while she wandered round again. She came up to that glass division and looked through.

'Can a person eat them eggs?' she asked. He answered excitedly. 'That's all right,' she said. 'No need to get worked up. I only asked didn't I?'

He muttered something.

'Oh all right I know you set great store by the birds,' she replied, 'an' if you took one half the trouble over yourself as you do with their layin' why you'd be a different person altogether,' she explained.

He got up, made after her. 'No,' she said, 'no,' but she did not move as he came grinning. He reached round her middle and drank her in a kiss like a man home after a journey. He pressed her back against the glass that fronted that huge cabinet. Through the opening behind could be seen those peacocks getting up with a sort of chittering as though alarmed. She sank into him as her knees gave way yet both of them stayed decent.

Out in the demesne Raunce said to Edith, 'I got to sit me down.'

'You got to sit down?' she echoed as he looked dull about him.

'I've come over queer,' he said. Indeed his face was now the colour of the pantry boy Albert's.

'Why you're not goin' to faint right off like I did surely,' she exclaimed and clucked with concern. 'Sit yourself on this stone,' she said, 'it's dry for one thing.'

He sat. He put his new terrible face into his hands. They stayed silent. The two children came up, stood and watched him.

'Run along,' she told them gentle. 'Go find Michael.'

When they were alone Raunce spoke. 'It must be the air,' he said.

She stood awkward at his side as though she could not

think what to do. Then she said, 'If we were inside I could fetch you a cup of tea.' She talked soft with concern. He groaned.

'It's me dyspepsia,' he said. 'It's coming away in the air 'as done it.'

'But you do go out,' she replied low, 'I saw you when we were by the doves that dinner time.'

'That was only for a minute,' was his answer. 'But this long stretch . . .' and he ended his sentence with a groan. By and by however he grew better while she stood helpless at his bowed shoulders. After a time he got up. Then they summoned the little girls, tenderly made their way back to the Castle.

'You should take more care,' she kept on repeating.

It was some days later they sat in the servants' hall talking with dread of the I.R.A. They were on their own now, with the lady and her daughter still over in England, and the feeling they had was that they stood in worse danger than ever.

Kate asked the lampman if he had heard any rumours. Paddy gabbled an answer. As he did so he did not meet their eyes in this low room of antlered heads along the walls, his back to the sideboard with red swans.

Raunce's neck was tied up in a white silk scarf of Mr Jack's. He seemed to turn his head with difficulty to ask Kate what the Irishman had said.

'He says not to believe all you're told.' 'I don't,' Raunce put in at once. 'And that they're not so busy by half as what they was,' Kate ended.

Edith anxiously regarded her Charley.

'I should hope not indeed,' Miss Burch informed the company. 'Though I will say for Mrs Welch she was dead right when she forbade her girls passing the time of day with those tradesmen. Just in case,' she added.

'And what about their afternoons off?' Mr Raunce enquired.

'What I always insist is that if you can't trust your girls,' Miss Burch replied, 'you might as soon give in your notice and go find yourself another place.' She turned to Edith. 'Now you never speak to none of the natives when you get outside?'

'Oh no Miss Burch,' they both replied, mum about Patrick with his fine set of teeth.

'That's right,' Raunce told them. 'You can't be too careful. There's a war on,' he said.

'Are you in a draught?' Edith asked him tenderly. 'You don't want to take risks.' And Kate looked as though she might start a giggle any minute.

'There is a draught,' Raunce answered grave. 'There's a draught in every corner of this room which is a danger to sit in.'

'Move over to the other side then,' Miss Burch suggested.

'Thank you,' he said, 'but it's the same whichever side you are. I don't know,' he went on, 'but with them away now I feel responsible.'

'And what about the Jerries?' Kate put in suddenly. 'What if they come over tell me that?'

'Kate Armstrong,' Edith cried, 'why I asked you that selfsame question not so long since and you said they were ordinary working folk same as us so wouldn't offer no incivilities.'

'And I'm not saying they would,' Kate answered, 'not that sort and kind. But it might go hard for a young girl in the first week perhaps.'

'Mercy on us you don't want to talk like that,' Miss Burch said.

'You think of nothing but men, there's the trouble. Though if it did happen it would naturally be the same for the older women. They're famished like a lion out in the desert them fighting men,' she announced.

'For land's sake,' Edith began but Paddy started to mouth something. It was so seldom he spoke at meals that all listened.

'What's he say?' Raunce asked when the lampman was done.

'He reckons the I.R.A. would see to the Jerries,' Kate translated.

'Holy smoke but he'll be getting me annoyed in a minute. First he says there aren't none then 'e pretends they can sort out a panzer division. What with? Bows and arrows?'

Paddy muttered a bit.

'He says,' and Kate gave a laugh, 'they got more'n pikes like those Home Guard over at home.'

'If you can snigger at that you would laugh over anything my gel,' Raunce announced with signs of temper. 'Why you've only to go down in Kinalty and see yourself. Every other house burned right out. Once they got started they'd be so occupied fightin' each other they'd never notice Jerry was in the hamlet even.'

Paddy gave a great braying laugh.

'Laugh?' Raunce shouted and sprang up. All except for Miss Burch wilted and his lad's jaw dropped. 'You would would you?' he went on but the lampman had returned to wooden silence and Raunce subsided back into his seat again. 'Well,' he went on, 'if it should ever come to it there's guns and ammo in the gunroom.'

Edith gave a cry and Kate looked serious. But Miss Burch displayed impatience.

'Whatever's come over you?' she asked. 'You're never thinking you could knock down one of the Mark something tanks as you would a rabbit with one of those shot guns they've got locked up here?' she said.

'What I had in mind was a cartridge each for you ladies,' he replied in a low voice. Utterly serious he was.

'Would you spare one for Mrs Welch?' Miss Burch enquired tart and Kate let out a yell of laughter. Edith laughed also and after a minute Raunce himself joined in shamefaced. Paddy stayed impassive.

'You want to go delicate you know,' Miss Burch went on, 'you've no game licence.'

'You mean you wouldn't hesitate . . . ?' Edith began to ask him seriously but Charley interrupted her.

'I'd like to see 'em up in Dublin issue a permit over Mrs Welch as they do with the salmon trout,' he said to Miss Burch. At this they all laughed once more when Kate broke in with,

'Speakin' for myself I'd rather have the Jerry.'

'Under 'er bed,' Raunce made comment and even Miss Burch teehee'd wholehearted.

'There's the telephone,' Raunce announced. Bert got up to answer it away in the pantry.

Miss Burch fixed a stern eye on Kate so much as to say a minute or so ago just now you were about to be actually coarse.

'Well I don't aim to be shot dead. On no account I don't,' the girl explained.

'There's worse things than death my girl,' Miss Burch repeated. 'As anyone can tell you who remembers the last war.'

'I saw in the papers they behave themselves most correct towards the French people,' Edith said, still looking at Charley.

'What can you believe in these Irish rags?' Raunce asked.

'Well, there's one thing,' Miss Burch told him, 'they're neutral enough, they print what both sides say against one another.'

'Ah,' said Raunce, 'that's nothing but propaganda these days. It's human nature you've got to keep count of. Why it stands to reason with an invadin' army . . .' he was going on as Edith watched him open eyed when Albert came back.

'It was a wire for you,' he said to Raunce.

'Where is it then?' this man asked.

'Well there ain't no telegram,' was the answer he got. 'They read it out over the phone.'

''Ow many times have I told you never to take nothin' over that instrument without you write it down,' Raunce demanded in rising tones. 'Why I remember once at a place I was in, that very thing occasioned the death of a certain Mrs Harris. There you are. Killed her it did as if she had been blown in smithereens with a shotgun.'

'Go on,' the boy said respectful.

'Don't give me no go ons,' Raunce almost shouted at him. 'D'you know what you're about?'

'Yes Mr Raunce.'

'All right then.' The authority Raunce seemed to have acquired since Mr Eldon's death must have impressed them all. Even Kate gave him earnest attention. 'Now,' he went on, 'take your time. Don't rush it. What did the thing say?'

'Staying on for a few days Tennant, Mr Raunce.'

'Ho,' said Raunce, 'stayin' on a few days eh? That would

be Mrs Tennant then. Mrs Jack she signs herself different. Staying over eh? Leavin' us to face the music that's about the long and short of it.'

'D'you consider there's something likely to occur then?' Edith asked.

'I feel responsible,' he replied.

'For two pins I'd give in my notice,' Kate told them.

'How would you do that?' Edith enquired, 'when they aren't here?'

'Why I'd send it by post or I'd put it on a post card if I was in the mood,' the girl answered and there was a pause. 'I'm game if you are Edie,' Kate added, giving Edith a look that seemed highly inquisitive. But long before she could get an answer Charley was speaking, had so to speak thrown himself into a breach to stop the rot.

'Here,' he cried, 'what's all this, tell me that, what is it? I know the name it could be given, runnin' away, that's two words for it make no mistake. We're British aren't we? Turn tail and flee?' he asked in a loud voice. He glanced in menacing fashion at the lampman.

'Is it running away to get back to your own country to lend a hand?' Miss Burch enquired almost with amusement.

'And block the roads getting there?' Raunce asked.

'Why certainly,' she said, 'and block the roads, why not? If it's in the path of the enemy,' she said.

'But suppose they wished to evacuate the Governor General? Or the gold in the Bank of Ireland?' Raunce objected.

Paddy murmured something.

'There 'e goes again,' Raunce said and looked at Kate. 'What is it this time?'

'He says the Governor General is an Irishman an' would never go to England.'

'That's a bloody lie,' Raunce announced with finality. 'There's always been a Britisher in that job. Excuse me,' he added to Miss Burch, 'I seem to have forgot myself. Well what d'you know?' he went on. 'There's that telephone again.' Bert left the room. This time they kept uneasy silence till he returned.

'Well?' Charley asked the lad when he got back. He was handed a scrap of paper. He examined it. 'I can't read this,' he said.

'You should write down the messages neatly on a proper bit of paper,' Miss Burch told Albert. Raunce sat staring at what he held. 'There's times I despair of you my lad,' he moaned. Kate winked at Albert. 'Well come on, don't stand there dumb,' Charley went on, 'I can tell it's from Mrs Jack an' that's all.'

'Not returning for few days Violet Tennant,' the lad recited.

A silence fell over them once more. Then Kate saw fit to comment with what seemed like satisfaction,

'And that's the last we shall see or even 'ear of her if you ask me.'

'Why Kate,' Edith said, 'I never heard such a thing.'

'It was uncalled for,' Miss Burch pronounced, 'and what's more I don't wish another word spoken,' she added very grim. Silence fell yet again. At last Raunce broke the spell.

'Left all on our own,' he said with genuine emotion, seeming to ignore the others. 'How do you like that?'

Edith appealed to the lampman,

'But the Irish would act the same as anyone surely?' she put it to him, 'they'd be busy looking after their own if Jerry came? They'd never bother to protect us. They wouldn't have the leisure?'

He made no reply. It was Charley gave her an answer.

'And what about the panzer grenadiers ?' he asked. 'When they come through this tight little island like a dose of Epsom salts will they bother with those hovels, with two pennorth of cotton? Not on your life. They'll make tracks straight for great mansions like we're in my girl.'

'Mr Raunce,' Miss Burch reproved him.

'I'll ask you to excuse me Miss Burch,' he said. 'I got carried away for a moment. It's you ladies I can't get off my mind.'

'I know what I'd say if one of those dirty Germans offered me an impoliteness,' Edith said.

'And what good would that do if he didn't speak English?' Kate wanted to be told.

'This much,' Edith answered. 'He wouldn't be left in two minds even if he was only familiar with his own language.'

'Now look girl,' Raunce broke in gently, 'it's not only a question of one but of a whole company. Not just one individual but of above a score. Get me?'

'Oo a hundred,' Edith moaned. 'I ought to get away from here.'

Paddy spoke again indistinct as ever.

'Well what is it now?' Charley asked Kate.

''E says not to worry, they won't never come over.'

'I will not allow myself to get upset,' Raunce announced with what appeared to be excessive good humour, 'I've promised my lad here. But can anyone tell me what's to stop 'em,' he went on.

Paddy replied readily in sibilants and gutturals. Kate did not wait to be asked. She translated at once.

'Because the country's too poor to tempt an army he reckons, all bog and stones he says.'

'I'm going to lie down for a spell before I sit by Miss Swift,' Agatha announced as she got up to leave by way of the scullery. For the nanny had taken to her bed. No one paid attention. They all stared at the lampman.

'But let 'im satisfy me in this respect,' Raunce cried, 'what the condition of Ireland has to do with it? For one thing if it wasn't rotten land fit only for spuds we'd've been 'ere to this day, our government I mean. No we gave Ireland back because we didn't want it, or this part anyway. Nor Jerry doesn't want it. Then what is 'e after? I'll tell you. What he requires is a stepping stone to invade the old country with. Like crossin' a stream to keep your feet dry.'

'D'you really think so Mr Raunce?' Edith asked.

'I'm dead certain,' he answered.

'Then what are we waitin' for?' Kate wanted to know. 'If Michael drove us down this afternoon we could cross over on the night boat.'

'Hold hard a minute,' Raunce advised her, 'you're drawin' your wages. Right? You're gettin' what you thought was fair I presume or you wouldn't have come nor taken the place?'

'I wanted to get away from 'ome,' she interrupted.

'You wanted to leave home so you went into service,' he echoed. 'All right. You've been here 'ow long? Sixteen months O.K. All that period you ate their grub, took your wage, and didn't give more in return than would cover a tanner. I'm not blaming, mind, I've done the same. Now then when they're entitled to a month's notice you want to welsh no offence to cook. Don't call her cook she don't like it,' he added referring to Mrs Welch, and seemingly in high good humour.

'Forty quid a year and all found then to have a hundred Jerries after me no thank you,' she said.

'Kate Armstrong,' Edith cried out.

'Send in your notice then,' Raunce went on, 'there's nothing and nobody to stop you. But give them the four weeks that's coming to 'em. And be called up in the Army when you land on the other side.'

'What d'you mean get called up?'

'Didn't you know? They've Army police waitin' where the travellers come off the boat. You'll be took straight off to the depot.'

'I wouldn't go.'

'Then if you resist it's the glass 'ouse for you my girl.'

'The glass 'ouse? What's that?'

'Army Detention Barracks ducks. It's rough in them places.'

'Well I don't know, you are cheerful aren't you,' Kate said.

'That's right you forget all about it,' he answered. He winked his bluest eye at Edith so Kate could not see him.

Looking round the corner into the great kitchen Miss Burch said, 'I was going to have a lie down for ten minutes but here I am.' Mrs Welch was alone with her notebook. She did not look up. She called out,

'Jane a cup of tea for Miss Burch.'

Agatha sat down across the table from her. She did not speak again until the tea was brought. Then she came out almost tragically dramatic, in a very different tone to the one she had used in the servants' hall.

'They're not either of them coming back now,' she said. 'There's been a telegram. They're staying over.'

'Not ever?' Mrs Welch enquired sharp, drawing a tumbler of what appeared to be water towards her.

'Oh I don't go so far as that Mrs Welch,' Miss Burch replied, 'I wouldn't like to say they were never returning, but here we are now on our own and there's Raunce in there over his dinner upsetting my girls with his talk of the war and this I.R.A. worry.'

'I never let that man into my kitchen.'

'You're one of the lucky ones Mrs Welch. You've a place you can call your own.'

'Ah,' this woman answered, 'but run over by two-legged mice.'

'Can't keep nothing safe,' she went on after a silence, and took a gulp out of the glass. 'It's me kidneys,' she explained.

'I wonder you don't take that hot,' Miss Burch commented.

'Hot?' Mrs Welch cried. 'Not on your life not with . . .' and then she checked herself. 'It's not natural to sup what's been heated except when it's soup or broth,' she went on careful. Miss Burch eyed the tumbler. On which Mrs Welch put her head back and drank what was left at one go, as if in defiance. 'There you are,' she said to Agatha in a thicker voice.

'Very soon if he carries on in the way he's doing,' Miss Burch began again rather quickly, 'I'll remain to do the work alone. Even now with Miss Swift taken bad there's only Edith to look after the children.'

At this Mrs Welch without warning let out a shout of, 'Who took my waterglass tell me that,' and leaned right across the table.

'Bless me,' Miss Burch said, hurriedly drinking up her tea. 'But it's not as if it was any more trouble takin' your Albert out for the afternoons I'm sure. The girl's bringing a third along doesn't amount to nothing,' she said.

At this point, as Agatha was getting up to go, Mary the scullery maid came in the door.

'I spoke to the butcher'm,' she said.

There was a heavy silence. At last Mrs Welch replied unctuously, 'So you spoke in spite of what I said.' From her voice she might have been pleased.

''E said Captain Davenport had left for England sudden. Jane and me's wonderin' if per'aps they've learned something about this invasion.'

'Maybe there's something you don't know Mary,' Miss Burch said, 'and which has nothing to do with wars or rumours of wars.'

'I won't wear it,' Mrs Welch suddenly shouted out thumping the table. 'You'll get us all butchered in our beds that's what I tell you.'

'I was only out by the larder when he rang the bell'm an' I 'id behind the monument like you said but 'e must've catched sight of my dress for he came behind.'

'Did he?' Miss Burch announced with dignity. 'There's no end to it nowadays,' she said. She stopped by the door, turned back towards Mrs Welch. 'And the Captain's gone over you say? I shall go and lie down.'

'Well don't stand there lookin' Mary, get on with your work,' Mrs Welch remarked as if exhausted and once she was alone got out the key, unlocked the cupboard, and poured another measure of gin.

'For why?' she asked herself aloud, 'because it ain't no use.'

When they broke up after dinner in the servants' hall Albert went to clear away in the nursery. Kate followed to help. Paddy returned to his lamproom. This gave Raunce a chance to say to Edith quite formal,

'Have you seen the pictures in my room?'

She called him every day now with his early tea. So she said, 'What d'you mean?'

'Why the pictures I've hanged on the walls.'

She had done this bedroom out these last five weeks and had carefully examined what he had put in place of Mr Eldon's Coronation likenesses of King Edward and his Danish Queen.

'What's that?' she asked.

'It's brought a big improvement you'll see,' he answered, leading the way. He said twice to himself, 'if I make it seem ordinary she'll follow,' and did not look round for he heard her come after. But his legs went shaky. Probably it was trying to counteract this that made him walk stiff.

'Mortal damp these passages are,' he remarked as their footfalls echoed.

'You want to take care with those swollen glands,' she replied.

'That's why I've got it well wrapped round,' he said. 'Trust little Charley.' It was not long before he was opening his door and entering in front of her.

'Well?' he asked, 'what d'you say to that? Brightens the old place up doesn't it?'

Making herself dainty she looked once more at the two colourful lithographs of Windsor Castle, and the late King George's Coronation Coach, a plain house photograph of Etonians including Mr Jack in tails, and the polychrome print of scarlet-coated soldiers marching in bearskins. The frames were black and matched.

'The British Grenadiers girl,' he said hearty. 'Grenadier Guardsmen they are,' he said. 'Finest soldiers in the world,' he added.

She let this pass, merely enquiring if the pictures were not out of Mr Jack's old playroom and if he did not think they would mind his taking them.

'I don't pay attention,' he announced.

'So I notice,' she said.

'Well what's the object?' he wanted to know. 'They can't remember what they've got.' He was getting almost brisk with her.

'No,' she replied, 'but that's not saying they would never recognize a picture which is hung on the wall.'

'All right,' he said, 'what then? They couldn't make out I'd took it could they when it's in the house all the time.'

'Oh I'm not talkin' of that old picture,' she replied, not looking at him. 'There's other matters I've noticed.'

'Really!' he asked as though he had not made up his mind whether or no to be sarcastic.

'Yes Mr Raunce,' she said.

'Aw come on now,' he objected, 'you don't need to call me Mr Raunce, not when we're like this. I'm Charley to you as we are.'

'All right, yes . . . Charley,' she murmured.

'Listen dear you don't want to bother your head with what you see,' he began again.

'Me?' she answered. 'I'm not worrying.'

'Well then what is it you take exception to?'

'Oh nothing,' she said as if she did not care what he did.

'Should it be the lamp wicks now why they're just my perks since I come into the place,' he explained. 'I know old Aggie Burch reckons she tumbled something the other day and I don't doubt she's talked. But you needn't run away with the notion I put new wicks down in my book and then buy none. Why it's to get them a stock up. One day they might turn round to find there won't be wicks being made no more for the duration. If I didn't tell Mrs T. they were required I couldn't get any for 'er could I?'

'It'll be all right till they find you out.'

'No one ever found out Charley Raunce. Lucky Charley they call me.'

'It's the lucky ones have furthest to fall,' she said low.

'But what's it to you?' he asked as though challenging her. 'It's nothing to you,' he said.

'I do care,' she said and turned away abruptly.

'What's this?' he enquired chuckling, a light in his eyes. Coming up behind he laid hold of her shoulders. 'Here give us a little kiss,' he said. For answer she burst into noisy tears. 'Now girlie,' he cried as if stricken, dropped his hands and sat heavily down on the bed. He seized her wrist and began rubbing the knuckles.

'Oh I don't know,' she broke out keeping her head turned so he should not see and blowing her nose, 'it's all this talk of invasion – an' the Jerries an' the Irish – then what I witnessed when I called my young lady – an' you makin' out I never seen what I did – oh it's disgustin' that's what this old place is, it's horrible,' she said.

'Why whatever's up?' Raunce asked abashed, still rubbing the back of her hand.

'First you blow hot then you blow cold,' Edith said and snuffled.

'Blow hot then cold?'

'One minute you say the Jerries are comm' over,' she complained, 'and next you won't have a body try to get over home while there's time.'

He pulled gently on her arm. 'Come and sit by father,' he said.

'Me?' she said in a brighter voice. 'What d'you take me for?'

'That's better,' he said although she was still standing there. 'The trouble with you is you take everything so dead serious.

'And how do you view things for the matter of that?' she enquired.

'Here,' he replied, 'we don't want you jumpin' on me into the bargain. No me,' he went on, 'I take things to 'eart.'

'Yes?' she said and sat down as though bemused.

'I take things right down inside me girl,' he said putting an arm lightly round her. 'When I feel whatever it is I feel it deep. I'm not like some,' he was going on when she turned her face so that he looked into her eyes which seemed now to have a curve of laughter in their brimming light.

'Oh baby,' he said, reached out with his face. He might have been about to kiss her. She twisted slightly, came out with a 'now then,' and he ceased. 'Look,' he went on and put his other arm round her waist so that he had her in a hoop of himself and was obliged to lean awkwardly to do this. 'Look,' he said again, 'it's what is to happen to you I can't get out of my system, that I think of all the time.'

'And so you should,' she said.

'What's that?' he asked and began to pull at her. She put one hand loose on his nearest arm, holding it between a small finger and thumb.

'Well,' she answered looking away at the rain through that pointed window so that he could not see her face which was smiling, 'the two ladies are gone. They're not coming back are they? We're all alone Charley. We've only you to look to, to know what's best.' He relaxed.

'And you'd rather have it that way, eh ducks?' he asked jovial. 'What can Mrs T. do for you?'

'She can ring up them green police can't she?' Edith said

loud and sudden and pushed and shook his arms off while he stayed limp. One of his arms fell across her lap. He lifted it off at once. 'They'd never come for us, not them Irish,' she said.

'Come what for?' he asked confused.

'Why to protect us if the Germans took this place for their billets,' she said.

'You don't want to pay no attention,' he told her.

'Is that so? Then what do you need to go talkin' round it for?'

'It's you I'm concerned about,' he said.

Again she took a short look at him. This time it was as if he could not understand the flash of rage on her face. He put an arm through hers. As she turned her head away he said almost hoarse,

'Here, give us a kiss.'

'Lucky we left the door open wasn't it?' she said.

'Just a small one?' he asked. She got up.

'Have you cleaned your teeth?' she enquired.

'Have I cleaned my what?'

'Oh nothing,' she said. She did not seem so pleasant.

'Why,' he remarked, 'I brush them every morning first thing.'

'Forget it,' she said and wandered over to that group photograph of Mr Jack which she peered into.

'I can't make you out at all,' he complained, getting up to follow her.

'You will,' she replied. 'You will when those Jerries come over and start murdering us or worse in our beds. When the police begin to fight one another like you said they would.'

He stood back making motions with his hands.

'But it's you I was concerned over love,' he said.

'Me?' she took him up. 'What have I got to lose by goin' home? I'll thank you to tell me that. While if I stay on here there's worse than death can come. It'll be too late then. I got my life still to live Mr Raunce. I'm not like many have had the best part of theirs.'

'Just lately I been wonderin' if my life weren't just starting.'

'Well even if you can't tell whether you're comm' or goin' I know the way I'm placed thank you.'

'Look dear I could fall for you in a big way,' he said and he saw her back stiffen as though she had begun to hear with intense attention. She said no word.

'I could,' he went on. 'For the matter of that I have.'

At this moment she flung round on him and his hangdog face was dazzled by the excitement and scorn which seemed to blaze from her. But all she said was,

'You tell that to them all Charley.'

He appeared to rally a trifle and was about to answer when she exclaimed,

'Why Badger you dirty thing whatever have you got then?'

He turned to find the greyhound wagging its tail at him, muddy nosed, and carrying a plucked carcass that stank.

'Get off out from my premises,' he cried at once, galvanized. 'No wait,' he said. 'What've you got there mate?' The dog wagged its tail.

'Why d'you bother?' she asked impatient. 'It's only one of them peacocks.'

'One of the peacocks?' he almost shouted. 'But there'll be murder over this. No,' he added, 'you're having me on.' He made a step towards the dog which started to growl.

'That's right,' she said, 'Mrs Welch buried it away where none should see.'

'You're crazy,' he said.

'I'll have you remember who you're speaking to Charley Raunce,' she broke out at him. 'Mrs Welch thinks nobody's learned but this bird aimed a peck at 'er Albert's little neck so the little chap upped and killed it. Then she buried it in such a way that no one shouldn't know. The children told me. But I wouldn't have that stinking thing lying around in my part no thank you. Badger,' she said, 'you be off you bad dog.'

On which the dog deposited this carcass at Raunce's feet.

'Holy Moses,' he said, 'the old cow.' 'Now then,' Edith interrupted. 'That's all right,' he went on, 'I'm thinkin' of you ducks. See?'

'No I don't.'

'Well she's got it in for you about that waterglass an' now we've something on her. Get me?'

A noise of high shrieks and the clapping of hands

announced Miss Evelyn and Miss Moira, tearing along towards them down passages.

'For land's sake the children,' Edith exclaimed. 'Why I declare I forgot all about . . .'

Meantime Raunce had dashed out into the pantry snapping his fingers at the dog. It picked up the dead peacock and followed. Raunce shut that further door behind them both. For a moment Edith was alone as those children raced towards her the other way. Then they had arrived. She was holding her breasts.

'Mercy,' Miss Evelyn exclaimed with a trace of Cockney accent, 'why Edith you do look thrilled at something.'

Raunce's Albert came out of the door Mr Raunce had closed. He shut it again after him, on the butler and the dog and its find it carried.

'Hello Bert,' Miss Moira said.

'Hullo Miss Moira,' he replied. He just stood looking pale and miserable.

'You coming with us?' Edith asked. 'It's your afternoon off isn't it?'

'Oh yes,' he said, and a smile broke over his wan face.

'I got to get ready,' she announced. 'I'll race you two all the way up to my hide out. One three go,' she shouted and they were gone. The boy got out a handkerchief, blew his nose. His weak eyes shone.

As the three of them ran the front way through all the magnificence and the gilt of that Castle Miss Evelyn looked back. She cried,

'Why couldn't Bert race with us?'

'Because he's too old,' Edith called back panting, and steadied herself round a turn of the Grand Staircase by holding the black hand of a life-sized negro boy of cast iron in a great red turban and in gold-painted clothes.

Albert went behind the door to the cellar, unhooked his mackintosh and put on the rubber boots he kept there. It was not long before the others were back ready dressed to meet showers. Edith's head was in a silk scarf Mrs Jack had given her which was red and which had for decoration the words 'I love you I love you' written all over in black longhand with rounded letters.

Albert stayed silent while the rest argued where to go. At last they decided on that walk to the temple. Miss Evelyn had a bag of scraps to feed the peacocks. When they went through Raunce's pantry to reach the back door this man and the dog were gone without trace.

But as soon as they were outside rain began to come down so thick that they hesitated. Edith said not unkind,

'That's a silly thing Bert to come without a hat.'

He looked back speechless and plastered his long streaming yellow hair down one cheek with a hand. While those two little girls argued where they should go next to get out of the wet Edith looked at the lad derisively. She added as if in answer to a question,

'Oh it does mine good, the soft water curls my hair.'

Then while he regarded her, and he was yearning in the rain, Miss Evelyn announced they'd decided that they'd go play in the Skullpier Gallery.

'All right if you want,' Edith replied, 'but not through the old premises or we'll dirty 'em wet as we are,' for this Gallery was built on to the far portion of the Castle beyond the part that was shut up. So they ran along a path round by the back past the dovecote and any number of doors set in the Castle's long high walls pierced with tall Gothic windows. Running they flashed along like in the reflection of a river on a grey day, and smashed through white puddles which spurted.

Squat under this great Gothic pile lay the complete copy of a Greek temple roofed, windowed and with two green bronze doors for entrance. The children dashed through an iron turnstile, which clicked into another darker daylight, into a vast hall lit by rain and dark skylights and which was filled with marble bronze and plaster statuary in rows.

'What shall we play?' the Misses Evelyn and Moira cried. Their sharp voices echoed, echoed. The place was damp. Albert kept his mackintosh on. Edith took off her scarf. She was brilliant, she glowed as she rang her curls like bells without a note.

'Blind man's buff,' she said. 'Oh let's,' the girls cried. It was plain this was what they had expected.

'You won't have no difficulty telling it's me,' Albert

brought out as if he held a grievance, 'it's me,' the walls repeated.

'You stay mum or we'd never have invited you. We're not playing for you,' Edith told him.

On this there came a kind of faint mewing from the back. Albert started but stayed where he was while those others went hand in hand to see. Away in the depths, out from behind a group of robed men kneeling with heads and arms raised to heaven something small minced out into half light. It was a peacock which had come in to get out of the wet. 'You see her off these premises,' Edith told Albert, 'we don't aim to catch her when we're blindfolded. We don't want another death, the sauce,' she explained. But it took Albert some time to get the creature out. He had to make it hop over that turnstile which caused it to squawk spinsterish. 'You'll have Paddy after you,' Edith called to him at the noise.

When he came back he found Miss Moira had been chosen, had had her eyes bound with the sopping 'I love you.' She stumbled about in flat spirals under a half-dressed lady that held a wreath at the end of her two long arms. Stifled with giggling Edith and Evelyn moved quiet on the outside circle while Albert stood numb. So that it was he was caught.

'Mr Raunce's Albert,' Miss Moira announced without hesitation, her short arms round his thighs. 'Kiss me,' she commanded. 'Kiss me,' the walls said back.

He bent down. His bang of yellow hair fell at right angles to his nose. He kissed her wet forehead over the scarf. Her child's skin was electric hot under a film of water.

Then it was his turn. There was only Edith tall enough to tie him and as 'I love you I love you' was knotted over his eyes he quietly drew a great breath perhaps to find out if Edith had left anything on this piece of stuff. He drew and drew again cautious as if he might be after a deep draught of her, of her skin, of herself. He was puffed already when his arms went out to go round and round and round her. But she was not there and for answer he had a storm of giggles which he could not tell one from the other and which went ricochetting from stone cold bosoms to damp streaming marble bellies, to and from huge oyster niches in the walls in which boys fought giant boas or idled with a flute, and which volleyed under green skylights empty in the ceiling. He went slow. He could hear feet slither. Then he turned in a flash. He had Edith. He stood awkward one hand on her stomach the other on the small of her back.

'Guess then,' he heard Miss Evelyn tell him out of sudden silence.

'Edith,' he said low.

'Kiss her then,' they shrieked disinterested, 'kiss her,' they shrieked again. In a tumult of these words re-echoed over and over from above from below and from all sides his hands began to grope awkward, not feeling at her body but more as if he wished to find his distance. 'Kiss her.'

'Come on then,' she said brisk. She stepped for the first time into his arms. Blinded as he was by those words knotted wet on his eyes he must have more than witnessed her as his head without direction went nuzzling to where hers came at him in a short contact, and in spite of being so short more brilliant more soft and warm perhaps than his thousand dreams.

'Crikey,' he said and took the scarf off in one piece. He seemed absolutely dazzled although it had become almost too dark to see his face.

'You tie it dear,' she said kneeling down to Miss Moira. 'He's that awkward,' she said in a cold voice.

But there was an interruption. As Edith knelt before the child a door in the wall opened with a grinding shriek of rusty hinge and Raunce entered upon a scene which this noise and perhaps also his presence had instantly turned to more stone.

'I figured this was where you could be found,' he said advancing smooth on Edith. She had raised a hand to her eyes as though to lift the scarf but she let her arm drop and faced him when he spoke, blind as any statue.

'Yes?' she said. 'What is it?'

'Won't you play Mr Raunce?' Miss Evelyn asked.

'Playin' eh?' he remarked to Albert.

'It's Thursday isn't it?' Edith enquired sharp. 'That's his half day off or always was. What's up?'

'Nothin',' he replied, 'only I just wondered how you might be getting along.'

'Is that all?' was her comment. At which Albert spoke for himself.

'We was havin' a game of blind man's buff,' he said.

'So I perceive Albert,' the butler remarked.

'Oh do come on do,' one of the little girls pleaded but Edith chose this moment to take that scarf off her eyes.

'You surely didn't pass through all that old part alone?' she asked.

'And why not?'

'Oh Charley I never could not in a month of Sundays. Not on my own.'

'Is that so?'

'You are pleasant I must say aren't you?' she said.

'Thanking you,' Raunce answered.

'Oh please come on Mr Raunce please,' the child entreated. 'Edith'll give you up her turn.'

'I'm past the age and that's a fact Miss Evelyn,' Raunce said almost nasty. 'For the matter of that I chucked this blind man's buff before I'd lived as many years as my lad here. In my time if we had nothing better to do than lark about on a half day we got on with our work.'

'Here,' Edith said, 'just a minute.' She led him aside. 'What's up Charley?'

'Nothing's up. What makes you ask?'

'You act so strange. Whatever's the matter then?'

'Oh honey,' he suddenly said low and urgent, 'I never seem to see you these days.'

'That's not a reason,' she objected. 'You know I've got to look after them with Miss Swift sick as she is.'

'Yes,' he said. 'There's always something or other in the way each time.'

'How's your neck dear?' she asked as she strolled away. She gradually led him nearer and nearer the door he had come in by.

'Oh it's bad,' he said. 'It hurts so Edith.'

'Well you shouldn't stand about in a damp place like here,' she replied. 'For land's sake I don't know how you managed those passages alone. They give me the creeps. And what's become of Badger with the peacock?'

'I gave that dog the slip. All the brains he's got is in his jaw. Once he's dropped anything 'e's lost that dog is. I put it away where they'll find it in the outside larder.'

She slapped a hand across her mouth. 'You hung it in the outside larder?'

He smiled for the first time. 'That's right,' he said.

'Lord,' she remarked, 'what'll old Mother Welch say when Jane or Mary tells 'er?' She began to giggle.

'Don't call 'er cook she don't like it,' Raunce replied broadly smiling.

'Now look you mustn't stay here Charley with that neck of yours. You get back out of this damp. I'll see if I can't manage to slip down after tea.'

'O.K. ducks. Give us a kiss.'

'Don't be daft,' she said, 'what in front of all of them?'

'O.K. then,' he ended, 'I'll be seeing you.' And he shut that door soft although the hinges shrieked and groaned. Then he came in once more, stared at the mechanism. 'Wants a drop of oil that does,' he remarked, winked and was gone again. As he walked off into grey dust-sheeted twilight he said two or three times to himself, 'How she has come on. You'd never know it was the same girlie,' he repeated.

'At last,' Miss Moira called out back in the Gallery, 'I thought we'd never get rid of him. Kneel Edith,' she said pulling that scarf out of Edith's pocket.

Once Edith was blinded the little girls let out piercing shrieks and dodged as in laughter she moved her arms as though swimming towards them. Their cries reverberated round the Gallery. Miss Evelyn hopped on one leg pressing her snub nose upwards with the palm of a hand. When Edith came near, Miss Moira would turn and slip by Edith's blind wrists looking round over a shoulder ready to dodge again after Miss Evelyn had ducked under. But Albert stood like a statue and must have hoped he would be found. As he was. Yet when her fingers knew him which they did at once she murmured 'I don't want you,' and to shrieks from the others of 'You'll never catch us,' this immemorial game went on before witnesses in bronze in marble and plaster, echoed up and down over and over again.

Back in his room Raunce unlocked the drawer in which he kept the red and black notebooks. He verified that they were there. Then he drew pencil and paper towards him, laboriously made out the date and the address then settled down to write to his mother.

'Dear Mother,' he began, 'I hope you are well. I am. There has been nothing fresh here. Mrs Tennant has gone to England to stay. While she is over she hopes to see Mr Jack who is on leave just at present. Mrs Jack has also gone to be with them. So we are on our own here now and will be for a bit I expect.

'Mother I am very worried over this bombing for you. Don't wait until he comes to get your Anderson shelter fixed. Get it done now Mother dear and it will be something off my mind.

'I often wish I was with you dear but you know the way I'm placed. Once I should leave this country then I'm in their power over there. There's the Labour Exchange with the Army waiting. It's hard to know what to do best.

'Mother what would you say to your coming here. Who knows but there might be a change in my situation one of these days. You've often said it was time I settled down. But not a word to anyone dear, there's nothing said yet. But I've my eye on a nice little place in the park what the married butler before Mr Eldon had. Think of it will you Mother. And mind not a word not even to my sister Bell.

'Well I must close now. But I certainly am worried about you with all this bombing. Tell her, that's Bell I mean, to be sure and look after you all right. Your loving son Charley.'

Then he inked it in. And he wrote the address with his pencil and then inked that. Finally he slipped in the Money Order. After he had stamped the envelope he laid his head down on his arms and dropped off to sleep at once.

When a few days later as she lay in bed Miss Swift was paid a call by Miss Burch she was able to cut short the thanks having expressed what was necessary on the first of two visits of sympathy Miss Burch had already paid. But on the subject of her symptoms she left nothing out.

'I wonder you don't ask Doctor Connolly to put his rule over you,' Miss Burch remarked at last.

'Poor nanny,' Miss Swift exclaimed. 'That man?' she added as if injured.

'There's not another within reaching distance only the native doctors and we won't speak about them. Now they've taken their petrol away that is.'

'You'd never expect me to see him, Miss Burch, after what we witnessed every one of us with Mr Eldon. Why it was no more than a crime if I'm to put a name to it.'

'Mr Eldon he died of a broken heart Miss Swift. There was a lot he told nobody.'

'I'm sure I trembled for him as he lay there Miss Burch but then you see I knew. What training I've had was the best even if I've never served with a hospital. I could tell you things. There was a place I was in, I had him from a baby. The doctors gave him up, gave him up dear and they had two in from Harley Street. It was simple enough really. There he was such a good little chap. Lancelot his name was, his mother was Lady Mercy Swinley. Well one night when they were all gone I was watching for I never left his side, day and night I watched him yes, so I leant forward and looked into his little face and I could see he was going before my very eyes. It was all or nothing Miss Burch. So I took him up and I shook him. Yes and I slapped hard. My heart was in my mouth but he gave a kind of convulsive heave of his whole body and brought it all up. I'd known all along there was something stuck in his gullet but there they wouldn't listen. He brought it up. It was black as pitch. Then after I'd changed his bed things he fell into such a sweet sleep. Something made me do it there you are. But I shook so afterwards I dropped the cup when I poured myself a cup of tea. That hospital nurse couldn't fathom it once she came back. But I knew better.'

'Well,' said Miss Burch. 'But wasn't that the lady I read about the other day, the mother I mean?'

'Yes,' the nanny answered, 'times are hard for a number of them now, there's big changes under way. I shouldn't wonder if things were never the same say what you will. But don't mistake me. I wouldn't put myself above a doctor. Though

103

we can all bear witness about Mr Eldon how that poor man lay calling on a name and Doctor Connolly no more than paid him a call every so often, when we all know what we had under our very eyes with him growing weaker each day that passed, I don't say but someone might have taken matters into their own hands. And I'm sure they could have made free with my medicine cupboard and welcome.'

'You'll excuse me,' Agatha gently said, 'but that's a topic I can't mention.'

'Why certainly,' Miss Swift said bright. 'You don't want to take notice. The truth is,' she said frank, 'I'm an old woman and I'm growing simple.'

'Now Miss Swift . . .'

'Thank you,' the nanny interrupted rather breathless, 'and perhaps it's understandable. After all there's not a woman after a life spent with her charges but doesn't get an eye for illness. It may start as no more than a snivel when you put 'em to bed and then before you've time to adjust yourself you're right in the middle of it, day and night nurses under your feet with oxygen bottles and all that flummery. Prevention is better than cure I say. And there's many a one I've saved when those others in stiff cuffs had their backs turned.'

'I dare hazard it's no different to what I am with a floor,' Miss Burch said conversationally. 'Take a good polished parquet, now, that they've let go. With my experience I can tell at a glance, tell at a glance,' she said.

'There you are,' the nanny exclaimed and lay back grey about the lips. She was wrapped round in the huge crocheted shawl Miss Burch had lent her on the first visit.

'And there's some won't learn their lesson,' Agatha went on. 'Take Raunce. There's a man gone forty, been in good places all his life but his silver's a disgrace. I know of houses, houses I've worked in mind, where he could never have lasted seven days.'

'I won't have Arthur in my nursery.'

'Mrs Welch won't let him enter her kitchen. But then you've both of you a place you can call your own. Not like me with no more than a door opening into the sink and a bit of a cupboard in all this mansion. Now there's one woman been very different lately. Hardly the same at all. Mrs Welch.'

'Time was I wouldn't even venture into her scullery,' the nanny said, 'but since her little Albert's been over there's a noticeable change. He's a sweet child if he may be a bit of a monkey.'

'I suspicion whether it's all the child Miss Swift.'

'I've seen so many,' Miss Swift said, 'oh dear such a number I've looked after and not one but has a soft spot in their hearts for old nanny.'

'I shouldn't wonder if it wasn't the gin again,' Miss Burch said grim.

'Oh dear oh no I wouldn't wish to listen. Why fancy. Oh no I'm an old woman. I've seen things you'd never believe but I wouldn't wish to hear such a thing.'

'It's true for all that,' Miss Burch announced with what seemed to be satisfaction.

'There now I've forgotten every bit of it poor nanny,' Miss Swift replied. 'I don't know I'm sure but you gave me quite a shock with what you just said. But there, I've forgotten all about it. Bless me yes.'

'There's things I wish I could forget,' Agatha said in a far-off voice.

Miss Swift squirmed in bed.

'Take Raunce,' Miss Burch began, then stopped.

'You think I should be told?' the nanny asked.

'You'd never guess what he's been up to now,' Miss Burch went on adamant.

'I'm not strong, leastways that's how I've felt lately, weak,' the nanny muttered.

'He's took that peacock little Albert killed, which Mrs Welch hid away, and he's hung it in the outside larder. Swarming with maggots over our meat. How do you like that Miss Swift? It's wicked or worse it is.'

'Little Albert killed?' the nanny cried with a sort of wail.

'No. One of the peacocks crossed 'is path so he up and killed the thing. That's a flea bite, there's plenty more of the creatures. But from what I can make out Mrs Welch must have took umbrage. And who is there to say she was mistaken if she thought her life in peril even with that mad Irishman with his ear to every keyhole? So she put it back of a piece of cheese cloth away in her kitchen. Then she thought she'd dispose of the thing after, one way or another, but the carcass turned up again in such a fashion as Raunce could get hold of it. Crawling with maggots all over which is what my girl Kate tells me. Can you imagine the like Miss Swift? Infecting all our food.'

'Oh dear,' the nanny said come over limp. 'Arthur. I see yes, Arthur.'

'But that's a trifle,' Miss Burch continued placid yet firm, her eyes on her knitting. 'Now I went into the Red Library after dinner to see to the fire. Mrs Tennant will have fires lit to keep the rooms right for the pictures. And d'you know what I found. Why Edith and that man, the impudence, sat back in the armchairs they'd drawn to the fender. As if they owned the Castle.'

'Oh dear,' Miss Swift moaned.

'"Why whatever's this," I said,' Miss Burch went on. ' "It's my neck," he answered me. "Your cheek my man," I said and then Edith she did have the grace to get up on her two feet after that. But he went on sitting there. "What's it to you?" he asked though I could see he was ashamed for both of them. "Just this," I said so he couldn't be in doubt upon it. "There's right and wrong," I says, "and there's no two ways about which this is," I said.'

'His neck?' Miss Swift asked faint. 'You never can tell. Oh dear perhaps if I could have a glance.'

'He's kept his neck wrapped up the last two weeks,' Miss Burch announced, 'he makes out the glands are enlarged. But it's his whole head has swelled.'

'They can be dangerous swollen glands can,' the nanny said firmer.

'Well if you ask me things will go from bad to worse if Mrs Tennant won't come home soon. And I love that girl of mine Edith, I love that child Miss Swift.'

'She's a good girl Miss Burch. The children will do anything for her.'

'There it is Miss Swift, she's had her eyes on him a long time and wishing's not likely to make things different. But I'm afraid for her with that man. He's up to no good,' Miss Burch pronounced and then paused.

The nanny did not seem anxious for more. She merely repeated once again, 'She's a good girl Edith is.'

'I've never had a better,' Miss Burch began afresh. 'There, I'll go so far as that, never a better under me,' she said. 'In this great rambling place we have a week's cleaning to do each day. But you can depend on her. And that's something can't be said of the other, Kate. Sometimes I even wish with that one I'd been given an Irish girl to train up instead.'

'No Roman Catholics thank you,' Miss Swift said sharp.

'Yes,' Miss Burch agreed, 'we don't want those fat priests about confessin' people or taking snuff.' She stared from her knitting at Miss Swift for a moment. 'Are you feeling quite well?' she asked.

'Me?' the nanny said in a quavering voice. 'Thank you I'm sure. Poor nanny . . .' she began as if about to continue but Agatha broke in, 'Then that's all right. But I'm sorry for the girls nowadays,' she announced. 'It puts me in mind of the South Africa war. They see the men going out to get killed and it makes them restless. I remember how it was with me at the time. Then they look at us old women and they say to themselves they don't wish to end up like us. I was the same at their age. It's only after they've lived a few years longer that they'll come to realize there's worse than sleeping alone in your own bed, with a fresh joint down in the larder for dinner every day.'

'And a pension at the end, not just the old age,' Miss Swift put in quite bright once more. 'It was a weight off poor old nanny's mind I can tell you when they asked nanny to come back to Miss Violet after she'd done for her from a baby. To take on her own child's sweet babies the little angels.'

'Ah Mrs Jack,' Miss Burch announced in a voice of doom.

Miss Swift looked askance. She hurriedly went on, 'And two of the best behaved little girls as ever I've had in my charge,' she said, 'so loving with their pretty little ways the lambs. There's but one thing I could wish which is that there were more children round about for them to play with. You know Miss Burch it's not right at the age they are and with their position in life to have none but themselves. I was right glad when Mrs Jack told me about this Albert.' She paused for breath.

'Ah Mrs Jack,' Miss Burch put in as though sorrowing.

The nanny set off again, more breathless still. 'Of course it's the times,' she said. 'Now even after the last war they would never have entertained it, the very idea. Why a boy like Albert, the cook's own nephew, dear me no. Never in your life. But it's come about. It's the shortage. Having no petrol,' she ended and lay back, blue about the lips.

'What was revealed came as a great shock to me,' Miss Burch said and paused to pick up a dropped stitch. The nanny rested herself with closed eyes. There was a silence. 'A great shock,' Miss Burch repeated getting up speed once more with her knitting. Miss Swift did not utter.

'They can do what they like after all,' Miss Burch went on, 'there's little or nothing we can say will make any difference when all's told. Yet I've got to consider my girls. It's not so much the example. Enough goes on in any farm yard. But there's the upset to a girl of Edith's age coming from a good home. I'm afraid for her.'

'She's a strong girl,' Miss Swift said faint, 'I can tell.'

'That's as may be,' Miss Burch replied, 'but going to call the lady and then to turn round after drawing those curtains to find the Captain Davenport in her bed as well why . . .' Miss Burch said and pursed her lips. There was no response so she looked up full at Miss Swift. This woman was lying back eyes closed or rather screwed shut in a wild look of alarm.

'There,' Agatha added and returned to her knitting, 'I never meant to tell you. It slipped out. These last days I've been afraid it would throw my Edith right off her balance. It's her I mind for.'

'They imagine things that's how it is,' the nanny murmured. 'I remember when I was a girl. Always imagining I was till I didn't rightly know.'

'I saw him don't worry,' Miss Burch said in a loud voice. 'Why I thought she was going to faint away into my arms when she came out. Of course the moment she told me I went straight in. And there she lay the young lady naked as the day she was born with him just putting his shirt on. It didn't take me long to come away again I can tell you.'

'She was all the time the sweetest child,' the nanny said in a stronger voice. Miss Burch looked at her quickly, saw her face was smooth now, that she seemed peaceful. 'Miss Violet had such lovely golden hair,' Miss Swift went on, 'the only child I knew to keep it always. On her wedding day it was the same, oh dear. What a number of years that is to be sure.'

'So I told Edith, Miss Swift, how she'd best be off out of it. The less said the better I told her. And the next time we were alone I insisted she shouldn't pay attention, that what they did was no concern of ours. But she's took it to heart. I know. There's times I feel desperate.'

'Such a picture in white when she come up the aisle. Dear me it's a strange thing but I feel quite tired. I fancy I'll take a little nap.'

'Are you sure there's nothing you'd like, a cup of tea or something?'

'No thank you Miss Burch all the same.'

Agatha got her knitting together. She cast another glance at Miss Swift who was very blue about the lips.

'You're sure there's nothing now?' she said once more. 'You wouldn't like me to change your hot-water bottle?'

'No I'm quite comfortable,' the nanny answered. 'I just wonder if I won't have a little nap that's all.' So Miss Burch left. As she closed the door she said to herself, 'Well she never thanked me for coming but then I shouldn't have let my tongue run on. But she never took it in even. We're both getting old women,' she repeated aloud as she went along the white linoleum in that corridor and walked to one side over the purple key pattern border.

Miss Burch never told the nanny that her protest to Raunce and Edith had been without effect. Edith it is true had risen to her feet when she left them but Charley had not stirred. And now as Agatha went slowly to her room with a pounding heart, Edith down in the Red Library was back in what used to be Mr Tennant's special easy chair. She hardly seemed comfortable however for she was protesting,

'. . . and, well, I don't like it.'

'Now ducks,' he said.

'I don't want to set her against me Charley. It's me has to work with her. Not you after all.'

'She's got nothing on us,' he replied, 'no one has.' At that a silence fell between them. Then she let out careless in a low voice,

'Charley I found the ring.'

'What ring?' he asked as though talking of daisy chains.

'Why,' she explained with sudden excitement, 'Mrs T.'s ring she mislaid before she went away. I chanced on it the other afternoon.'

'She's always losin' valuables,' he remarked casual, 'the wonder is she gets them back so often.'

'That's what I mean,' she said.

'I don't get you.'

'Suppose she didn't get this ring back?'

'Well you're goin' to give it her surely? You don't want to hand it over to our Agatha so she claims all the credit. Stand up for yourself love. You found the object. You hand it back and gather the reward though I'm afraid you'll be unlucky there you know.'

'What I was wondering was suppose I never offered the old ring back?'

'Here,' he said, 'easy on. Knock the ring off you mean?'

'Keep it,' she agreed. She seemed overexcited.

'Where is it?' he asked.

'Hid here in the lining,' she replied and got up. She forked the thing out of a tear with her finger. Her hands trembled.

'Let's have a look,' he said. 'You know you want to go steady with suggestions like the one you've just put forward. See,' he said holding the ring on a level with his chin. It winked and glittered at him. He smiled on it. 'Christ,' he said low.

'Well Charley what d'you say?'

'I tell you this won't do,' he answered. 'Put'm back where you found'm.'

'Put it back where I found it,' she echoed as though dumbfounded.

110

'Yes so they can't discover the old loot on you and call that stealing by finding. Go on,' he said, 'I hate to do this but put'm back.'

'An' then what?' she wanted to know and pouted.

'The minute Mrs T. returns you go up to her and say you came by it as you were doing this room out.'

'I thought you'd have a better use for it than that,' she said.

'I don't follow you,' he said extremely cautious.

'What d'you keep writin' in those notebooks then?' she asked.

'I have to make up my accounts I put before Mrs Tennant each month,' he replied in an educated voice.

'Oh yeah?' she said.

'You've got to understand,' he said.

'It'll take a lot of understandin', Charley.'

'Listen I'm not makin' out I can be accurate down to the last cork or that when someone comes to stay they don't forget to put back a pencil they've taken off one of the tables.'

'You're telling me,' she said.

'But there's no place for valuables like this object,' he went on. 'You've got to see that dear. Why you'd gum up the whole works.'

'I can't fathom you,' she said. 'Here's a ring may be worth hundreds. It's been missed. It's lost and you want me to hand it back. There's no sense in a thing like that.'

'What would you do then?'

'I'd sell it an' save the money for a rainy day,' and she gave him a look as if to say the sky always rained at weddings.

'You're crazy,' he said.

'I'm crazy am I,' she cried, 'right then I'll act like I was,' and snatching that ring from his fingers she threw it in the fire.

'Now look what you've done,' he said going down on his knees. He fished it out with a pair of tongs. 'That'll need cleanin' that will. You leave me.'

'Leave what to you not very likely,' she said as though beside herself. 'I wouldn't trust you no further than that fender. Give here.' She grabbed the ring back again.

'Ouch it's hot,' she said dropping the thing on the rug. They stood looking down and from the droop of her shoulders it could be assumed that her rage had subsided.

'For land's sake I do feel awful,' she brought out.

'Now honey you don't want to take things so awkward,' he said putting an arm round her shoulders. 'There's nothing to get wrought up over,' he explained. 'I was only goin' to give it a rub so that when you gave it back to Mrs T. she wouldn't notice the difference. And look,' he said, 'you've no sense of proportion. If I make me a few shillings each week fiddlin' the monthly books that don't mean I can go and knock off valuables. That's dangerous that is. Besides what I'm on to is steady, ducks, get me? While I hold down this job I can put by something all the time.'

'What do you put by?' she asked not looking at him. There was a short silence during which she seemed to listen intently.

'Why a bit here and a bit there,' he said.

'And I don't suppose it's worth the small risk there is in it,' she broke out sudden.

'I don't know love but maybe there's two or three hundred a year one way or another all told.'

'Pounds?' she asked making her eyes big.

'Lovely British Bradbury's,' he answered.

'Oh Charley,' she said in admiration, 'so that's what you're on to?'

'And that's a sight less than old Eldon drew. But he was at the receiving end of some very special money.'

'What d'you mean?'

'He'd kept his eyes open. He wasn't so slow. Tell you the truth I never did give him credit till I come upon it the other day. He'd got your Captain weighed up.'

'The Captain?' she asked eyes shining.

'Those were my words.'

'But I mean that's worse than takin' a ring ain't it Charley?'

'Depends how you mean worse,' he replied. 'All I know is it's secure.'

'D'you stand there an' tell me Mr Eldon had come upon them some time? Just as I did? That she sat up in bed with her fronts bobblin' at him like a pair of geese the way she did to me? Is that what you're sayin' ?' She was so excited again that she fairly danced before him.

'Oh I don't know,' he replied cautious and as if he was shy.

'There she sits up at me . . .' Edith ran on, eyes sparkling. And he had to listen to the whole thing again, and with embellishments that he had never heard, that even he must have doubted.

Raunce's Albert, Edith, Kate, the little girls and Mrs Welch's lad chose for their picnic a place just off the beach. While those children ran screaming down to where great rollers diminished to fans of milk new from the udder upon pressed sand, Albert laid himself under a hedge all over which red fuchsia bells swung without a note in the wind the sure travelling sea brought with its low heavy swell. He could watch the light blue heave between their donkey Peter's legs and his ears were crowded with the thunder of the ocean.

'Fat lot of use you are,' Kate shouted to him as she began to unstow the panniers on Peter's back.

'Ain't there a glare,' he called.

'For land's sake you're not goin' sick on me surely like Charley did when I brought him out?'

'Don't he look pale?' Kate echoed Edith.

'Never mind let him be,' Edith went on, 'and we'll allow he may light the Primus.' She laughed, probably because it would never start up without a deal of coaxing.

'Did you remember your matches?' Kate yelled. On which he got to his feet to bring out a packet of cigarettes.

'Lawks we've took a man along,' Kate mocked. He offered them round. As he cupped his hands to shield the flame and Edith bent her lovely head he lowered his yellow one over hers. She giggled which blew the match out. 'One thing at a time thank you,' she remarked looking him in the eye from close. He blushed painfully. Then the wind sent her hair over her vast double-surfaced eyes with their two depths. As she watched him thus, he might have felt this was how she could wear herself in bed for him, screened but open, open terribly.

'Come on,' she said, 'snap out of it.'

Then all three huddled round as if over a live bird sat between his palms till their fags were lit. He collapsed back onto the ground.

'You wouldn't be looking up our legs by any chance now would you?' Kate enquired in an educated voice. For answer he rolled over onto his stomach and faced inland, all Ireland flat on a level with his clouded eyes.

'Let him be,' Edith said again. The wind blew a sickle of black hair down the opening of her dress.

'It tickles,' she said giggling, and swung her head back to let that breeze carry the curls off. 'Oh this wind,' she added. And it drove the girls' dresses onto them like statues as they lifted rectangles of white cartridge paper tied in string out of the panniers to lay these where sand joined that moss short grass. Then Edith stopped to gently pull Peter's ears.

'Aw come on,' Kate called to Albert, 'you don't want to go sulking away there. Why I daresay she'd never've minded if you had of 'ad a peep.'

'Now Kate,' Edith repeated, 'why can't you let him alone.'

'I never,' the lad cried turning over to face them, 'honest I never.'

'Well then don't act like you wished you did.'

'Katie,' Edith said and bent down to kiss the donkey's nose. She seemed altogether indifferent. At this moment little Albert interrupted.

'Can I take the shrimpin' net'm. There's 'undreds down there in that pool we're at.'

And so the long afternoon started. Then when they had had cup after cup of tea Albert in lighting Kate another cigarette set fire to a thin curl of her fair hair. She took this in good part, did no more than exclaim at the smell.

''Er peacock didn't half cause a stink,' he told them. The wind had dropped. They no longer had to shout. But the roar of that Atlantic swell was heavy.

'What peacock?' she asked.

'Why the one old Charley put back in the outside larder. Mrs Welch must've bided her time when there was nobody in the pantry so as to slip down and stuff 'im in my boiler.'

'In your boiler?' Edith shrieked. 'Whoever's heard?'

'Didn't you smell it at that?' the lad enquired.

'It's the first I've known,' Kate said.

'He created something alarming Charley did,' his lad

continued. 'He said there was enough to give us asthma and 'e went about coughin' for two days.'

'She's up to a lark then,' Edith said seemingly delighted. 'Bless us,' she added, 'look what he's after now,' she exclaimed. All three saw little Albert hopping round and round with a fair-sized crab fastened onto a toe of his sandshoes. The excited shrieks that came back from the children blanketed a screaming from gulls fighting over the waste food which they had thrown away although Raunce's Albert still had some scraps in a paper bag.

'Let 'em,' Kate said and closed her eyes again. 'I've got what I've had to digest yet,' she added. Then just as Edith was about to get up to help that crab fell off. The children began to stone it, driving it blow upon blow into a grave its own shape in the sand. At which Peter put his ears back and snatched the scraps out of Albert's hand, swallowed them bag and all.

'Why you ugly bastard,' Albert said scrambling out of the way.

'Now Albert,' Edith remarked indifferent.

'I thought 'e was asleep,' the boy explained.

'Which is what I would be if you'd only shut down,' Kate said from behind closed eyes. Her eyelids were pink. The sun warm.

As he was about to settle again Edith invited him to use part of the mackintosh on which she was seated adding that he would only spoil his indoor suit. He was dressed in the blue serge double-breasted outfit a livery tailor had made him on Mrs Tennant's instructions.

'You do look a sight,' was her comment, 'got up as you are like you were goin' in Hyde Park.'

He lay down at her side while she sat bolt upright to keep an eye on the children.

'I got a sister over at home,' he said low.

'What's that?' she asked careless. 'I can't hear you with the sea.'

'I got a sister works in an airplane factory,' he began. If she heard him she gave no indication. 'Madge we call her. They's terrible the hours she puts in.'

He lay on his stomach facing inland while Edith watched the ocean.

'I've only her and mum left now,' he went on. 'Dad, 'e died a month or two afore I came here. He worked in a fruiterer's in Albany Place. It was a cancer took 'im.'

When he broke off the heavy Atlantic reverberated in their ears

'Now Mr Raunce writes to his,' he continued, 'and can't never get a reply. And there's me writes to mine, every week I do since this terrible bombing started but I don't ever seem to receive no answers though every time 'e comes over I'm afeared mum an' sis must've got theirs. To read the papers you wouldn't think there was anything left of the old town.'

'That young Albert,' Edith yelled against the sea, 'I regret we took him along.'

Raunce's Albert looked over his shoulder on the side away from Edith but could not see how his namesake was misbehaving.

'You see with dad gone I feel responsible,' he tried again loud. 'I know I'm only young but I'm earnin' and there's times I consider I ought to be back to look after them. Not that I don't send the best part of me wages each week. I do that of course.'

A silence fell.

'What did you say your sister's name was?' Edith asked.

'Mum had her christened Madge,' the lad replied. He tried a glance at Edith but she was not regarding him. 'To tell you the truth,' he continued, 'I did wonder what's the right thing? I thought maybe you could advise me?' He looked at her again. This time she was indeed contemplating him though he could not make out the expression in her enormous eyes behind the black yew branch of windblown hair.

He turned away once more. He spoke in what seemed to be bitterness.

'Of course I'm only young I know,' he said.

'Well it's not as if they'd written for you is it?' she announced, on which he turned over and lay on his side to face her. She was looking out to sea again.

'No but then they're like that. Mum always reckoned she'd

116

rather scrub the house out than take a pen. Madge's the same. It's 'ard to know what's for the best,' he ended.

'I should stay put,' she said, speaking impartially. 'You're learnin' a trade after all. If they should ever come for you into the Army you could be an officer's servant. We're all right here.'

'Then you don't reckon there's much in what they say about this invasion? If there's one thing I don't aim at it's being interned by the Jerries.'

'Oh that's all a lot of talk in my opinion,' she answered. 'You don't want to pay no attention. Oh me oh my,' she said, 'but isn't it slow for a picnic. Here,' and at this she leant over him, 'let's see if we can't set old Kate goin'.'

She picked up a stray bit of spent straw which was lying on his other side then lowered all the upper part of her body down onto his, resting her elbow between him and the sleeping girl. Her mouth was open in a soundless laugh so that he could see the wet scarlet roof as she reached over to tickle Kate's sand-coloured eyebrows.

Kate's face twitched. Her arm that was stretched white palm upwards along deep green moss struggled to lift itself as though caught on the surface of a morass. Then still asleep she turned away abrupt till the other cheek showed dented with what she was lain on. She muttered once out loud 'Paddy.'

At this Edith burst into giggles bringing her hand still with its bit of straw up to her mouth as, eyes welling, she looked direct into Albert's below her. He lay quiet and yellow in a simper. This brought her up sharp.

'Can't you even have a joke?' she asked.

'Well you're a pretty pair no mistake,' Kate said and yawned. They found she was sitting to rearrange her tow locks.

'Not so comical as you, you believe me,' Edith answered removing herself from off Albert. He turned over onto his stomach again, facing Ireland.

'What have I done now then?' Kate wanted to know. 'Can't a girl treat herself a nap?'

'Forget it dear,' Edith told her.

117

'I don't know as I want to forget,' Kate replied. 'It's not nice finding people makin' fun of you when you're asleep.'

'It's only what you brought out love,' Edith sweetly said.

'What was that then?'

'You called a name.'

'Is that all,' Kate announced and blushed, which was unusual with her. 'Why from the fuss you two made lain right in each other's arms you'd imagine it might be something serious.'

'We wasn't,' Albert said sharp, twisting his head towards her. His eyes did not seem to see.

'Oh all right let it pass,' Kate replied. Her blush had gone. 'But you can take it from me what I witnessed was sufficient to make them precious children look twice if they'd noticed.'

'Just let 'im be,' Edith said indifferent.

'There's one thing I won't have,' Kate quoted looking with malice at Edith, 'an' that is the children bein' worried by it the little lambs.'

Edith gave a short laugh.

'Why who said that?' Albert asked.

'Miss Swift.'

'What for?' he enquired.

'And I say she's an old duck stickin' up for them,' Edith interrupted. 'They don't want to be bothered with what I witnessed, not yet awhiles any old how. They got plenty of time to learn.'

'You mean what you saw when you called Mrs Jack?' the lad said scornful. 'That old tale?'

''E won't believe it yet,' Kate announced as if delighted.

'Call it a tale if you will,' Edith answered. 'There's many a time I've wished I hadn't been the one. But you ask Agatha Burch if you disbelieve me. Stark naked she sat up in bed as the day she was born.'

'Get out?' Albert politely said.

'Well she's right Miss Swift is,' Edith added above the boy's head. 'Their mother's everything to them I should hope? Nor you'd never get 'em to believe if you did tell them. Not like you and someone I could mention.'

'That's enough,' Kate said violent. 'I've had all I can stomach from . . .'

'Land's sakes,' Edith called scrambling to her feet, 'will you just look what they're at now all three,' she cried making off at a run down to the ocean.

'Come on,' Kate said, 'give us a kiss when she's not lookin'.'

But he would not, did not even bother to reply. Yet the moment Edith came back he rolled over to ask if she had forgotten she had still to return him that gauntlet glove.

'What glove?' she asked as she sat down once more. 'Why the one you had full of eggs it must be six weeks since.'

'I got one or two things of hers when Mrs T. arrives,' she said. 'How's that Edie?' Kate asked opening her gimlet eyes.

'Oh nothing dear, nothing which is to say that concerns you, Edith sweetly answered. 'It's only that she will leave things lying idle.'

'Like her ring,' Kate commented shrewd. 'Which was worth more than an old king's ransom I'll be bound.'

'Which ring?' the lad enquired.

'Why Albert I will admit you're chronic,' Edith said. 'You mean to lie there and tell us you never heard of Mrs Tennant's ring that was mislaid.'

'I never heard nothing.'

'No more he would,' Kate announced. 'He's simple that's all.'

'Well,' Edith said, 'I made sure you must have. It was only that she's lost another valuable, a ring this time. But I chanced to come upon it the other day.'

'You did?' Kate exclaimed sitting up, 'an' you never told me.'

'Oh I've got it hid away trust little Edith,' Edith announced dully. 'They're never goin' to pin a thing on me they can call stealing by findin'. Once she gets back I'll tell her just where she'll come upon it,' she said.

'An object like that,' was Kate's comment.

'It's hid well away. There's only Miss Moira I've showed to an' she'd never tell. I worship that child,' Edith said.

'There you go again,' Kate exclaimed, 'when she's right under the thumb of Mrs Welch's precious lad. They both are. After what 'e done to that peacock one or two sapphires in a ring would be mincemeat for 'im.'

'So you've seen it,' Edith asked suddenly intense.

'Me?' Kate wanted to be told. 'Not me I never.'

'How do you come to know it was a sapphire ring then?'

'Because I've got eyes in my head, silly. I've seen 'er wear it.'

'Oh if that's all,' Edith pronounced turning away again. 'From the way you talked I thought you must've known.'

'So you 'id the ring away then?' Albert said.

'Well what else could I do, use your sense do. I didn't want to hand that over to Agatha Burch so she could get the credit did I?'

'She'd've told you were the person that came across it.'

'That's what you think Albert. You talk like one of these Irishmen you're so innocent but then there's more behind what they say than they let on to. If you want to know they're an improvement.'

'Edie,' Kate said in an admiring voice, 'you've changed.'

'Too true I have,' Edith answered, 'but there you are you see. Circumstances alter cases,' she said.

'Over at Clancarty,' Kate began, 'that Captain Davenport strips 'is men naked when their day's work diggin' is done to see they don't take nothing. Paddy says the priest 'as taken the matter up.'

'I bet you wishes you was there,' Albert surprisingly remarked.

In reply Kate fetched him a swipe with the back of her hand across his cheek. He scrambled up while she sat on fists clenched, ready to fight and get the better of him. But he walked off and did not say a word. The dejected donkey followed at his heels. Against the everlastingly hurrying ocean with its bright glare from the beginning of the world, he wandered with the donkey drooped to his tracks as if he was a journeying choirboy.

'The sauce,' Kate said.

''E's only a kid,' Edith remarked and lay back along the sand after spreading out 'I love you' for her head. She looked straight up at the sky without wrinkling the skin about her eyes.

'There's times I could go scatty in this old country,' Kate

announced calm as though nothing had occurred, 'I could really. Come on let's have one of them talks like we used to. Now what about you for a start? You tell your own girl what it's like to be loved.'

'Kate you are awful.'

'Come on now there's no one to hear with this sea. Your boy friend is in the sulks along of 'is precious donkey. You tell your Kate.'

'Oh him,' Edith said, 'you want to go easy with him. What you let slip when we woke you upset Bert.'

'What d'you mean?'

'Oh I wasn't referring to that name you mentioned.'

'Then what you're gettin' at Edie is my poking fun at you lyin' over 'im to reach me?'

'That's right. You see Kate 'e's touchy. It's calf love.'

'Don't make me laugh,' Kate said scornful. 'Calf love you call that? Why you talk like you was your young lady. We got no time for calf love dear as you call it. We're ordinary workin' folk. 'E'll be going off in a faint next.'

'Just because when I see a mouse caught by its little leg in a wheel and he opens a great mouth at me . . .'

'Now then,' Kate interrupted, ''old on. I wasn't gettin' at you. I don't know why we can't be like we used to I'm sure but nowadays we don't seem able ever to do anything but go sarky at one another.'

Edith turned away from her once more. 'O.K. let it pass,' she said.

'But surely you don't intend to permit that lad to go moonin' after you like a drowned duck?'

'Well what d'you want me to do then?' Edith asked her.

'You should've seen 'is face when you was leant over. It was enough to make me bring up my dinner. And you lookin' down into his eyes as though you liked it.'

'If he'd so much as touched me I'd've shown him dear I can tell you,' Edith said. 'I'd've given a lesson he'd remember all his life,' she added.

'Well if you want my advice that's what I'd learn the kid before this day is done.'

'Why,' asked Edith, 'you don't suppose I relish his goin'

mushy surely? A child like that? He wants his old mother, that's his trouble. But live an' let live is what I always say.'

'Then don't you keep on about me and you know who,' Kate said.

'O.K. dear. Now let's have a nap,' said Edith.

And in no time both were well away. The children got wet through.

Raunce's Albert crept back followed by the donkey that he could not rid himself of. He sat down by Edith. He never took his eyes off her body.

Edith found out that Agatha had a cup of tea most days with Mrs Welch. So she persuaded Miss Burch to put forward a claim to tea all round after dinner, a privilege not enjoyed by the others since before the war. Everyone was surprised when the cook agreed. But that was not all. Edith feared for Raunce's neck. She said those draughts in the servant's hall might harm him. Now coal was so short it was only a small peat fire she could lay each morning in the butler's room, and she insisted that the grate Raunce had was too narrow for peat. This no doubt could be her excuse to get him to take his cup along with her to one of the living rooms where huge fires were kept stoked all day to condition the old masters.

So it came about next afternoon that Charley and Edith had drawn up deep leather armchairs of purple in the Red Library. A ledge of more purple leather on the fender supported Raunce's heels next his you-and-me in a gold Worcester cup and saucer. Pointed french windows were open onto the lawn about which peacocks stood pat in the dry as though enchanted. A light summer air played in from over massed geraniums, toyed with Edith's curls a trifle. Between the books the walls were covered cool in green silk. But she seemed to have no thought to the draught.

'You ever noticed that little place this side of the East Gate?' he was asking.

'Well I can't say I've looked over it if that's what you're after,' she replied. He hooked a finger into the bandage round his throat as though to ease himself.

'Next time you pass that way you have a look, see.'

'Why Charley ?'

'It's empty that's why.'

'It's empty is it?' she echoed dull but with a sharp glance.

'The married butlers used to live there at one time,' he explained. Then he lied. 'Yesterday mornin',' he went on canny, 'Michael stopped me as he came out of the kitchen. You'll never guess what he was onto.'

'Not something for one of his family again?' she enquired.

'That's right,' he said. 'It was only he's goin' to ask Mrs T. for it when she gets back, that's all. The roof of their pig sty of a hovel 'as gone an' fallen on 'is blessed sister-in-law's head and's crushed a finger of one of their kids.'

'The cheek,' she exclaimed.

'A horrid liar the man is,' Charley commented. 'But it's not the truth that matters. It's what's believed,' he added.

'You think she'll credit such a tale?' Edith wanted to know.

'Now love,' he began then paused. He was dressed in black trousers and a stiff shirt with no jacket, the only colour being in his footman's livery waistcoat of pink and white stripes. He wore no collar on account of his neck. Lying back he squinted into the blushing rose of that huge turf fire as it glowed, his bluer eye azure on which was a crescent rose reflection. 'Love,' he went on toneless, 'what about you an' me getting married? There I've said it.'

'That'll want thinking over Charley,' she replied at once. Her eyes left his face and with what seemed a quadrupling in depth came following his to rest on those rectangles of warmth alive like blood. From this peat light her great eyes became invested with rose incandescence that was soft and soft and soft.

'There's none of this love nonsense,' he began again appearing to strain so as not to look at her. 'It's logical dear that's what. You see I thought to get my old mother over out of the bombers.'

'And quite right too,' she answered prompt.

'I'm glad you see it my way,' he took her up. 'Oh honey you don't know what that means.'

'I've always said a wife that can't make a home for her man's mother doesn't merit a place of her own,' she announced gentle.

'Then you don't say no?' he asked glancing her way at last. His white face was shot with green from the lawn.

'I haven't said yes have I?' she countered and looked straight at him, her heart opening about her lips. Seated as she was back to the light he could see only a blinding space for her head framed in dark hair and inhabited by those great eyes on her, fathoms deep.

'No that's right,' he murmured obviously lost.

'I'll need to think over it,' she gently said. Folding hands she returned her gaze into the peat fire.

'She's a good woman,' Raunce began again. 'She worked hard to raise us when dad died. There were six in our family. She had a struggle.'

Edith sat on quiet.

'Now we're scattered all over,' he went on. 'There's only my sister Bell with the old lady these days. There's her to consider,' he said.

'The one working in the gun factory?' she asked.

'That's right,' he replied. Then he waited.

'Well I don't know as she'd need to come to Ireland,' Edith said at last. 'She's got her job all right? I'd hardly reckon to make the change myself if I was in her position.'

'You have it any way you want,' Raunce explained. 'I thought to just mention her that's all. Mrs Charley Raunce,' he announced in educated accents. 'There you are eh?' He seemed to be gathering confidence.

She suddenly got up half turned from him.

'I'm not sayin' one way or the other, Charley. Not yet awhile.'

'But it's not no for a start,' he said, also rising.

'No,' she replied. She began to blush. Seeing this he grinned with an absurd look of sweet pain. 'No,' she went on, 'I don't say I couldn't.' And all at once her mood appeared to change. She whirled about and made a dive at the cushion of the chair she had been using.

'What's more I'll wear this old ring for the engagement,' she crowed, 'oh let me it won't only be for a minute.' He approached doltish while she hooked with her finger in the tear. 'That's funny,' she said. 'Why it can't have,' she murmured. 'But it has,' she announced drawing herself up to look him in the face. 'It's gone,' she said.

'What's gone?'

'Mrs Tennant's ring,' she said.

'It can't have,' he objected. 'Give here,' and he took that cushion, ripped the seam open. 'Must've slipped inside that's about the long and short of it,' he said as he worked.

'I don't know about can't have gone,' she said looking intently at him with something in her voice, 'but it's not there that's all.'

He felt round the edges.

'You're right,' he pronounced, 'there's nothing.'

'Yet a ring wouldn't have wings now would it?' she said meaningly.

'Edie,' he said, 'if you think I took that you must consider me worse than the lowest thing which crawls.'

'No,' she murmured, 'I don't,' and leant over to give him a light kiss.

'Then you ain't never found nothing, see,' he said putting his arms round her. 'Oh honey . . .' he began when both heard a car turn towards the Castle over the ha-ha.

'Look sharp,' he brought out as if she had been kissing him. 'That must be Mrs Tancy,' he said and turned to go. 'Holy smoke,' he added, 'but I can't answer the door dressed as I am.' While Raunce hastened out she went on her knees it might be to make believe she was only in the room to do the fire.

His training probably induced Charley to close the door soft after him and it was not until he had reached his quarters, when he was out of earshot, that he began to yell for Bert. So nobody saw this car drive up but Edith. She noted in it not the lady above referred to but a stranger, a man, a grey homburg hat.

His boy came running in a green baize apron. At that moment the bell rang. 'The front door,' Raunce said as the indicator chocked, 'I'm wrongly dressed. Put 'er in the Red Library an' don't leave till I come or something might go missing. Not like that,' he almost shouted as Albert made off tied in green, 'let's 'ave that down,' he cried as he twitched at

the bow it was knotted with, 'an' where's your jacket?'
Raunce got the lad away at last discreetly clad, calling out to
him, 'I won't be a minute while I dress.'

So it was Albert received Michael Mathewson at the
entrance, who took this man's business card when he asked
for Mrs Tennant. The lad held it upsidedown. In consequence
he could not read the name or the line in Irish below,
underneath which came a translation between brackets which
went, 'Irish Regina Assurance.' There was finally a Dublin
address in the right-hand corner.

'This way please,' Albert said the way he had been
taught. He led the man over the chequered marble floor.
Mike Mathewson followed fat and short and bald with blue
spats.

'That's to say they're not here,' the boy piped over his
shoulder.

'It'th O.K. thon,' Mike lisped.

So it was Albert showed him in where Edith was still on her
knees after a proposal of marriage, as if tidying. As
Mathewson passed Albert probably remembered twice for he
sang out again. 'This way please.'

'Thankth thon,' the man replied. Edith turned away from
them and began a fit of giggling.

'Nithe plathe you've got,' he remarked bright in her
direction. Albert closed the door gently, stood so it seemed
unobserved and ill at ease. He licked a palm of his hand then
smarmed his yellow hair.

'The familieth away?' Mr Mathewson enquired picking up
the paper-knife with the agate handle.

'Yes sir,' Edith made answer. She looked for a second time
full at him seriously with her raving beauty.

'That'th all right girlie,' he brought out and goggled a trifle.
Then he put that paper-knife down. He came near.

'I'll do thomething for you,' he announced soft, 'I'll put you
in the way to make a fool out of Mike. That'th me. There'th
my bithueth card he holdth. It'th thith way. We'll maybe have
a little bet on thith. I'll wager thixpenth you can never gueth
my bithneth.'

On this she rose to her feet, back to the fire. Her eyes were large as she smoothed her dress. He turned round as though to give her time.

'You're in on thith thon,' he called urgent, soft, but the lad made no move.

'It's Mr Raunce you want,' she interrupted.

'That'th all right,' he answered, 'I'm not thelling anything. I gave up thelling when trade got thlack. I'm an enquiry agent,' he brought out sharp, turning to her close.

'What?' she muttered and began to blush.

'Yeth that'th a thurprithe ain't it,' he went on seemingly delighted. 'Now you'd never have guethed ith'nt that right without you'd theen my bithneth card. Mike Mathewthonth the name. Jutht had a tooth out that'th why I thpeak like thith,' he excused then laid a hand genteel across his mouth. He took it away at once to finger the spotted tie. He was now very near indeed. He smelled of acid of violets.

'I come down when they claim a loss,' he brought out sharp, not lisping.

'Oh,' she said faint.

'I reprethent the Inthuranth Company,' he explained again.

At this precise moment out by the dovecote little Albert was with Mrs Jack's little girls. He knelt down while Miss Evelyn and Miss Moira stood dappled by leaf sunshine. The lad himself was shaded by that pierced tower of Pisa inside which a hundred ruby eyes were round.

'You're not ever goin' to bury it Bert?' Miss Evelyn enquired.

'Naw,' he replied picking up half an empty eggshell.

The sisters squatted. Opening his fist he displayed the ring, a small blaze of blue. He scooped it into that eggshell which he then placed with the unbroken end upwards, a pale bell over the jewel, under a tuft of sharp grass.

'You won't leave that out in the open?' Miss Moira asked.

'It's on account of them birds pinch rings,' he answered. 'If Mr Raunce come to find'm then we don't know a thing, the pigeons took'm see.'

'But doves don't steal rings Albert, you mean jackdaws.'

'Don't be so soft,' he said. 'Everyone knows doves will,' he ended.

'You'll lose it,' Miss Evelyn announced wondering.

'Rings don't walk,' he said, 'an' this shell's so them birds won't rout'm out,' he explained. 'They'd never think to turn an egg that's broken.'

'Well you are clever,' Miss Moira told him and meant it.

'I'm smart don't fear,' he said, 'only I didn't ought to let you girls in on this. You'd never keep a secret. So you'll 'ave to take a oath see.'

'An oath?'

'That's right. You're to swear you won't never tell. It'll be special. This is 'ow it goes. While I break a cock's egg over your mouth you say, "My lips is sealed may I drop dead."'

'Cock's eggs?'

'Peacock's softy. I'll fetch me a couple.' As he ran off to that door he had seen Raunce come out of on another occasion he called back as he stumbled with urgency, 'Don't you stir from where you be.' He had picked up countrified expressions when he was evacuated.

'Well it's wicked I know,' Miss Moira said with satisfaction.

'How will you swear so the egg doesn't get in your mouth?' Miss Evelyn asked.

But they waited. In almost no time the lad was back. Then one of the girls objected. She said she wasn't going to stand for having that filthy sticky stuff on her face. The other wanted to know who she considered she was to think she couldn't, when Edith had hundreds of these eggs put away in waterglass against the time she might want them for her skin. And little Albert heard. And then made them both go through with it. They seemed delighted.

Meantime the assessor had been asking questions. Edith did not know so she said. Or she could not tell for certain she was sure. Mike Mathewson was getting nowhere. Albert kept silence. Then Raunce at last arrived, in his dark suit and without the bandage. He came quiet and Mike Mathewson did not hear him. He had to clear his throat to make this man turn round.

'Yes sir?' Charley asked.

'That'th all right my man,' Mike answered. 'Making a few enquirieth that'th all.'

It might have been Raunce thought Edith looked upset. Not moving from the door he took a line.

'I'm sure Mrs Tennant would not wish for questions asked,' he said.

'Precithely why I wath thent,' Mr Mathewson replied, a green high light following out his nose.

'I'm afraid we can't have this,' Charley said firm. 'Mrs Tennant would never allow it.'

'Is it so?' Mike said grim, not lisping.

'I will have to ask you to leave that's all,' Charley went on and did not call him sir.

'But I have been thent.'

'Who by?'

Then Edith must have forgot herself. She interrupted.

'It's about the ring,' she said in a small voice.

'What ring?' Raunce wanted to know without a sign of any kind.

'Let'th thee,' Mike suggested. 'When Mr Tennant wath alive you uthed to be hith man I take it.'

'No I was not.'

'And you never heard of a ring being gone?' Mike asked in menacing fashion.

''Ow d'you mean?' Raunce enquired in a less educated voice.

'That'th thtrange,' Mathewson said almost genial, 'nobody theemth to know nothing.'

'What's strange about that?' Charley asked and began to squint. 'Come on you tell me. Who might you be for a start?'

'You're the butler?'

'What's that got to do with you? It's you we're talkin' about. Who're you?'

Edith broke in again.

'He's come about the insurance,' she explained and appealed.

'Nobody asked you,' her Charley said sharp but with a soft glance in her direction. 'You don't know nothing,' he added.

'Know nothing?' Mr Mathewson echoed. 'Mark what I'm thaying now. I never inthinuated thith young lady knew anything.' He spoke gently as if to ingratiate.

'In – what?' Charley asked.

'Inferred,' Mike Mathewson explained and now he spoke sharp. 'Don't try and be thmart with me. You'll find it don't work.'

'I wouldn't know what you're referrin' to,' Raunce said a bit daunted.

'The ring,' the assessor replied soft. 'The thapphire cluthter my company inthured on.'

'Is Mrs Tennant acquainted with you?' Raunce asked.

'She called us in,' the man said very sharp, again without lisping. 'Now is that sufficient?'

'She called you in?' Raunce echoed.

'You do know about the ring then?'

'Know about it? I've 'eard Mrs Tennant mislaid one.'

'Then why tell me jutht now you never did,' Mike asked him very quiet.

Raunce began to bluster. 'Me?' he cried, 'me tell you that? I never made any such statement and this girl and my lad here's my witnesses. What I very likely said was I didn't know your business an' I say I don't know it now any more than I did at the start. There you are.' He glanced as though for support at Edith. She was gazing at the seat of the armchair. She seemed distracted.

'Will you anthwer a fair quethtion?' Mr Mathewson began again. 'That'th above board ain't it?' he said almost friendly.

'Reply to a question? Well I don't know before you ask me do I?' Raunce replied.

'Then you won't anthwer?'

'I never said that. What are you tryin'? To trap someone?'

'Who mentioned a trap? I'm here to trathe a ring.'

'What's that got to do with me?' Raunce enquired.

'I don't know yet,' Mike replied gentle.

'Well get this then. I don't know nothin' an' I'm not sayin' nothin' without Mrs Tennant gives permission. So now have you got that straight?'

They stared at each other. Edith went down on her knees again. She began to polish the bright steel fire irons with a leather. Catching Charley's eye behind Mike's back she shook her head urgent at him. Albert stood as though transfixed.

'Mithith Tennant thent for me to come over before she got

130

back,' Mr Mathewson began again. This time he appeared to speak to Albert.

'Mrs Tennant's comin' back?' Raunce cried.

'Tho I'm led to underthtand.'

'Then thank God for that,' Raunce said relieved. 'She can clear a whole lot up Mrs Tennant can. But if she don't all I'll say is she can have my notice. Arriving down 'ere to bully the girls, then treatin' me like I was a criminal.'

'Lithten,' Mike began again as if tired. 'A ring'th been mithed. A very valuable thapphire cluthter. My company'th been called on to dithburthe. I've come down to invethtigate. I've driven a hundred mileth. Now do you underthtand?'

'O.K.,' Raunce answered. 'And now you can tell me something. What's all this to do with me?'

'I'm asking you that's all,' the assessor said with sudden venom. Again they stood and stared at one another. Then Raunce's Albert spoke.

'I got it,' he confessed.

'You what?' Raunce shouted. Edith jumped to her feet. Raunce swallowed three times and began an, 'I tell you,' when Mike Mathewson brought him up sharp, fairly hissing.

'I've had about enough d'you hear me? Now then my lad we're getting placeth. You got it?'

Albert was trembling but he stood his ground.

'Come on then,' Mike continued. 'Nothing to be afraid of. Where've you got what?'

The boy was silent in a palsy. There was a sort of lull. Edith went over and knelt by him, arms by her sides, as though he was very small and was to tie the scarf over her eyes. Until she turned on the assessor, blushing dark.

'He got an idea he meant an' who may you be to come scarin' honest folk that earn a living?' She spoke loud. 'You get off h'out, there's the best place for you. We don't want none of your sort here, frightenin' his wits out of the lad. How should we care about her old ring? If I was a man I'd show him off the premises,' she said panting to Raunce.

'That's an idea,' this man replied. He began to move slowly over to the assessor who started to say, 'What idea did the young chap have?' Only to break off with a 'now then,' as he moved backwards to the open french windows away from Charley.

'Plantin' words into people's mouths like it was evidence,' Raunce almost chanted as he advanced. 'When a lad says he got an idea makin' out he got the ring.'

'Well what wath the idea?'

'It's a disgrace that's all,' Charley said, now very close. 'You go on off see?'

'All right I'm on my way,' Mr Mathewson announced. Then he had the last word. 'But get this. We're not paying,' he said and went.

'Wait till 'e's gone,' Raunce warned the others.

And Mike Mathewson drove off quick.

As soon as the car had cleared the ha-ha Raunce rounded on Albert. He was shouting in passion, dead white with a wild squint.

'So you got it,' he yelled, 'you got what? I got it,' he shrieked in falsetto. 'And you can have at that. 'Ere you are then 'and over.' He came at Albert who seemed paralysed. 'Where is it then?' he cried like an epileptic as he shook him. 'Where is it?' Albert's head swung back and forth, his yellow shock of hair flopping. But the lad kept silent.

'That's enough Charley,' Edith said. 'He's never had it.'

'But 'e might 'ave,' Raunce answered desisting. His rages never lasted. '''E's capable of anything that lad is. Why there was none spoke to 'im. I don't suppose there was one of us in this room remembered 'is presence. An' then what must 'e go an' do. Why bless my soul if 'e doesn't feel the need to sing out 'e's got the miserable object. Holy Moses,' Charley ended, apparently in better humour. 'But that was smart of you love to think that one up. It was you had the idea all right. Now don't start snivellin',' he said to Albert who began to cry in the painful way boys do when they are too old for tears.

'Charley,' she said, 'what did that mean when 'e said his company wouldn't even pay.'

Mr Raunce explained. Albert's sobs grew louder but they paid no attention.

'Then that's awkward Charley. I mean it may come back on Mrs Tennant.'

'Well she's lost so much, girl, I shouldn't wonder if the Insurance Company would never take her on a second time. Once one refuses her I don't suppose she'll get any to insure her jewellery again. That's the way it goes.'

'Yes but look here then that's serious that is Charley.'

'Serious you bet the thing is serious,' he replied. 'But you wait until I get this lad of mine to meself. Just give me two minutes alone with him.'

'Oh him,' she said indifferent, 'don't trouble your mind over him.'

'And why wouldn't I when 'e knows? My God what an afternoon.'

'He never took it,' she told him without so much as a glance at Albert. 'He did what he done for me. He thought that inspector was makin' out I'd had it.'

'He what?'

'He was,' she said. Albert sobbed suddenly unrestrained as though somehow he had come unstoppered. 'You don't understand these things, I do,' she said. Then she bent down. Before Raunce's eyes she kissed the lad's cheek. 'There, thanks kid,' she said. But Albert, not looking, made a move to strike her away without however hitting her.

'Did you see what 'e done then?' Raunce asked low. 'I'll learn 'im.'

'Let him be dearest,' she advised and the boy ran out. Raunce shut the door Albert had left open.

'Well I don't know,' he began, taking her by the shoulders. She looked into his face. 'The dirty tyke,' he said. 'But we got to find it.'

'All right,' she replied, 'an' I'm goin' to start with my Miss Moira. You go off, I'll handle this best alone. And don't you lay hands on that Albert. It's the other I have my suspicions of,' she ended.

When Raunce was gone she went to the window. She called the child.

The little girl came running, stood moist in the sun before Edith.

'Where've you been Miss Moira?' She asked sweet.

'Why out by the dovecote Edith.'

'Look at you then,' Edith scolded gently and squatted down. 'Just see the state you're in. You'll be landin' me in such trouble if you don't take good care when your grandma gets back.'

'Is grandma coming?'

'She is that,' Edith said smiling as she began to clear up the child's glowing face with her own grubby handkerchief.

'Is mummy too?'

'I couldn't say love. Whatever've you been at to get in such a state?'

'I hope mummy doesn't come.'

'Hark at you,' Edith said letting it go.

'I do. 'Cos that Captain Davenport will be over all the time when she does.'

'Hush dear,' Edith said sharp, 'someone'll hear. And you shouldn't mention such a thing even to your own Edith.'

'I don't like him.'

'It's not for us to like or not like. You're too little.'

'Darling Edith why are you looking so excited?'

Edith giggled. 'Am I?' she asked, wiping away at stains on Miss Moira's deep blue skirt.

'You should see yourself.'

'Well I expect I've had a day and a half. But what've you been up to? That's what I want to be told thanks.'

'Edith why are you?'

'Can you keep secrets ducky?' Edith asked in reply.

'A secret oo how lovely,' Miss Moira exclaimed.

'I don't suppose you know how.'

'Oh I promise. Let my lips be sealed,' the child said. May I drop dead she added to herself.

'Well then. Only don't breathe to nobody mind. Your Edith's had a proposal.'

'Oh Edith has Albert at last? And are you going to marry him?' Edith put the handkerchief away and kissed her.

'There that's better,' she said.

'Do tell,' the child pleaded warm.

'One secret for another,' Edith announced. 'You say what you've been along of.'

'Will you marry him then?'

'Look I've told you my secret. Now you come out with yours. Fair's fair,' Edith said.

'We've been with Albert.'

'That's no secret.'

'It was.'

'What's dark about that then?' Edith wanted to know.

'He's got my grandma's ring. The one she lost.'

'Has he so? And what's he done with it?' Edith enquired casual.

'I don't know,' the little girl lied, on account of dropping dead perhaps.

'Which Albert, yours or mine?' Edith asked soft.

'Mine,' Miss Moira answered. 'Oh I do love him.'

'Are you goin' to be married?'

'Of course.'

'Isn't that lovely,' Edith said. 'But what's he been up to with that ring meantime?' she went on carefully disinterested.

'I don't know, honest I don't,' the child lied once more. And Edith let it go. And the day laden with sunshine, with the noise of bees broke in upon their silence. There was a sharp smell of geraniums.

'Well I must be off now,' Miss Moira said. She ran away stepping high.

'I don't know,' Charley grumbled good natured again at Albert in the pantry as the lad washed his face, 'I don't rightly know what to make of you an' that's a fact. Speakin' out of turn like you did. There's times I ask myself if you'll ever learn.'

'I'm sorry Mr Raunce.'

'That's O.K. my lad,' said Charley unexpectedly mild. 'Today of all days I wouldn't wish to have a disagreement with nobody. But you must use your best endeavours. 'Owever hard it may seem to keep mum for 'eaven's sake keep mum. That's your place and in a manner of speakin' it's mine. You've no knowledge of this ring, nor I have, we none of us know. What's more it's no concern of ours. When Mrs T. made a rumpus soon as she first lost it well then it was up to anyone she spoke to to make a search. She's always puttin' things down where she can't find 'em. But after the first upset let sleepin' dogs lie. D'you get me?'

'Yes Mr Raunce.'

'It did your heart credit to speak up when you did, mind. But you'll discover it don't pay to have a heart on most occasions. Anyway not with a man of his stamp. Where did 'e say 'e come from? What's 'is trade card?'

Albert picked up the man's bit of pasteboard and handed it to Charley.

'Not with wet fingers,' Mr Raunce began again. ''Ow many times do I have to tell you, wipe your hands when you pass anything and clean your teeth before you have to do with a woman. Holy Jesus', he sang out without warning, 'holy Moses,' he corrected himself, 'what's this?'

'What's the matter Mr Raunce?'

'Why the Insurance Company. I knew it all along. See 'ere. "Irish Regina Assurance." Don't you read that the way I do.'

'No Mr Raunce.'

'Why spell me out those letters. Irish Regina Assurance. I.R.A. boy. So 'e was one of their scouts, must a' been.'

'I.R.A.?'

'Where's my girl?' Raunce asked and dashed out.

A few days passed. Then one morning while they were at their dinner in the servants' hall that telephone began to ring away in the pantry. Albert came back with a message he had written out in block letters.

'Returning Monday, Tennant,' Raunce read aloud into a silence. 'Well thank God for it,' he added, 'and about time if you ask me.'

'I never knew you so keen to start work again,' Agatha remarked malicious.

'That's all right Miss Burch,' he said.

'There's more in this than meets the eye,' she suggested.

'Why I've not said a word,' he began as Edith watched him anxiously and as though disapproving. Then he went on, 'I've not let on about it because I wouldn't have you bothered. We've all of us got our worries with this bombin' over the other side to mention just the one item. So I thought I'll keep it to meself. Your own back's broad enough I said.'

'Thanks I'm sure,' Miss Burch announced, putting a small

slice of potato dainty into her mouth. Then she raised a crooked finger as if to scratch under the wig but thought better perhaps for she picked up the fork again.

'There's things occur which you'd never believe,' he went on.

'Now Charley,' Edith said. It was the first time, as Kate's eyes showed, that the girl had called him in public by his christian name. 'You don't want to bring all that up,' she ended weak.

'Well we're all one family in this place, there's how I see the situation,' he started. Kate began to giggle. But she got no encouragement from Edith. 'We can share,' he continued, still sentimental. 'Now Mrs T. is comm' back she can clear this little matter up. It was something occurred not more than five days ago.'

'No Charley,' Edith interrupted.

'Bless me,' Miss Burch said staring at her, 'if it's known to another it should be known to me I hope.'

'She couldn't help herself,' Raunce put in. 'She was present when 'e called along with my Albert here.'

'Who called?' Miss Burch enquired.

'The I.R.A. man,' Raunce announced as though with an ultimatum.

'Mercy,' Miss Burch exclaimed, 'and are we going to have that old nonsense all over again?'

'Nonsense it may be to you Miss Burch but you'll excuse me, I know different,' he said.

'Then I'd best learn more,' she suggested.

'It was about the ring,' Edith put in.

'That was 'is pretext right enough,' Raunce said, 'that was how he got past Albert here at the door. It was my bandage,' he explained. 'I couldn't answer the bell dressed as I was. So I sent the lad. If it had been me opened the door to him then with my experience I'd've told within a second, like in the twinklin' of an eye,' he said serious.

'Mrs Tennant's ring she mislaid?' Agatha enquired.

'That was no more than the way he chose to put it,' Charley began again when Miss Burch surprisingly broke out as follows.

'Then they'll needs must dig the drains up,' she cried in what seemed to be great agitation, 'I've said so all along now haven't I?'

'Come, come,' Raunce said, 'there's no call to take things that far,' he said and frowned. 'She's always mislayin' possessions.'

Paddy spoke.

'What's 'e say?' Raunce asked.

'He says that weren't no I.R.A. man if 'e came to the front door,' translated Kate. 'They only use the back entrance those gentry he reckons.'

'Hark at 'im,' Raunce announced.

'Well how d'you know he's mistaken?' Kate wanted to be told.

'Now then,' Raunce said to her. 'We don't want none of your backchat my gel thank you.'

'You leave my girls out of it,' Miss Burch ordered but in a weak voice as though about to faint.

'I told you,' Edith said to her Charley.

'I don't know,' Charley said, 'there's times I can't fathom any one of you an' that's a fact. What is all this?'

'What is all this?' Miss Burch echoed in a shrill voice. 'You ask me that? When you're telling us we've had a I.R.A. man actually call at the Castle?'

'But I thought you were on about the drains.'

'Oh you men,' Miss Burch replied faint once more, 'you will never understand even the simplest thing.'

'It was only an insurance inspector came about the ring,' Edith explained. 'I don't know where Mr Raunce got it he was from the I.R.A. I'm sure,' she said.

'You mean he said that ring was stolen?' Miss Burch cried, plainly beside herself again.

'Not on your life,' Charley took her up. 'You ladies will always jump at conclusions.'

'Well what was he here for then?' Miss Burch enquired.

'Why to see 'ow much his Insurance Company could do about it,' Raunce replied. But Miss Burch, who seemed really agitated, was not having any.

'You said just now he was an I.R.A. man,' she objected

quavering. 'Well maybe he was both,' Raunce said. 'They've got to live like everyone else when all's said and done.'

'And we never had the drains up,' Miss Burch wailed. 'Oh dear. Now Mrs Tennant's coming back when it will be too late. Only the other day Mrs Welch was tellin' me they should be dug on account of the children. She's nervous for her Albert.'

'The drains?' Edith asked.

'The drains?' Charley echoed. 'You'll pardon me but you don't dig drains again.'

'Well clean them out then, do whatever you do with the things,' Miss Burch answered a trifle sharper. 'They're unhealthy as they are now if they aren't worse.'

'We're livin' under a shadow these days,' Raunce announced, 'that's the way it is with all of us. There's matters you mightn't take account of in normal times get you down now.'

Kate began to giggle cautious and looked for support to Edith. Edith however appeared grave. So did Albert who was watching her. Then Edith said to Raunce,

'I don't know, I can't seem to take any account of it,' she said.

'Oh you're young,' Miss Burch told her.

'She's gone and hit the nail right on the head Miss Burch has,' Raunce announced agitated in his turn. 'An I.R.A. man now. An inspector from the Insurance Company. Then the drains an' all on top of all this bombing not to mention the invasion with Jerry set to cross over with drawn swords, it's plenty to get anyone down.'

At this point Albert spoke. His face was dead white.

'Well I'm crossing over the other side to enlist,' he said.

'What?' Edith sighed.

'Oh?' Raunce shouted. 'Enlist? You at your age? Enlist in what will you oblige me?'

'I'm goin' to be a air gunner,' the lad said.

'An air gunner eh?' Raunce chortled but you could tell he was distracted. 'But you aren't of an age boy. Besides that's the most dangerous of all bloody jobs boy. You'll be killed.'

Edith and Kate had gone pale. Miss Burch's eyes filled with

tears. They all stared at Albert except Paddy who went on with his food. Edith said,

'But what about your mum Bert?'

'Sis'll look after her and I'll be home while I'm waiting till I'm old enough. I wish to get me out of here, then go an' fight,' he said. Miss Burch burst into tears.

'Why you poor dear,' Edith murmured going round the table to her.

'Now look what you done,' Raunce said.

'I'm sorry Mr Raunce I never intended . . .' the lad mumbled.

'You've no thought for others that's the trouble,' Raunce complained his eyes anxious on Agatha, 'speaking up like you did, sayin' this that and the other. But there it's your age.'

'You let me fetch you a nice cup of tea,' Edith was telling Miss Burch who sat bowed with her face in her hands. 'Oh dear oh dear,' Agatha moaned.

'Gawd strewth look what you done,' Raunce said once more at which Albert got to his feet, moved over to the door. He stood for a moment before he went out.

'I'm sorry Miss Burch I'm sure. I'm goin' to be a air gunner,' he said white, as though defiant.

When the door was shut Miss Burch looked up between her fingers.

'How old would he be?' she asked.

'My Albert?' Raunce replied. 'Not above sixteen I'll be bound.'

'He's eighteen,' Edith said.

'Eighteen?' Raunce cried. 'Why you've only to look at 'im. No girl, I've got it somewhere in my desk, the letter 'e come with I mean, he can't be a day more than I just said.'

'He's eighteen. That was his birthday the other week,' Edith insisted calmly.

'Oh this war,' Miss Burch wailed, then hid her face again.

'You run and carry her a cup of tea,' Edith asked Kate.

'All right I'll go,' the girl replied unwilling.

But Miss Burch would not stay. She said she had best lie down for a spell. So Edith slipped out to the kitchen to ask Kate to fetch that cup to Agatha's room. When she got back in the hall she found Raunce seated on his own there. Paddy had probably gone back to his peacocks. So she sat down alongside him although this must have seemed rather noticeable, seeing that it was nearly time to start work.

Charley barely glanced at her. 'Eighteen?' he muttered. 'Is he that much? I could've sworn he was two year younger.'

'Well dear,' she said, 'you did put your foot right in it.'

'In what way?' he asked.

'I'll say you opened your mouth. That ring's not found yet even if I do fancy I know who's got it.'

'It's you honey,' he explained. 'I was worried over you. Then when I received the wire I thought to myself now everything will come right once Mrs T. gets back. It seemed to loose my tongue,' he said.

'Something loosed it dear. But there's nothing gained by speakin' of that ring until we hold it safe.'

'You never took the ring,' he said reaching over for her hand. 'You found a valuable yes but you put that back right where you came across it. And what else could you do? Tell me? You've no lock up. Of course there's the strongroom back in my quarters. But we can't have that shut all day and the things which are kept in it might as well be laid out on the drive for all the safety they're in of a daytime in this barracks of a hole. So you couldn't count on the old strongroom. Then what did you do? You put it back where for all you could speak to Mrs Tennant had hid the thing in security. In the finish someone or other pinched it from there. That's all.'

'What's on your mind then Charley?'

'Nothing,' he answered not looking at her.

'Oh yes there is. I can tell,' she returned. 'Besides you said just now you was worried over me.'

'Oh honey,' he broke out sudden, 'I do love you so.'

'Of course,' she replied bright.

'Give us a kiss dear please.'

'What here?' she asked. 'Where someone will come in any minute?'

'I didn't realize I could love anyone the way I love you. I thought I'd lived too long.'

'You thought you'd lived too long?' and she laughed in her throat.

'I can't properly see myself these days,' Raunce went on looking sideways past her at the red eye of a deer's stuffed head. 'Why I'm altogether changed,' he said. 'But look love, no man's younger than his age. There's more'n twenty years between us.'

'I like a man that's a man and not a lad,' she murmured.

'Yes but the years fly fast,' he answered. 'To think of Albert old enough to enlist.'

'He's upset you your lad has isn't that right?'

'Yes Edie,' Raunce said wondering. 'It did give me a turn I must confess.'

'Why?' she asked grim.

'Well it looks like we're out of it over in Eire as we are or whatever they call this country of savages. D'you get me? I can't seem able to express myself but there you are. Away from it somehow.'

'That's what we want to be surely?'

'Yes dear.'

'I mean you're too old. They'd never take you could they?'

'They'd never take me over here. Not if de Valera keeps 'em out.'

'Well we're not crossin' over to the other side are we?' She looked sharp at him. He seemed dreamy.

'No,' he answered, 'we're not. Not so long as we can find that ring,' he said. 'And keep the house from bein' burned down over our heads. Or Mrs Jack from running off with the Captain so Mrs Tennant goes over for good to England.'

'Why Charley,' she objected soft, 'there's other places.'

'Not without we find that ring,' he said.

'But I thought you was bringing your mother across,' she said and seemed bitter. She was about to go on when Kate stuck her head in at the door.

'Ho,' this girl announced, 'so you're still 'ere. An' what about the work?' she asked Edith. 'I'm not carryin' on alone let me tell you.'

'I won't be a minute,' Edith answered.

'I know your minutes. I've 'ad some,' Kate remarked.

'And there's the children,' Edith said remembering. 'They'll want their walk.'

'Then I fancy I'll lay me down on my bed. I feel faint,' Kate suggested in Agatha's voice.

'What?' Raunce asked as though confused. 'And with Mrs Tennant returning the day after to-morrow?'

'Oh go drown yourself,' Kate said and slammed the door.

'Holy smoke look what we're coming to,' Raunce muttered under his breath.

But Edith laughed. 'Come on slow coach,' she invited giving him a light kiss on his forehead as she got up. 'Here wait a tick,' he cried as if waking. 'Come to father beautiful,' he called. Only by the time he was on his feet she was gone.

He began to clear away the dinner things for his lad Albert. He surprised himself doing it.

When later that afternoon Edith came into Raunce's room to find him unconscious with his feet on the other chair, he awoke with a start. 'Why me love here I am,' he remarked as if to say you see I don't come out of a good sleep bad-tempered.

'It's me that's worried now all right,' she announced.

'How's that?' he asked.

'They won't tell where they've hid the ring.' He was wide awake at once.

'You're certain they've got it?'

'I know that for sure,' she answered, 'Miss Moira wouldn't lie to me.'

'You give me just five minutes alone with young Albert.'

'No dear,' she said, 'we don't want more trouble with Mrs Welch.'

'Just five minutes. That's all I need.'

'It won't do dear. If only I had more time. But she'll be back Monday.'

'Mrs Tennant you mean?' he asked. 'Well all I can say is if 'er own grandchildren have took it the little thieves I don't see what she can say to us.'

'Then what were you on about when you came out at dinnertime that if we couldn't discover the ring we'd never get another place in Ireland?'

'Did I say that?'

'You did dear,' she told him. 'An' you went on that they'd clap you in the Army soon as ever you stepped off the boat over in Britain.'

'Look,' he said, 'don't you worry your head. We'll think of a way. Of course it would be best if we found where they've 'id it particularly after the visit we've been paid. That's what I must've intended. It has made things more awkward that man turning up. And then Albert sayin' what 'e did. And now he wants to go and be killed just to get his own back for speaking out of turn I shouldn't wonder.'

'No Charley you don't understand.'

'I don't. That's a fact. I never will I shouldn't be surprised. But I'll say this. You'll live to regret having a kid like that fallen in love over you.'

'He's not,' she lied, it may have been to protect the lad.

'And they say nothing gets past a woman,' Raunce said heavy. 'Why it stands out a mile he is.'

'You're imaginin' Charley,' she said soft.

'Imagining my eye,' he replied. 'But if 'e just wanted to fight for the old country I could agree with the lad.'

She sat up.

'You mean to say you're even considerin' such a step?' she asked.

He answered in a low voice. 'I'm bewitched and bewildered I am really,' he said. 'I don't know what I'm after.'

'Thanks I'm sure,' was her bitter comment.

'Here wait a minute, not so fast,' he exclaimed and leaning forward he got hold of one of her hands on the arm of the other chair. 'Don't get me wrong,' he said. 'That's dam all to do with you an' me.'

'And your old mother you were so keen to get over?' Edith wanted to know.

'Oh her,' Raunce answered.

There was a miserable pause. Then Edith began again,

'Then what did you intend a week or two back when you made out our place was where we are now and Miss Burch said that about blocking the roads? The time Paddy got the wrong side of you?'

144

'I expect I had in mind what they told us in the newspapers about stayin' put where you happen to be in an invasion.'

'You don't sound very sure,' she said.

'It's Albert,' he explained. 'My Albert to want to do a thing like that. Why it's almost as if 'e was me own son.'

'I wish he could hear you now after the way you bawl him out.'

'Me?' Raunce said, 'Why I just give him the rough side of my tongue on occasion so that he'll learn a trade,' he said. 'Here give us a kiss,' he added smiling at last.

This time she actually got up in haste and did no less than sit on his knee.

'You don't love me,' she murmured. When he kissed her she kissed him back with such passion, all of her hard as a board, that he flopped back flabbergasted, having caught a glimpse of what was in her waiting for him.

When the other Albert came to the kitchen for his tea that same afternoon he found Mrs Welch asleep with her head on the massive table. Labouring she lifted heavy bloodshot eyes in his direction.

'Well?' she asked.

'I been out,' he answered sly.

'Out where?'

'We was round the back,' he said.

'And who's we?' she wanted to know as she scratched a vast soft thigh. She gave a wide yawn.

'The young leddies,' he replied. He passed a hand over his forehead as if he could tidy his hair with that one gesture and came to sit quiet opposite auntie.

'Not with that Edith?' she enquired sharp.

'Oh no'm.'

'You're positive?' and Mrs Welch leant across. 'For you know what I told you?'

'Yes'm.'

'What was that then?'

'That I weren't to have nothing more to do with 'er ever,' the boy repeated.

'That's right,' Mrs Welch rejoined. She leant back again and left her arms straight out from her bosom resting on closed fists upon the kitchen table. Her dark hair straggled across her face. 'You wouldn't lie to me?' she asked.

'Oh no'm.'

'Because I daren't abandon this kitchen day or night, not till I go to me bed when day is done that is and then I double lock the door. On guard I am,' she announced in a loud voice. 'Because that Edith's no more'n a thief I tell you an' my girls are hand in glove with 'er, I don't need to be told.' She came to a stop and although glaring at him she seemed rather at a loss.

'Yes'm,' he said respectful.

'An' they're in league with the tradesmen, the I.R.A. merchants, the whole lot are,' she went on a bit wild. 'You mark my words,' she finished and closed anguished eyes.

There was a pause. Then he asked a question with such a glance of malice as must have frightened her if she had caught it.

'What's a I.R.A. man auntie?' he enquired.

'Thieves and murderers,' she said half under her breath as though her thoughts were elsewhere.

'Blimey,' he said. If she had looked she would have seen he mocked.

'Makin' out she's too good to have anything to do with us,' Mrs Welch began again. She opened her eyes. 'Sayin' she won't take you along of Miss Moira and Miss Evelyn.' Mrs Welch heaved herself back to the table, propping her head on the palms of her hands. 'The lousy bitch,' she said soft, 'runnin' in double 'arness with that Raunce into the bargain. Oh,' she suddenly yelled, 'if I catch you I'll tan the 'ide right off of you d'you understand?'

Out in the scullery Jane and Mary nodded at one another, at the rise and fall of this thick voice.

'Tan the 'ide off me what for?' the lad asked.

'What for you bastard imp?' she shouted and lumbering while still on her seat she made a slow grab which he easily dodged.

'I ain't done nothing,' he pretended to whine.

'Ah they're in a society with them tradesmen,' she cried out. 'Don't I know it. Why only the other day Jane was got be'ind the monument by one. I made out I never noticed when she told me,' Mrs Welch explained lowering her voice, 'but I marked it well. And I shan't forget,' she added although she seemed short of breath, 'I weren't born yesterday,' she said.

'Can I 'ave my tea'm?' he requested.

'Can you 'ave your tea?' she replied with scorn and made no move. 'Yes,' she went on dark, 'I've watched their thievin'. Raunce an' that Edith. Not to mention Kate with what she gets up to. . . . As I've witnessed times without number from me larder windows. So don't you never 'ave nothin' to do with any one of 'em see. 'Ave you got that straight?' she asked hoarse, glaring right through him. Without waiting for an answer she called out, 'Jane, Master Albert's tea.' She was perfectly serious.

'And may your ladyship's heart be asy on her to get back to the Castle,' Michael said from the driver's seat as obviously excited, grinning in his idiot way, he at once drove off to the stables leaving Mrs Tennant dumped down in front of her own front door surrounded by the luggage.

'Michael,' she called after him to a wisp of blue smoke.

Then she reached for the latch which was a bullock's horn bound in bronze. But these great portals were barred. She gave the ordinary bell a vicious jab.

'What's this Arthur I mean Raunce?' she asked when Charley opened.

'I am very sorry I'm sure Madam. I had no idea the boat would be punctual. I was just putting on my coat to come to look out for you Madam.'

'But why the locked door?' she asked as she entered.

'We had an unwelcome visitor Madam,' he replied, a suitcase already in each hand.

'What do you mean Raunce? Really do try and talk sense. Such a trying journey which it always is now one can't fly and then this.' Charley's Albert came hurrying for the other bags. Mrs Tennant seemed to watch the lad. Raunce had his eye cautious on her.

'Is nobody even going to say good afternoon to me then?' she enquired without warning. 'Raunce I'm sure you don't mean to be unfriendly but when one comes home one does

147

expect a little something. Eldon when he was alive always had a word of welcome.'

'Well all I can say is Madam thank God you are back,' Raunce burst out.

'I suppose that means you've all been at each other's throats again? Very well put those bags of mine down and tell me about it. I might have known,' she added as she went into the Red Library. He followed after.

She sat down where he had rested his heels a day or so before. She took off her gloves.

'Have you had much rain here?' she enquired.

'Hardly any at all Madam.'

'I do hope the wells don't run dry then. Now Raunce what is all this?'

'Well Madam we had an unwelcome visitor on the Saturday.' There he stopped short although she could tell from his manner that he had thoroughly prepared what he meant to say.

'So you said a minute ago,' was Mrs Tennant's comment.

'It was about your ring Madam,' he went on taking his time. He gazed at her as though hypnotized.

'Good heavens had he found it?'

'No Madam. To tell you the truth he came to enquire if we had come across the ring.'

'Well has anyone?'

'No Madam, we haven't and that's a fact.'

'It is a shame. It was rather a beautiful one too,' she said. 'And d'you know Raunce I've never had a word of sympathy from any of you? Just a single word would have made all the difference.'

'I'm very sorry Madam. We were all very disturbed when you lost the ring I'm sure.'

'Very well then. Now what has made you so thankful that I'm back?'

'It was not very pleasant Madam. Indeed this individual seemed to take the attitude one of us might have had the ring.'

'You can go now Albert,' Mrs Tennant sang out to the lad through the open door. 'This doesn't concern you. Just take my bags up for Agatha to unpack do you mind?'

148

'I regret to inform you Miss Burch is indisposed Madam. And Miss Swift is no better I'm sorry to add,' Raunce told her.

'What's the matter with Agatha then?'

'I couldn't say I'm sure but I don't think she has anything serious Madam.'

'All right then. I don't want to be difficult. I'll unpack for myself. Now you surely aren't going to tell me that an insurance inspector calling to make the usual enquiries has set the household at sixes and sevens?'

'Well this was not exactly a pleasant experience Madam. More like the third degree Madam. And it seemed to throw my boy Albert right off his balance, Madam.'

'Raunce may I say something?'

'Yes Madam.'

'Don't Madam me quite as much as you do. Put in one now and again for politeness but repeating a thing over and over rather seems to take away from the value,' and she gave him a sweet smile really.

'Very good Madam.'

'Well go on.'

'It seemed as I say to put my lad right off his balance. I was astounded Madam there is no other word. The first thing anyone knew while this individual was making his enquiries was that Albert said he had it.'

'Had what?'

'Well I suppose the ring Madam.'

'Albert has it?' Mrs Tennant echoed brightly. 'Why on earth doesn't he hand over then?'

'Oh no Madam I'm sure he's never even seen the ring. It was only he completely lost his head Madam.'

'Stuff and nonsense Raunce if the boy said he had it and you heard him, very well then he's had it and he's a miserable little thief isn't he?'

'I do assure you Madam Albert could never do such a thing.'

'But you told me yourself he'd said he had it. You heard him.'

'That was the inspector from the insurance people.'

'All right then what on earth did the insurance man say to make Albert go out of his mind? Because this is what you're asking me to believe isn't it, that Albert's had a breakdown or what?'

Raunce answered with what appeared to be reluctance.

'He said the company would not meet the claim I'm sorry to tell Madam.'

'Not meet the claim? Really Raunce this is too detestable. Are you sure?'

'Yes Madam.'

'It's not the money I'm worried about, the thing had memories for me that money couldn't buy. No what I'm thinking is that I shan't get any insurance company to insure me if we don't get this cleared up. Oh how aggravating you all of you are. Why the whole thing's distasteful. Here am I have got to suffer because you can't control your pantry boy. You do see that don't you Raunce? Then tell me this. What on earth would you advise me to do now?'

'Well Madam if I may say so Albert is a good lad. In fact I can't believe he can know the least thing. If you would give me another few days Madam I'm positive I can sift to the bottom of it for you.'

However Mrs Tennant decided that she must see Albert for herself. As Raunce went to fetch the lad she called him back.

'But what are you thanking God for that I'm here if things are in the state they're in?' she asked.

'It's the uncertainty,' he replied straight out and went.

Mrs Tennant did not have a satisfactory little talk with Bert. He readily explained that he had told the assessor he'd got it but he would not admit to her that he had the ring. He just stood there upright and yellow, refusing to answer most of the time. She told him it was despicable to take refuge in silence but this had no effect, any more than it did when she meaningly said she would have to think it over. Indeed he chose that moment to say he wished to give in his notice.

'I won't accept it,' she said at once.

He could not have thought of this for his jaw dropped in a ludicrous look of surprise.

'It wouldn't be fair to you Albert, not with this hanging over you.'

'I want to be a air gunner'm,' he blurted out.

'Stuff and nonsense. Speak to Raunce and ask him to get some sense into you. I'm very displeased. I'm very displeased indeed and I shall have to consider what I'm going to do. Run along at once. You've stolen a ring and now you want to be a hero. Yes that's all. Run along.'

He did not cry as he went to the servants' hall, he shook with rage. He was repeating to himself 'I won't ever speak to one of 'em in this bloody 'ouse not ever again.'

Meantime Raunce had hurried back to his room where Edith was waiting. 'Any sign yet?' he asked urgent. She shook her head. She was biting her nails.

'Why don't you change your mind an' let me 'ave a go at that precious lad?' he appealed. 'Honest Edie dear we've no time. Mrs T.'s just sent for my Albert. There's no tellin' what 'e'll say. He's just a bundle of nerves that kid. Because if we don't find the ring this afternoon we'll be in a proper pickle.'

'I tell you you'll never get anything out of them children by fright. I understand them and you don't.'

'That's all fine and dandy,' Raunce answered, 'but there's nothing come of your method these last two days and now I warn you it's desperate dear,' he appealed. 'Lord but I do wish you'd never found the object.'

'What lies on your mind so Charley?' she asked. 'You're that nervous you've got me upset. You tell me this then you tell me the other till I'm all confused.'

'Look this is the way I see the situation,' he explained. 'I must've been crazy not to tumble it in the first place. The minute Mrs Welch's Albert goes to cash in on that ring an' they ask the kid where he got a valuable like it, all 'e'll say is that 'e found what you'd hid away. He'll drag you in see?'

'But listen,' she objected, 'the young ladies'd never allow him.'

'Allow him?' Raunce echoed intense, 'but how could they prevent it? There's one thing about evacuees,' he said. 'No matter what the homes are they've come from they're like fiends straight up from hell honey after they've been a month or more down in the country districts. And comm' as 'e does from that woman's sister before 'e even left London, well what else can you expect? There's only one language those little merchants understand an' that's a kind of morse spelt out with a belt on their backsides.'

'No Charley,' she appealed looking up at him round-eyed from where she sat in his chair, 'you leave me my own way till nightfall at any rate. Because I know Miss Evelyn and Miss Moira like I've read them in a book. If they get frighted then there's nothing in this world will make them say a word.' Came a knock on the door. 'This is it.' And Miss Moira entered.

'Oh hullo Mr Raunce,' the child said, standing as though uncertain.

'Hullo Miss Moira,' he said very loud.

'Are you come about our secret?' Edith asked. The little girl nodded. 'Then you can tell in front of Mr Raunce, he's in it along with us,' she explained. But Miss Moira stood hands behind her back, shifting from one foot to the other, and looked from Raunce to Edith then back again.

'Tell Edith,' the maid gently persuaded.

'I got it,' Miss Moira piped at last.

'You got what darlin'?' Edith asked through Raunce's heavy breathing.

'Why your wedding present of course,' the child replied. 'Just what you said you wanted. But from me, not from Evelyn or Albert. It's my special present,' she explained.

'Oh isn't that kind,' Edith exclaimed softly. 'When can I see it?'

'Here,' the child said. And she whipped out another of Mrs Tennant's rings heavy with uncut rubies worth perhaps two hundred pounds.

'Christ,' Raunce muttered half under his breath. Edith let the thing drop through her fingers and began to cry. Her crying was genuine, even became noisy.

'Now Miss Moira if I was you I'd run along,' Raunce began, stepping awkwardly up to Edith. But Edith clutched his arm in such a grip he took it for a warning. Then she held her arms out blind to the child who ran into them.

'Why darling Edith don't cry,' she said, 'darling don't, darling.'

'It's Albert,' Edith wailed, 'Albert and me'd set our hearts on the blue one.'

'Then why ever didn't you say?' Miss Moira asked with her lips at Edith's ear. 'I won't be a minute.'

'You'll take this one back,' Edith said beginning to recover. 'You won't let your grandma know it's been missed.'

Miss Moira grabbed the ruby ring. 'Of course not,' she said.

'She's about this minute, Miss Moira. You'll never let her catch sight of you?' Raunce asked. Edith clutched his arm again so that he kept silent

'You do fuss so,' the child pouted. 'Goodbye for now.'

'And you'll let me have my blue one?' Edith begged. 'We've made our minds up to have that, honest we have dear.'

'Don't be so terribly impatient,' Miss Moira replied reproving. 'I told you I won't be a minute. And it's a great lot to do for anyone even if it is a wedding present,' she added as though bitter, and then was gone.

'Oh my Christ,' Raunce uttered, 'did you ever know the like?'

'Hush dear don't swear everything'll come right in a jiffy,' Edith answered as she began to dry her face. 'But where did the child come across those rubies?'

'Where else but in Mrs T.'s room,' Raunce answered gloomy. 'Even when she goes over to London they lie there open in a drawer. Will that child bring the blue one d'you suppose?'

'It's all right now don't worry,' Edith said.

'I hope,' he said. 'An' so that's what you told Miss Moira,' he went on. 'You're deep you are. Which Albert is it you're goin' to be wife to? Mine or Mrs Welch's?'

'Don't be silly it was yours I told her of course.'

'I don't get that,' he pointed out. 'I mean I don't see the reason.'

'I had to so she could understand. I've been obliged to do a lot I didn't like.'

'Women are deep,' he said. He bent down and kissed her. She put her arms slack about his neck. She did not kiss him. He straightened up.

'And now where are we?' he asked beginning to pace up and down. 'Before we're much older we'll be caught with all her bloody jewellery in this room red 'anded.'

'Be quiet,' Edith said. 'Ring or no ring I don't aim for Mrs Tennant to find me if she thought to come through this way to the kitchen. But it'll be all right now you'll see. Miss Moira'll fetch the right ring this time. I worship that child,' she added. Raunce halted when he heard this. He looked at her almost in alarm.

After she had done with Charley's Albert Mrs Tennant went straight upstairs, took off her hat, washed her hands, murmured to herself 'better get it over,' came down again and went to the kitchen by a way which did not lead through the pantry.

The cook lumbered to her feet on Mrs Tennant's entry.

'Well mum I do 'ope you had a enjoyable visit and that the young gentleman was in good health as well as in good spirits in spite of this terrible war,' Mrs Welch said.

'You are a dear, Mrs Welch,' Mrs T. replied. 'D'you know you're the first person has greeted me since I got back as though they had ever seen me before, not counting Michael. I don't count him. You can't believe these Irishmen can you?'

Mrs Welch let out a deep, cavernous chuckle. She behaved like an established favourite.

'Gawd save us from 'em, they're foreigners after all,' she announced. 'What's more I won't allow my girls to have nothing to do with 'em,' she announced, beginning to grow mysterious.

'I'm sure you're right,' Mrs Tennant agreed brightly.

'Now it's strange your mentioning that mum but I had an example only the other day,' Mrs Welch went on fast. 'I happened to be stood by the larder windows when I 'ad a terrible stench of drains very sudden. Quite took my breath away. Just like those Irish I said to myself as I stood there, never to clean a thing out.'

'You don't imagine . . .?' Mrs Tennant began to ask. She sat down on a kitchen chair.

'A terrible stench of drains,' Mrs Welch repeated. 'And me

154

that had thought we were goin' to have them all up while you was away with Mrs Jack.'

'The drains?' Mrs Tennant echoed.

'That's what was said,' Mrs Welch insisted.

'Who said? I never gave orders.'

'No mum I'd be the last to say you did seein' you knew nothing. Only when that lovely cluster ring you had was lost, an' what a terrible thing to 'appen, there was one or two did mention that takin' 'em up was the only thing.'

'Down the drain?' Mrs Tennant cried. 'How fantastic.'

'Ah I could've told them they'd never get away with that,' Mrs Welch rejoined as though triumphant. 'Fantastic's the word beggin' your pardon. Down the plumbin' indeed when it was all the time right where I'll be bound it is this moment if it's not already been come upon.'

'No,' Mrs Tennant said guarded, 'there's no trace.'

'Ah there you are,' Mrs Welch replied profound.

'Now Mrs Welch I don't think we shall get anywhere like this,' Mrs Tennant gently expostulated.

'Just as you please mum,' the cook answered calm. 'And what would you fancy for your luncheon?'

'That is to say what I really came for was to ask your advice,' Mrs Tennant countered, looking again to make sure the kitchen door was shut.

'I shouldn't think twice about the stench of drains,' Mrs Welch put in, 'that was likely nothin' really. Probably the way the wind lay or something.'

'I haven't had you with me all these years without getting to know when I'm to take you seriously,' Mrs Tennant replied. 'No it's about Albert.'

'Albert?' Mrs Welch echoed with a set look on her face. ''Ave they been on to you about Albert?'

'Well you know he's admitted it.'

'Admitted what I'd like to be told?' cried Mrs Welch.

'Why he did to me only a quarter of an hour ago.'

'What about?' Mrs Welch asked grim.

'Well what we've been discussing, my sapphire cluster ring,' Mrs Tennant answered.

'Your lovely sapphire cluster,' Mrs Welch echoed

anguished. 'Why the lyin' lot of . . . no I won't say it, that would be too good for 'em.'

'D'you think the others have had a part in this then?'

'I don't think. I know mum,' Mrs Welch announced.

'But they would hardly have told him what to say to incriminate himself?'

'Criminal?' Mrs Welch replied, her voice rising. 'That's just it mum. For this is what those two are, that Raunce and his Edith. I don't say nothin' about their being lain all day in each other's arms, and the best part of the night too very likely though I can't speak to the night time, I must take my rest on guard and watch as I am while it's light outside, lain right in each other's arms,' she resumed, 'the almighty lovers they make out they are but no more than fornicators when all's said and done if you'll excuse the expression, where was I? Yes. "Love" this an' "dear" that, so they go on day and night yet they're no better than a pair of thieves mum, misappropriatin' your goods behind your back.'

'Mrs Welch,' Mrs T. protested rising to her feet with a deep look of distaste. 'I won't listen,' she was going on but the cook interrupted.

'I'm sorry mum but you must allow me my say. There's been insinuations made and it's only right I should have the privilege to cast 'em back in the teeth of those that's made it. They're like a pair of squirrels before the winter layin' in a store with your property mum against their marriage if they ever find a parson to be joined in matrimony which I take leave to doubt. And it's not your ring alone. Did you ever look to the cellar mum? Why you hadn't been gone over into England more than a few hours when I chanced to look into that jar where I keep my waterglass. I was just goin' over my stores as I do regular every so often. Believe it or not there was above a quart gone. So I made my enquiry. You'll never credit this'm. It seems that Edith has been makin' away with the peacock's eggs to store them. There you are. But that's child's play. Listen to this.'

'Peacock's eggs? Whatever for?'

'Because they're starvin' over the other side the ordinary common people are begging your pardon mum.'

156

'Really Mrs Welch,' Mrs Tennant began again peremptory.

'I'm sorry I'm sure,' the cook insisted, 'but a few dozen eggs and a gallon or two of that stuff is child's play. Take the dead peacock. Stuffed 'im in my larder Raunce did all a'crawlin' with maggots over the lovely bit of meat I'd got for their supper. And what for you'll ask? As well you might. Ah you'd never believe their wickedness. It's to set that I.R.A. man Conor against me, that devil everyone's afeared for their life of in this place. And they're in it the two of them over your corn that's fed to the birds, Raunce an' that mad Irishman is. Like it was over the gravel between Raunce again an' Michael. The diabolical plunderers,' she said and paused to take breath, her face a dark purple.

'I'm not going to listen. I shall leave you till you're in a fit state. . . .' Mrs Tennant insisted wearily but Mrs Welch cut her short by shambling forward between her mistress and the door.

'Yet when they grow bold to come forward with their lying tales,' she went on, and grew hoarse, 'when they say cruel lies about the innocent, their fingers winkin' with your rings once your back is turned, then the honest shan't stay silent. If I should let myself dwell on what they told you, that my Albert, my sister's own son, so much as set eyes on that ring of yours or anything which belongs to you an' you don't know how to look after, then that's slander and libel, that there is, which is punishable by law.'

'All this is too absurd,' Mrs Tennant said cold. 'What's more I shouldn't be a bit surprised if you hadn't been drinking. I've wondered now for some time. In any case it never was a question of your Albert but of the pantry boy.'

'Gin?' Mrs Welch cried, 'I've not come upon any yet in this benighted island and you'll excuse me mum but I know who was intended, which Albert . . .'

'Now then,' Mrs Tennant cut her short in a voice that carried. Jane and Mary went crimson outside, began to giggle. 'Out of my way.' Mrs Welch leant back against the dresser. Her face was congested. She was in difficulty with her breathing.

'An' my pots and pans,' she began once more but this time in a mutter.

'We won't say any more about this,' Mrs Tennant went on, 'but if I ever find you like it another time you'll go on the next boat d'you hear me, even if I have to cook for the whole lot of you myself. Good mornin' to you. Oh I forgot what I really came about,' she added turning back. 'Mr Jack's been given embarkation leave now so Mrs Jack is bringing him home by the day boat to-morrow.' And on that she left.

As she came out of that swing door which bounded Mrs Welch's kingdom she found Raunce waiting bent forward in obvious suspense and excitement.

'It's been recovered Madam,' he announced.

'What has Arthur?'

'Why your sapphire ring Madam.'

'Thank you,' she said as though she had not heard. Taking it from him she slipped it on a finger. As she walked away she said half under her breath but loud enough for him to hear,

'And now perhaps you'll tell me what I'm to say to the Insurance Company?'

He was absolutely stunned. His jaw hung open.

'Oh Raunce,' she called over her shoulder. He stood up straight. Perhaps he simply could not make a sound.

'Who found it?' she asked.

He seemed to pull himself together.

'It was Edith,' he answered at random and probably forgot at once whom he had named.

Even then she had the last word. She turned round when she was some way off down the passage.

'Oh Raunce,' she said, 'I'm afraid your luncheon to-day may be burned,' gave a short laugh, then was gone.

Young Mrs Tennant came into the Red Library where her mother-in-law was seated at the desk which had a flat sloping top of rhinoceros hide supported on gold fluted pillars of wood.

'Where's Jack?' she asked.

'Fishing of course dear.'

'I shouldn't have thought there was enough water in the river.'

'Oh Violet,' Mrs Tennant replied, 'that reminds me. Ask tomorrow if I've told Raunce the servants can't have any more baths, so that I shan't forget. Or not more than one a week anyway until we can be sure the wells won't go dry.'

'I will. Was he always as fond of fishing?'

'Always. But tell me Violet. Oughtn't we to do something about him in the evenings? Get someone over I mean. Another man so that he needn't sit over his port alone.'

'But who is there now they've stopped the petrol?' the young woman asked. 'Anyway I'd have thought a girl would have been better.'

'Oh no we don't want anything like that do we? In any case they're all Roman Catholics. No I was thinking of Captain Davenport?'

'Not him,' Mrs Jack answered too quickly.

'Why not Violet? He used to be such a companion of yours?'

'Well I don't think Jack likes him.'

'Oh I shouldn't pay any attention,' Mrs Tennant said vaguely. 'I've so often noticed that if they can talk salmon trout they never go as far as disliking one another. Ring him up.'

'You're sure? I mean I don't want to crowd the house out just when you've got Jack home.'

'Oh really Violet,' her mother-in-law replied. 'That's perfectly sweet of you but in this great barn of a place with the servants simply eating their heads off it's a breath of fresh air to see someone new. Oh the servants, Violet darling,' Mrs Tennant said in tragic tones. She turned her leather Spanish stool round to face the younger woman.

'Have they been tiresome again?'

'Did I tell you I'd got my ring back?' Mrs Tennant enquired.

'No. How splendid.'

'My dear it was quite fantastic. When I arrived I found all the servants up in arms about it with not a trace of the ring. They were going round in small circles accusing each other.'

'Good lord,' her daughter-in-law remarked looking almost rudely out of the open window on the edge of which she was perched.

'Whether it's never having been educated or whether it's

just plain downright stupidity I don't know,' the elder Mrs Tennant went on, 'but there's been the most detestable muddle about my sapphire ring.'

'Your sapphire cluster ring?'

'Yes I lost it just before we crossed over for Jack's leave. You know I told you. I was wearing the thing one day and the next I knew it was gone. I must have taken it off to wash my hands. Anyway suddenly it had disappeared into thin air. Such a lovely one too that Jack's Aunt Emily gave me.'

'You never said,' Mrs Jack complained limp.

'Didn't I darling? Well there it is. And the moment I got inside the house three days ago I found Raunce crossing and uncrossing his fingers obviously most terribly nervous about something. Well I let him get it off his chest and what d'you think? It seems that when the insurance inspector came down after I'd reported the loss the pantry Albert all at once went mad and said he'd got it whatever that means. What would you say?'

'Why I suppose he'd picked the thing up somewhere.'

'My dear that's just what I thought at the time. But not at all. Oh no Raunce took the trouble to explain the boy had never even seen my ring. In the meantime of course the inspector had gone back to Dublin and I received a rather odd letter from them, everything considered, and only this morning to say that in view of the circumstances they could not regard the thing as lost. Well that's quite right because I'm wearing it now. But what I can't and shall never understand is what the boy thought he had or had got, whichever it was. Now d'you think I ought to take all this further?'

'It's so complicated,' Mrs Jack complained.

'Would you advise me to have Raunce in and get to the bottom of things I mean?'

At this question the younger woman suddenly displayed unusual animation. She got up, stood with her back to the light, and began to smooth her skirts.

'Not if I were you,' she said. 'Let sleeping dogs lie.'

This answer probably made Mrs Tennant obstinate. 'But I should at least like to know where it was found,' she cried.

'Why there is Edith. Edith,' she summoned her shrilly, 'come here a moment I want you.'

The girl came modest through the open portals. She did not look at Mrs Jack.

'Where did you find my sapphire ring in the end Edith?'

'Me Madam?' she replied almost sharp, 'I never found your ring Madam.'

'But Raunce told me you did when he gave it back.'

'Not me Madam,' Edith said looking at the floor.

'Then who did find it then?'

'I couldn't say Madam.'

'Oh why is there all this mystery Edith? The whole thing's most unsatisfactory.'

The housemaid stayed silent, calm and composed.

'Yes that's all now you can go,' Mrs Tennant said as though exasperated. 'Shut the door will you please?'

When they were alone again Mrs Tennant raised a hand to her ear which she tugged.

'Well there you are Violet. What d'you think?'

'I expect you heard wrong. Perhaps Raunce said someone else.'

'Oh no I'm not deaf yet. I know he named Edith.'

'Darling,' Mrs Jack entreated, 'I'm sure you're not. At all events you've got your ring back haven't you?'

'Yes but I don't like having things hang over me.'

'Hanging over you?'

'When there's something unexplained. Don't you ever feel somehow that you must get whatever it is cleared up? And then I don't think I can afford to keep the insurance going. It comes so frightfully expensive these days. But if I feel that there is someone not quite honest who perhaps was caught out by the servants and made to give the thing back then I do think it would be madness to let the insurance drop. Violet don't you find that everything now is the most frightful dilemma always? But I don't suppose you do. You're so wonderfully calm all the time dear.'

'I'm not if you only knew. But you've got so many worries with everything you have to manage.'

'That's just it. And when you feel there's someone in the

house you can't trust matters become almost impossible.'

'Someone you can't trust?' the young woman asked in an agitated voice so that Mrs Tennant looked but could not see her expression, standing as she was against the light.

'Why yes,' Mrs Tennant said, 'because that ring must have been somewhere to have been found.'

'Oh of course.'

'Then Violet you don't really consider I need do any more?'

'Well I don't see why. I'd let sleeping dogs rest,' the young woman repeated.

'Well perhaps you're right. Oh and darling Violet there's this other thing. You know Agatha is ill now so that with Nanny Swift that makes two trays for every meal. As a matter of fact Jane and Mary are being very good and I've been able to ease things for the pantry by telling Raunce to discontinue the fires now it's so much warmer. The pictures won't come to any harm for the weather really is quite hot. At the same time it makes rather a lot for Edith when she has to take the children out. There's all the cleaning still to be done as usual. So I was wondering Violet darling if you could possibly take on the children a bit more after Jack's leave is up but only in the afternoons of course.'

As soon as the children were mentioned the younger woman relaxed, sat down again. There came over her face the expression of a spoiled child.

'Why of course,' she said. 'I was going to anyway.'

'You are a brick Violet. One knows one can always rely on you. Things are really becoming detestable in these big houses. I must have a word with Doctor Connolly. It's all very well I shall tell him his killing off poor Eldon but he must be more careful over Agatha,' and Mrs Tennant tittered at herself. 'We simply can't afford to lose her I shall tell him. Or nanny for that matter, though of course if there was anyone to take her place she would almost be pensionable now.'

'Oh I think she's still very good,' Mrs Jack objected. Miss Swift was her own servant.

'She's excellent Violet, quite excellent. I only meant she was getting older as I am. But that's the dilemma nowadays. Whether to have matters out with the servants and then to see them all give notice, or to carry on anyhow so to speak with the existing staff and have some idea in the back of one's mind that things may change for the better? What would you do?'

'My dear I think you manage wonderfully,' Mrs Jack said in a reassuring voice.

'Well I don't know about that,' Mrs Tennant replied. 'It seems we're living pretty well from hand to mouth when I hardly dare ask anyone over to a meal even for fear one or more of the creatures will give notice. You will remember to ring up that Captain Davenport won't you? But in a way I regard this as my war work, maintaining the place I mean. Because we're practically in enemy country here you know and I do consider it so important from the morale point of view to keep up appearances. This country has been ruined by people who did not live on their estates. It might be different if de Valera had a use for places of the kind. Why he doesn't offer Ireland as a hospital base I can't imagine. Then one could hand over a house like this with an easy conscience. Because after all as I always say there are the children to consider. I look on myself simply as a steward. We could shut Kinalty up to-morrow and go and live in one of the cottages. But if I once did that would your darlings ever be able to live here again? I wonder.'

'Did Jack's stepfather live here much before he died?'

'Edward would never be away from the place when he first rented it,' Mrs Tennant replied. 'But once he bought outright he seemed to tire. Still he was a sick man then and most of the time he stayed in London to be near the doctors.'

'Well anyway I think you are doing a perfectly marvellous job,' Mrs Jack murmured.

'Thank you darling. You are a great comfort. I love this house. It's my life now. If only there wasn't this feeling of distrust hanging over one.'

'Distrust?' Mrs Jack enquired rather sharply again.

'This business about my ring,' her mother-in-law replied. 'What I always say is, if one can't trust the people about you where is one?'

'Oh but I'm sure you can? Of course Edith's very much in

love with Raunce, we all know that, which makes her a bit funny and imaginative sometimes. Still I'm sure she's absolutely reliable otherwise.'

'Imaginative my dear?'

'Well you know how it is. She's trying to land Raunce. My God that man's a cold fish. I'm glad it isn't me.'

'Let them marry, let them live in sin if they like so long as we keep them but my dear,' the elder Mrs Tennant said, 'what do we know about the servants? Why,' she added, 'there's Jack. Whatever can be the matter to make him leave the river at this hour? Hullo Jack,' she called, 'done any good?' She had moved over to the open window with this man's wife and stuck her rather astounding head with its blue-washed silver hair out into the day as though she were a parrot embarrassed at finding itself not tied to a perch and which had turned its back on the cage. He waved. He came over. He was in grey flannel trousers with an open red-and-white checked shirt. He looked too young for service in a war.

'I ran out of fags,' he explained looking mildly at his wife who smiled faintly indulgent at him.

'Oh Jack,' his mother said, 'we're asking Captain Davenport, do you remember him, over for dinner to-night?'

'Him?' the young man asked. 'Has he got back then?'

'I didn't know he'd been away,' Mrs Tennant said. Her daughter-in-law stayed very quiet.

'Oh we saw quite a lot of him in London this time didn't we Doll,' he remarked casually to his wife.

'Well there's no one else in this desert of a place so you'll simply have to see him again that's all,' Mrs Tennant said sharp but cheerful and all three drifted off on their separate ways without another word.

The evenings were fast lengthening. Charley and Edith slipped out after supper that same day to be with each other on the very seat by the dovecote where Miss Swift that first afternoon of spring had told her charges a fairy story while they watched the birds love-making. These, up in the air in declining light, were all now engaged on a last turn round before going back inside the leaning tower to hood their eyes in feathers.

Edith laid her lovely head on Raunce's nearest shoulder and above them, above the great shadows laid by trees those white birds wheeled in a sky of eggshell blue and pink with a remote sound of applause as, circling, they clapped their stretched, starched wings in flight.

That side of Edith's face open to the reflection of the sky was a deep red.

'She passed my books all right this mornin',' he murmured.

'What books?' she asked low and sleepy.

'Me monthly accounts,' he replied.

'Did she?' Edith sighed content. They fell silent. At some distance peacocks called to one another, shriek upon far shriek.

'That'll mean a bit more put away for when we are together,' he went on and pressed her arm. She settled closer to him.

'You're wonderful,' she said so low he hardly heard.

'I love you,' he answered.

Her left hand came up to lie against his cheek.

'An' did you ask about our little house we're going to have?' she enquired.

'I did that. But Mrs T. couldn't seem to take it in. She said yes and no and went on about Michael being tiresome. But of course I didn't come straight out about it's being for us dear.'

'You wouldn't,' she made comment dreamily.

'Ah you want to move too fast in some things you do. Slow but sure that's me,' and he chuckled. 'I get 'em so they think it's their idea.'

'You're smart!' she murmured in admiration.

'Clever Charley's the name,' he echoed and kissed her forehead. 'You see girl you want to go soft. A bit at a time.'

'What's it worth to you?' she wanted to know, the hand she had against his cheek stiffening up his face. 'This job I mean,' she added.

'Why you know the money I draw dear? I've made no secret.'

'Yes but the extra on the books?'

'Oh maybe two or three quid a week.'

'Here,' she said drawing her face slightly away, 'it was

more like five or six pounds when you told me a week or two back.'

'Not on your life,' he said in a louder voice. 'You've got it wrong. I couldn't have.'

'You did,' she insisted.

'All you women are the same,' he announced calm, 'you ask so many questions you get a man tied in knots. Then you never forget but bring it up later. Why it couldn't have been that much dear. Mrs T. would notice. She's not short-sighted let me tell you.'

'You wouldn't hold out on me would you Charley?' Edith asked sweet, but looking at him.

'Come off it,' he murmured and kissed her mouth.

'I don't know but I do love you,' she said when she could. After a time he rather unexpectedly tried her out with some news, sitting back as though to watch the effect.

'The Captain was at dinner,' he said.

'Captain Davenport? Oh him,' and she laughed.

'What's comical about that?' he enquired. 'I thought you might consider it a trifle strange so soon after you know what.'

She just lay on him without replying.

'A bit thick it looked to me after he'd followed her right over to England,' he went on.

'Captain Davenport?' she repeated. 'You just put that silliness out of your mind.'

'Women are a mystery,' he added. He kissed her avidly. Some minutes later he spoke once more. 'Was that right what you said about Mr Jack taking liberties?' he asked.

'Wouldn't you like to know,' she replied.

'No girl,' he objected drawing a bit away from her again, 'I got the right to learn now I hope.'

'You don't have to worry your head about him either,' she said.

'I'm the best judge of that,' he muttered.

'Why Charley you're not ever goin' to be jealous of a stuck-up useless card like him surely?'

'You've got such peculiar notions,' he said. 'It'd be hard to tell what you consider is right or wrong.'

'Say that a second time,' she demanded.

'Now sweet'eart,' he said, 'don't go ridin' your high horse.'

'I'm not ridin' nothing.'

'Then what's it all about?' he asked.

'Seems to me you're trying to make out I gave that boy encouragement.'

'Yes they do take 'em young for the army,' he replied.

'Were you?' she went on. 'Because I won't stand for it Charley.' But she was only grumbling.

'Who me?' he said. 'Not on your life. You wouldn't reply to my question.'

'What girl would?' she enquired sweet.

'I'd have thought any woman could give a straight answer if she was asked whether a certain individual had offered . . . well offered . . .' and he seemed at a loss.

'Offered what?' she murmured obviously amused.

'Well all right then, tried to kiss her?' he ended.

'An' I should never've thought there was a man breathing would be so easy as to expect he'd be told the truth.'

'Oho so that's the old game,' he laughed. 'Keeping me on a string is it, to leave me to picture this that and the other to do with you and him?'

'If you can bring your imagination to such a level you're to be pitied,' she answered tart.

'All I did was to ask,' he objected.

'You're free to picture what you please,' she replied. 'I've got no hold on your old imagination, not yet I haven't.'

'What d'you mean not yet?'

'I mean after we're married,' she whispered, her voice gone husky. 'After we're married I'll see to it that you don't have no imagination. I'll make everything you want of me now so much more than you ever dreamed that you'll be quit imaginin' for the rest of your life.'

'Oh honey,' he said in a sort of cry and kissed her passionately. But a rustling noise interrupted them.

'What's that?' he asked violent.

'Hush dear,' she said, 'it'th only the peacockth.'

And indeed a line of these birds one after the other and

hardly visible in this dusk was making tracks back to the stables.

'Whatever brought you to think of that cow son at a time like this,' he asked awkward.

'There'th a lot you'd like to know ithn't there,' she answered.

'Oh give us a kiss do,' he begged.

'If you behave yourthelf,' she said.

After tea one afternoon Edith went up to her room to lie down. She was tired. Agatha and Miss Swift were still confined to bed. The extra work this caused was hard.

She found Kate stretched out already. The rain pattered on ivy round their opened window.

'I'm dead beat I am,' this girl said to Edith who answered,

'Well I don't suppose hard work ever did anyone any harm.'

'But don't it keep pilin' up against you dear all the time,' Kate remarked. Then she added as Edith sat to roll down her stockings. 'There's one thing we still get you can't buy the other side.'

'What's that?'

'Silk stockings,' Kate explained.

'It certainly is a change to hear you have a good word for this place,' Edith said.

Kate let it pass. 'Why don't we have the talks we used to Edie?' she asked.

'Land's sakes I expect it's we're too tired for anything when we do get up in the old room,' Edith answered.

'We used to have some lovely talks Edie.'

'Maybe we've got past talkin'.'

'What d'you mean by that?'

'Well things is different now Kate.'

'If you're referring to the fact that you've an understandin' with Mr Raunce that's no reason to tell me nothing about you, or about him for that matter, is it?'

Edith laughed at this.

'O.K. dear,' she said, 'you win. You go on asking then?'

'You are going to be married Edie?'

'We are that,' Edith said, lying down full length. Both girls looked up at the ceiling, stretched out on their backs airing their feet.

'Well I wish you all I could wish meself,' Kate said in a low voice.

'Thanks love,' Edith replied matter of fact.

'When's it going to be?'

'As soon as I've got me a few pretties together I shouldn't wonder,' Edith answered.

At this a sort of snorting sob came from the other bed. Edith rolled to look, then sat up. 'Why you're crying,' she exclaimed. She came across and sat on the edge of Kate's eiderdown.

'Whatever for? You are silly,' she added gentle. 'Here,' she said, 'look at you right on top of the quilting. Let's get you comfortable.' She began to roll Kate across to one side to get the eiderdown from underneath her. Kate was limp. 'Oh Edie' she wailed and started to cry noisily.

'Hush dear,' Edith murmured, 'someone'll hear.' She began to ease Kate's clothes off.

'Oh Edie,' Kate moaned. Edith stopped to wipe the girl's face which was damp with tears.

'There,' Edith said. 'Now don't you pay attention love. They're nothin' but an old lot of muddlers every one.' She covered Kate's greenish body up.

Kate's violent crying passed to hiccups.

'Why,' she asked turning so that she could watch Edith, 'has one of them spoken about me?'

'No not a word.'

'I got the hiccups,' Kate announced, almost started a giggle. She brightened. ''Cause you'd've known what to tell 'em if they had?'

'Of course I would dear,' Edith was stroking the nape of Kate's neck.

'Oh that's nice love,' this girl said. She blew her nose on the handkerchief Edith had left ready to hand. 'You don't know what a lot of good that's doin'.'

'And so it should,' Edith answered.

'Thanks duck. And now we're like we used to be isn't that right?'

'That's right.'

'I can't make out what came over me,' Kate went on. 'Honest I can't.'

'It's a hard bloody world.'

'Why Edith I never thought to hear you swear of all people, I didn't that.'

'It's the truth Kate just the same.'

'You're right it is,' Kate said. 'Look I've got rid of my 'iccups. That's one good thing. Yes there's times I could bust right out with it all. It gets you down. An' then your tellin' me about you an' Mr Raunce.'

'I thought you said once you'd never give him a Mr.'

'Oh Edie that's different. Now you're to be married I must show my respect.'

'I don't know dear. I'm sure you can call him Charley for all I care.'

'Have it any way you want,' said Kate peaceably. 'An' where will you live? Are you planning to stay in Kinalty?'

'Yes we got our eye on that little place in the demesne.'

'Oh isn't that lovely.'

'And we're thinking of gettin' his mother to come over to be with us so she will be out of the bombin'.'

'Oh isn't that nice,' Kate said and seemed to choke. She began to cry silently again, great tears welling from her shut eyes.

'Why love,' Edith asked, 'is anything the matter?'

'No,' Kate wailed.

'You're sure now?' Edith went on. Then she asked, 'There's nothing going to happen to you is there?'

'Me?' Kate echoed, suddenly quiet. 'You mean on account of Paddy don't you?'

'Then there is,' Edith said. Her eyes opened wide.

'Why Edie,' Kate replied serious, 'you wouldn't ever believe that surely?'

'That's all right then.'

'Never in your life,' Kate went on. 'So you guessed?'

'It was Albert told my young ladies. That little bastard had it from Mrs Welch. There's no other word to describe the lad.'

'She calls 'im that 'erself so Jane told me. She heard her.'

'Would you believe it?' Edith murmured.

'But Paddy's not what you suppose dear,' Kate said as if she had given Edith's last remark a certain meaning. 'You've no need to bother yourself about that between Paddy an' me. I'm not goin' to have nothing don't worry. No it was everything got me down all of a sudden.'

'You weren't thinkin' of him in such a way then?'

'Well there's not much else to think of is there Edie?'

'Why he's a Roman.'

'That don't make no difference.'

'I don't suppose it should. But these Irish are not like us.'

'Once I get Paddy smartened up you'd never recognize him for one.'

'But what about his speech, Kate?'

'Yes I know that's a problem. It'll be the hardest thing to alter.'

'So you are considering him?' Edith asked.

'There's nobody else. A girl gets lonely,' Kate answered beginning to cry once more. 'And I think you're not bein' gracious about it,' she added.

'There dear,' Edith said, 'you're upset.'

'Don't go,' Kate muttered between sobs.

'I'm not goin' love. You quiet yourself. Life's not easy.'

'You're tellin' me,' Kate agreed and pulled herself together to blow her nose. 'Now d'you know what's come about?'

'What's that?' Edith asked as she began to stroke her again.

'He's in a terrible state about them eggs.'

'What eggs?'

'Why the eggs you put away under waterglass in this very room,' Kate answered.

'But that was months ago. However did he come to learn?'

'It was young Albert again who else? I promise I never told 'im nothin'. I wouldn't do such a thing. And then in addition Mr Raunce went and informed about that peacock Mrs Welch had in the larder. Oh Edie 'e got in such a state. I was frighted.'

'I'll speak of this to Charley,' Edith said grim.

'It's as you like,' Kate replied, 'but 'e worships the birds, there you are love, he fair worships 'em. There's nothing I can do. And what he's just learned has made 'im act so strange. I don't know what to think, honest I don't.'

'Then what does he say he'll do?' Edith enquired.

'Why 'e talks as if 'e was goin' to lock 'em up and never let the things out any more. Can you tell me how Mrs Tennant'll see that?'

'I'd forgotten all about those old eggs,' Edith said. Then she added in a wondering voice, 'I suppose it was me knowin' I had no more use for 'em.'

'What d'you mean no more use? You used to reckon they'd still be good for your skin even if they had been stood in that stuff.'

'Yes,' Edith said. 'it's not that I've no need any more for my face which'll still come in handy I don't doubt. But the fact is now Raunce an' me's come to an understanding I got no time for charms.'

'I shouldn't wonder if he didn't find time for yours even if you shouldn't,' Kate remarked archly.

Edith blushed.

'Look,' Kate cried and seemed far more cheery, 'you're blushin'.'

'It's not that kind you mention,' Edith said. 'I meant like crossing a gipsy's palm with silver at the fair. A charm to make you seem different,' she explained.

'Would they do the same for me d'you suppose?'

'I don't know Kate seein' I've never tried.'

'But if 'e came upon it Edie 'e'd strangle me.'

'Like little Albert did to one of his peacocks?' Edith was smiling.

'You don't know 'im Edie, there's no one could tell what action 'e'd take.'

'Why should he ever learn?' Edith asked.

'There's not much is kept mum in this house love.'

'O.K. then. But it's only the children after all, Kate, as we've found since little Albert came. They'll never discover. I shan't tell.'

'But d'you think it's real what you believed about the things?'

'There's this to it Kate. He loves the birds, you've just said so. If you used their eggs and he was ignorant then it might do something to him.'

'Just imagine me smarming that muck over my face and chest to please. What we girls do have to put up with.'

'Go on,' Edith said, 'that's nothing.' Both began to giggle. Edith put the heel of her hand up to cover her mouth. 'For land's sake,' she cried.

'And when they come at you . . .' Kate began then stopped. She started laughing helplessly all of a sudden. Edith joined in. Within a minute they were exchanging breathless and indistinct accounts of the antics men get up to, in between shrieks of giggling.

Later that afternoon came over dark with a storm outside. Edith had filled a polished copper jug and was hurrying down the Long Passage to lay the hot water in Mrs Jack's washbasin when she saw something move in an open doorway into the dressing room next door. She stopped dead, raised her free hand to her heart. But it was Raunce.

'You Charley,' she said low when she saw him, 'why I nearly spilled it.'

'Sorry ducks,' he answered, whispering also, 'I was only puttin' out his things.'

'Whatever for?' she asked. 'You don't do that so early do you?'

'Well if you're speaking of the hour I'll wager this hot water you're carryin' will go cold before she comes to use it.'

'There's a cover I put over the jug stupid,' she replied. 'Are you goin' to tell me you didn't know that after all the years you've been here?'

'I don't like to let you out of my sight.'

'Why Charley,' she said warm, 'you don't mean to say you've got him on your mind again?'

'Well it's not right when he might come across you in his own bedroom.'

'Have you ever heard?' she muttered in a delighted voice and went inside Mrs Jack's room. He followed after.

'I don't know,' he said, 'but I gave you a bit of a start. I saw.'

'Oh these jugs,' she began, 'they will tarnish. And when we're shorthanded like we are.'

'You give'm to me in the morning an' I'll rub'm up for you.'

'Not if you set Albert to it I won't.'

'Where did you get that notion?' he enquired. He was looking at her as he usually did nowadays, like a spaniel dog.

'I move around,' she answered.

'No. What I do for you I do for you,' he announced. 'Who'd you take me for?'

'Take you for? You're not so easily mistaken for anyone.'

'Just now,' he explained, 'you thought I was someone else.'

'You do want to know a great deal.' She was smiling. They stood close to each other. Then she reached up to finger a button on his coat. She poked at it as though at a bell. He did not seem to dare touching her.

'I'll have to be on hand each time you come up that's all,' he said.

'But what about your work?'

'Only when it's like now, when there's none of us about dear,' he appealed.

'You are silly,' she replied and gave him a quick kiss.

'But did he ever?' he asked still rigid.

'See here,' she said, 'you may have your Albert to do everything for you but I've not, I'm on my own.' She crossed over to the bed. 'Look,' she said. She took a black silk transparent nightdress out of its embroidered case. 'What d'you say to that Charley?'

He gazed, obviously struck dumb. She held it up in front of her. She put a hand in at the neck so that he could see the veiled skin. He began to breathe heavy.

'It's wicked that's all,' he announced at last while she watched. 'What?' she echoed. 'Not more than it was with mam'selle surely?'

''Ow d'you mean Edie?'

'"There's many a time I'd give her a long bong jour,"' she quoted.

'I never,' he said and took a step forward.

'That's you men all over,' she went on.

'Her?' he protested. He had gone quite white. 'Why you're crackers. That two pennorth of French sweat rag?'

'Now you're being disgustin' dear.'

'I can't make you out,' he said coming towards her.

'No,' she cried, 'you stop where you are. I'm goin' to punish you. What d'you say if we took this for when we are married? How would I look eh Charley?' And she held that nightdress before her face.

'Punishment eh?' he laughed. If it had been a spell then he seemed to be out of it for the moment. 'That's all you girls think of. Why holy Moses,' he added as if trying to appear gay, 'that piece of cobweb ain't for us.'

'Don't you reckon I'd look nice in it then?' She lowered the nightdress till he could see she was pouting.

'You'd appear like a bloody tart,' he said, then broadly smiled. She stamped her foot.

'Don't you swear at me of all people Charley.'

'O.K.,' he said.

'Why,' she went on, returning to the charge, 'not above a minute or two ago you were puffin' like a grampus.'

'What's a grampus honey?' he asked and looked a bit daunted.

'Wouldn't you like to know?' she teased him.

'I can't make out why you want all this mystification,' he said. 'Honest you've got me so I'm anyhow.'

'An' so you should be Charley dearest.'

'Oh Edie,' he gasped moving forward. The room had grown immeasurably dark from the storm massed outside. Their two bodies flowed into one as he put his arms about her. The shape they made was crowned with his head, on top of a white sharp curved neck, dominating and cruel over the blur that was her mass of hair through which her lips sucked at him warm and heady.

'Edie,' he muttered breaking away only to drive his face down into hers once more. But he was pressing her back into a bow shape. 'Edie,' he called again.

With a violent shove and twist she pushed him off. As she wiped her mouth on the back of a hand she remarked as though wondering,

'You aren't like this first thing are you?'

This must have been a reference to the fact that when she called him with a cup of tea in the mornings he never kissed her then as he lay in bed. Or he must have understood it as such because, standing as he was like he had been drained of blood, he actually moaned.

'Why,' he said, 'that wouldn't be right.'

'Don't you love me in the early hours then?'

'Sweetheart,' he protested.

'With me carryin' you a cup of tea and all?'

'Well it's usually half cold at that,' he said, seeming to pull himself together.

'Oho,' she cried and began to do her hair with Mrs Jack's comb. 'Then I won't bring no more.'

'I'd been intending to speak to you about that very point,' he began shamefaced. 'I don't know that you should continue with the practice. It might lead to talk,' he said.

'Charley you don't say I'm not to,' she appealed and seemed really hurt. 'Why, don't you like me fetchin' your tea?'

'It's not that dear.'

She turned vast reproachful eyes on him.

'I was kidding myself you would fancy me above any other to open your eyes on first thing,' she repeated softly grumbling.

'It's the rest,' he moaned.

'Just because I'm keeping myself for you on our wedding night you reckon they'd think you're free with me?' she asked as though he had hit her.

'Well that's what would happen isn't it, being as they are?' he enquired.

'Oh Charley,' she went on gentle but reproachful, 'that's cowardly so it is?'

'You know I love you don't you?' he entreated and took hold of her hands. She was limp.

'Yes.'

'Well then,' he went on, 'we don't want no chitter chatter do we?'

'You mean no one shouldn't know in case you change your

mind about our being married?' she asked. There was laughter now in her voice.

'What's comical in that when you've just spoken a lie?' he demanded.

'All right then I'll not bring your old tea again that's all.' She laid her arms round his neck and gave him a powerful kiss. Putting his hands against her shoulders he pushed her away.

'You said yourself we were on a good thing an' didn't want to lose this place,' he explained.

'I never imagined you could do without me pulling your curtains. So the first you set eyes on every new day should be me.'

'I love you that's why honey,' he said.

'O.K.,' she said, 'but you're to do the explainin' with Mother Burch mind.'

'That's a good girl. Holy smoke,' he exclaimed, 'an' there's my lad forgotten to lay their table I'll be bound. I'll be seeing you,' he said. He fairly stumbled out.

Some days later Mrs Jack unexpectedly entered the Blue Drawing Room to find her mother-in-law in tears beneath a vaulted roof painted to represent the evening sky at dusk. Mrs Tennant immediately turned her face away to hide her state. She was seated forlorn, plumb centre of this chamber, on an antique Gothic imitation of a hammock slung between four black marble columns and cunningly fashioned out of gold wire. But she had not concealed her tears in time. Mrs Jack saw. She went across at once.

'Why you poor thing,' she said rubbing the point of Mrs Tennant's shoulder with the palm of a hand.

'I'm sorry to make such a fool of myself Violet,' this older woman said from between gritted teeth and got out a handkerchief.

'I think you've been perfectly wonderful dear,' Mrs Jack suggested.

'Really I don't know how your generation bears it,' Mrs Tennant went on. She blew her nose while Mrs Jack stood ill at ease.

As she rubbed the shoulder of her husband's mother she was surrounded by milking stools, pails, clogs, the cow byre furniture all in gilded wood which was disposed around to create the most celebrated eighteenth-century folly in Eire that had still to be burned down.

'You've been absolutely magnificent Violet,' Mrs T. continued. 'Here he's been gone three days God knows where on active service if he hasn't already sailed. There's been not a whimper out of you once.'

'Don't,' his wife said sharp and gripped that shoulder in such a way as to hurt the older woman.

'No you must let me,' Mrs Tennant began again but calmer as though the pain was what she needed. 'It's so hard for my generation to talk to yours about the things one really feels. I never seem to have the chance to speak up over the great admiration I hold you in my dear.'

'You mustn't.'

Her mother-in-law ignored this though she must have recognized that it had been uttered in anguish. 'I grant you,' she went on, looking straight in front of her, 'your contemporaries have all got this amazing control of yourselves. Never showing I mean. So I just wanted to say once more if I never say it again. Violet dear I think you are perfectly wonderful and Jack's a very lucky man.'

Violet stood as if frozen. Mrs Tennant used her handkerchief.

'There,' Mrs T. said, 'I feel better for that. I'm sorry I've been such an idiot. Oh and Violet could you let go of me. You are hurting rather.'

'Good heavens,' the young woman exclaimed gazing at the impression her nails had made on Mrs Tennant's shirt and with trembling lips.

'It's my fault entirely Violet because I invaded your privacy,' Mrs Tennant said with a positive note of satisfaction in her voice. 'Oh your generation's hard,' she added.

'But he'll be all right you'll see,' Mrs Jack began, then did not seem able to go on while she smoothed the silk where her nails had dug in. 'He'll come back,' she said finally.

'Of course he will,' Mrs Tennant agreed at once, all of a

sudden brisk with assurance. But under her breath with an agony of shame the younger woman was repeating I will write to Dermot and say my darling I must never see you again never in my life my darling.

'You must forgive me for just now Violet,' the older woman said not in the least apologetic.

My darling my darling my darling, her daughter-in-law prayed in her heart to the Captain, never ever again.

'I think everything's partly to do with the servants,' Mrs Tennant announced as if drawing a logical conclusion.

'The servants?' Mrs Jack echoed, it might have been from a great distance.

'Well one gets no rest. It's always on one's mind Violet.' She got up. She began to search for dust, smelling her wetted forefinger as though there could be a smell. 'This last trouble over my cluster ring now. I spoke to Raunce again but it was most unsatisfactory.'

'I shouldn't have,' Mrs Jack murmured a trifle louder.

'I know Violet. But you do see one can't stand things hanging over one? This hateful business round the pantry boy. There's no two ways about it. Either you can trust people or you can't and if you can't then they're distasteful to live with.'

'Yes,' Mrs Jack agreed simply. All at once she seemed to recollect. 'What d'you mean quite?' she asked sharp almost in spite of herself.

'Well he said he had it, he told Raunce so.'

'Had what?' Mrs Jack demanded suddenly frantic.

Mrs Tennant swung round to face her daughter-in-law who did not raise her blue eyes. There was something hard and glittering beyond the stone of age in that other pair below the blue waved tresses. And then Mrs Tennant turned away once more.

'Why my cluster ring Violet,' she said going over to an imitation pint measure also in gilded wood and in which peacock's feathers were arranged. She lifted this off the white marble mantelpiece that was a triumph of sculptured reliefs depicting on small plaques various unlikely animals, even in one instance a snake, sucking milk out of full udders and then

179

she blew at it delicately through pursed lips.

'Besides there's another thing,' Mrs Tennant went on, moving around amongst the historic pieces which made up this fabulous dairy of a drawing room. 'The peacocks,' she said. 'Now yesterday was perfectly dry without a drop of rain yet I couldn't see one of the birds all morning.'

'Perhaps they thought it was going to rain,' Mrs Jack proposed and drifted over to the windows. 'They don't like getting wet.'

'My dear Violet please tell me when does it ever not threaten rain in this climate? No I made enquiries. Like everything else in this house it was quite different. Not the natural explanation at all. Just as I'd feared. Because I had Raunce in and I asked him. Of course he pretended to know nothing as the servants always do,' and at this Mrs Jack winced, 'but I can't stand lies. D'you know what he wanted me to believe?'

'You said he was lying?' Mrs Jack asked faint over her shoulder.

'Well he must have been my dear. Now look at this pitchfork or lamp standard or whatever they call it.' Mrs Tennant was halted before a gold instrument cunningly fixed as so to appear leant against the wall and which had been adapted to take an oil lamp between its prongs. 'The damp has settled on the metal part which is all peeling. In spite of the fire I have kept up on account of the Cuyps. Isn't that provoking? And of course it's a museum piece. Or that's what they say when they come down. They simply exclaim out loud when they see this room.' But her daughter-in-law did not look. 'It's all French you know,' Mrs Tennant continued, 'they say it came from France, which is why I try to impress it on the servants that they really must be careful. There'll be so little left when this war's finished. But Raunce is hopeless. D'you know what he said to me?'

'No?'

'Well Violet I'd asked him to have a word with O'Conor. You know how extremely difficult that man is. Then it came out,' and Mrs Jack drew her breath sharp, 'or not everything, just a bit probably. You see he said O'Conor had locked the

180

peacocks up in their quarters as he termed it. Now that's very unsatisfactory of course. After all they are my peacocks as I pointed out to Raunce. I have a right to see them I should hope. They're a part of the decoration of the place. But he told me he thought O'Conor was afraid of something or other.'

'How ridiculous,' Mrs Jack exclaimed. She turned to face her mother-in-law with a look which appeared stiff with apprehension. But if Mrs Tennant noticed this she gave no sign.

'Exactly,' she said. 'Frightened of what I'd like to know? I put it to Raunce. But he couldn't or wouldn't say.'

'Which is just like the man,' the younger woman interrupted. 'Always hinting.'

'But that wasn't the lie,' Mrs Tennant said soft. 'When it came it was much more direct than that. You see as I said before I asked him to speak to O'Conor. D'you know what he answered? Sheer impertinence really. He had the cheek to stand where you are now and tell me that it was no use his going to interrogate the lampman, can't you hear him, because he couldn't understand a word he said.'

'I don't quite see,' Mrs Jack put in livelier. 'I can't catch what he says myself.'

'No more can I. That's why I wanted someone else to go. But my dear it's not for us to understand O'Conor,' Mrs Tennant explained as she replaced into its niche a fly-whisk carved out of a block of sandalwood, the handle enamelled with a reddish silver. 'We don't have to live with the servants. Not yet. It's they who condescend to stay with us nowadays. No but you're not telling me that they pass all their huge meals in utter silence. He eats with them you know. Of course Raunce was lying. He understands perfectly what O'Conor says. There's something behind all this Violet. It's detestable.'

'Raunce told you that O'Conor shut the peacocks up? But that's too extraordinary,' Mrs Jack remarked in a confident voice. She was tracing patterns on the window-pane with a purple finger nail.

'I shall get to the bottom of it,' Mrs Tennant announced. For an instant she sent a grim smile at her daughter-in-law's back. 'I shall bide my time though,' she said, then quietly left that chamber the walls of which were hung with blue silk. Mrs Jack swung round but the room was empty.

That night the servants all sat down to supper together. Mrs Welch had asked for and been granted leave to stay in Dublin overnight to consult a doctor. Her Albert had been sent to bed. By this time he was probably running naked on the steeply sloping roofs high up. Mrs Jack now looked after her children who ate with their mother and the grandparent while Miss Swift died inch by inch in the bedroom off the nursery. And because Miss Burch was still indisposed Edith as though by right took this woman's place at table.

'Well what are we waiting for?' she asked quite natural in Agatha's manner.

'Bert's just bringing in the cold joint,' Mary replied. 'Jane's lending a hand. My,' she went on, 'this certainly is nice for us girls to have company. It's a thought we both of us appreciate Mr Raunce to be invited to your supper.'

'You're welcome,' the man replied as he sharpened his carving knife against a fork. He spoke moodily.

'Come on Bert do,' Edith remarked keen to the lad when, followed by Jane carrying vegetables in Worcester dishes, he came struggling under a great weight of best beef. He cast a reproachful look in her direction but made no reply.

'If it wasn't for O'Conor being absent this could be termed a reunion,' Raunce announced pompous. 'With Miss Swift and Miss Burch confined to their quarters as they are by sickness we won't count them. Nor Mrs Welch thanks be with her 'ardening of the kidneys.'

'Charley,' Edith remonstrated.

'Pardon,' he said. He sent her a glance that seemed saturated with despair.

'I'm sure we're very happy to have you with us,' Edith said in Jane's direction. Kate watched. Her gimlet eyes narrowed.

'Because if Paddy turns up I've been charged to speak to him,' Raunce began heavy as he set about carving the joint.

'Well you know right well where he is the sad soul,' Kate replied. 'Locked up with them birds 'e's been the past ten days and only gettin' what I fetch out. Not that I defend it,' she ended.

'We can excuse him. I'd be the very last to question 'is motives,' Raunce answered who without doubt had his own reasons for leaving Paddy alone if only that he cannot have been anxious to implicate Edith in the affair of the eggs. 'Matter of that,' he continued, 'Mrs Tennant's got a lot she wants me to say and not to our friend alone. Oh no,' he said. 'For she's on about her ring still.'

'And how would that be Mr Raunce since she got it back didn't she?' Mary enquired.

'There you are,' he answered with as good reasons perhaps for not pursuing this one either. 'There you are you've said it,' he repeated rather lamely.

'It was only that man who came down upset her,' Edith explained while Albert watched. 'And you can't wonder after all. Setting everyone about the place at sixes and sevens as he did. But all's well that ends well,' she concluded.

'If it has ended,' Raunce remarked. 'A sewer rat like him should never be permitted to harass honest folk. Is that right or isn't it? What'th that you thay. Lithping like a tothpot,' he added in a wild and sudden good humour.

'Charley,' Edith called. She began to go red.

'You should have seen the expression you wore,' he said complacent, 'you should really. When he had the impudence to ask you if you'd theen a thertain thomething. D'you recollect?'

'I certainly don't,' Edith said and pouted.

But Kate took this up. 'You don't thay he thpoke like thith thurely,' she asked letting out a shriek of amusement. All of them started to laugh or giggle except Edith and Raunce's Albert.

'It's a lot of foolishness,' Edith reproved them.

'Foolithneth perhapth,' Raunce said roguish. 'But you're dead right. Whatever it may have been it was uncalled for.'

'Why Charley,' Edith went on, 'you're not going to starve yourself again. You will have your supper to-night surely?'

'No girl,' he answered but with a soft look. 'Truth is I don't feel equal to it.'

'The spuds are nice. I cooked 'em myself,' Jane explained and the girls all clucked with sympathy at him except Kate who went on with the lisping.

'If he'd 'a lithped at me I'm dead thure I'd 'a lithped back. I couldn't help mythelf.' Mary giggled. 'Oh Kate you don't thay tho,' she cried.

'Holy thmoke but you've got me goin' now,' Raunce laughed. They all began giggling once more, even Edith. But Albert simpered.

'The whole thing'th too dithtathteful,' Raunce quoted. ''Ere I can't get my tongue round it. Dithtasteful,' he tried again. 'No that won't do.' In a moment most of them were attempting this.

'Detethtable,' he shouted out into the hubbub then doubled up with laughter.

'Hush dear they'll hear you,' Edith giggled.

'And what do I care?' he asked. 'Now if you'd said "Huth" I might've harkened. But detethtable's right. It is detestable and distasteful if you like, to have been put through what we've been as if we were criminals,' he said.

'What d'you mean Mr Raunce?' Mary asked.

'Why over this ring she mislaid. Had an investigator sent down and all she did,' he explained. 'Got hold of my lad here then drove 'im half out of his mind with the cunning queries he put till there was Bert sayin' the first thing that came into 'is head. Proper upset you didn't he?' Raunce said to the boy who kept quiet. 'No, but it's wrong,' Raunce told the others, 'it didn't ought to be allowed. Why matters went so far he got 'im talkin' of joining up to get killed. There you are. Not but what we'd all be better off over on the other side.'

'Charley,' Edith called as though he had turned his back on her.

'Upset me too that merchant did. There's been something wrong with my interior from that day to this. I can't seem able to digest my food.'

'You want to take care,' Jane chipped in solicitous. 'Now if I was to put you together a nice bowl of hot broth,' she suggested.

'Thank you,' Raunce replied lordly. 'Thank you but I'd best give my economy a half holiday. It's me dyspepsia,' he explained. 'Dythpepthia,' he added gay on a sudden.

'Don't be disgusting,' Edith reproved him. 'And I'll do all

the looking after you need,' she said glancing jealous at Jane.

Kate began to blush deeply.

'Holy Motheth,' Raunce crowed, 'now see what you've been and done Edie. You've set our Kate goin'.'

'Things is getting out of hand if you ask me,' Edith remarked. She looked desperate. At that Kate rose, left the room absolutely scarlet.

'Why whatever's the matter with her then?' Mary asked but if Charley was about to reply he never managed it because he was taken by a violent fit of coughing. Edith went to his side. A volley of suggestions was directed at him. Only Albert sat back apart.

'I choked,' he excused himself when he had recovered. 'I don't feel very grand. But you'll agree it's not good enough. It's not right this cross questionin'. Men entering the house without leave and then every sort and kind of question asked. I know she lost a valuable,' he went on, 'but it was not worth that much, couldn't have been, or she would never have gone over to England.' Then he corrected himself. 'Well I don't know,' he said. 'It's a fact Jack had his week's leave right enough but that's not to say she should permit this individual to come nosing round. Conditions are bad enough as it is with all the buzzes and rumours over the invasion,' and all this time the others listened to Raunce with deference, 'not to mention talk of the I.R.A. Because we're at the mercy of any 'ooligan, German or Irish, situated as we are. With Mrs Tennant away we've no influence none whatever.' He paused to cough, not so violently. 'For two pins I'd throw the place up. And one reason is I got a feelin' I'm not appreciated. My work I mean.'

'I don't suppose she was in a position to help herself,' Edith pointed out reasonably. 'Once she claimed on her insurance it would be a thing the company in Dublin would do in the ordinary run, to send down and investigate.'

'I'm not disputing that,' Raunce countered, 'but what I say is Mrs T. should've been here to receive 'im. We're plain honest folk we are. This is not the first position of trust we've held down. We've come out of our places with a good reference each time or she would never have engaged us. No,' he insisted with authority, 'there's a right and a wrong way to go about matters of this sort. There you are, it's 'ighly dithtrething,' he ended as though, having noticed Edith's expression, he now intended to turn all this off into a joke. If that was his intention it was immediately successful. Like a class at school when given the signal to break up they all with one accord burst out lisping, with the exception of Raunce's Albert. In no time their hilarity had grown until each effort was received with shrieks, Edith's this time amongst the loudest.

Charley began to laugh unrestrained as he held his side which seemed to pain him. Yet he let himself go.

'There'th a tanner in thith for you altho,' he shouted to Edith above the din, quoting her description of Mike Mathewson's proceedings.

'Thankth thon,' she called back. He doubled up again.

'Well thith evening'th a big differenth I mutht thay,' Jane shrieked to Mary. 'Not what we uthually have to look forward to duckth, ith it?' she yelled. At this Kate who had slipped back again began to laugh so much she dribbled. 'Mith Burthch,' she squealed, 'Mitheth Welcheth,' Mary screamed, 'oh Burcheth Welhech,' Raunce echoed and pandemonium reigned. But in his convulsions of laughter Charley was noticeably paler even. For the past fortnight he had been looking very ill. 'Landth thakes Mith Thwift,' howled Edith. By now everyone bar Albert was crying. All wore a look of agony, or as though they were in a close finish to a race over a hundred yards. 'Jethuth,' Raunce moaned.

'Hush dear,' Edith said at once. 'That's not comical dear,' and they began to sober down.

'Moses,' he corrected himself.

'There,' Jane announced between gasps, 'I feel like I'd been emptied.'

'What of duckth?' Kate asked and there blew up another gust of giggling. 'Oh me,' someone remarked weak. 'It's my side,' another said. Then they quietened.

'Well nobody can say we don't have our fun on occasions,' Edith made comment as she dabbed at her great eyes.

'It'd be all right if we was like this every night,' Jane murmured.

186

'Oh it's not so bad after all.'

'I don't know Edith,' Mary answered. 'You've not got Mrs Welch although I shouldn't mention names.'

'We ain't got her Albert,' Raunce put in.

'It's not him so much,' Jane explained. 'He's well enough conducted indoors in the kitchen,' she said. 'It's Mrs Welch is the matter. Oh I know I shouldn't but she drinks. All the time she drinks. She's only gone in to Dublin to get another crate. She's like the wells, she's runnin' dry. There you are. That's right isn't it Mary or isn't it?'

'It's the honest truth,' Mary said.

'Go on,' Raunce objected, 'but then 'ow does she get the stuff delivered will you oblige me with that? Because I don't need to tell you she's not drawin' a drop out of my cellar. I don't hold with this fiddling like you'll come across in some households.'

'Why,' Jane disclosed in a hushed voice, 'it's the tradesmen. You know she won't 'ave one of us pass the time of day with 'em even. Well you'd never guess what's behind it. I tell you they drop a case of the stuff with the meat and another with the groceries. And the price all included in the monthly books, isn't that so Mary?'

'That's right,' this girl replied.

'The artful old cow,' Raunce exclaimed.

'Charley,' Edith said firm.

'Pardon I'm sure,' he answered gravely, 'but did you ever hear anything to touch this? Fiddlin' 'er monthly books. No. You know that's serious this is.' He was solemn.

'You're tellin' me,' Kate muttered.

'What?' he asked at once and sharp. 'Bless me my gel but you seem to grow more and more sarky every day which passes. What's come over you?'

'Nothin' Mr Raunce.'

'You let her be, Charley,' Edith reproved him. 'She was only agreein'.'

'No offence intended I'm sure,' he assured her. 'But is that what Mrs Welch is up to? Would you believe it?' he enquired of all and sundry in an astounded tone of voice.

'The wickedness there is in this world,' Mary said.

'The wickedness?' he asked gentle but with a sharp look.

'Because that's thievin' that is,' Jane concluded like a little girl put through her catechism.

'You've said it,' Raunce agreed and relaxed. It had plainly been the right answer. 'That's the very word.' Then he quoted Miss Burch with solemnity. 'And the wicked shall flourish even as a green bay tree,' he intoned. Everyone bar Albert seemed to approve.

A few days afterwards Edith entered Charley's room as she was coming on her way from tea in the servants' hall.

'Come on out and feed the peacockth,' she proposed, for Paddy had at last consented to free these birds again. She waved a bag she had filled with scraps.

'Steady,' he replied. 'That's no light matter.'

'Why what's up Charley?'

'Nothing,' he answered.

'I know there is,' she said.

'I'm not right,' he went on. 'I vomited this morning another time.'

'Oh dear that's bad,' she said lightly.

'I shouldn't wonder if you made fun of this as you've done before but I love you so much my stomach's all upset an' there you are.'

'So it should be,' she countered as though determined not to worry.

'Yes but what's to be the end?' he asked low. 'I can't go on the way I am. I'm in bad shape. Honest, dear.'

'You wait till we're married love. I'll take care you're never sick then.'

'Oh the worry of it all,' he broke out.

'Now just you come along with me,' she said. 'Getting out in the air for a while will do you more good than any other thing.'

'I've no time.'

'No time Charley? How's that?'

'I must lay the dinner dear. Now my Albert's left, everything falls back on me you know.'

'But surely you've never forgotten how they're over to

188

Clancarty for dinner with the Captain. Why you've a free evenin'.'

'There I go again,' he said bewildered. 'It had clean slipped my memory. Well perhaps I will at that.'

'That's right Charley,' she coaxed as she took his arm. She laid her body up against his shoulder. 'We'll sit us down by the old dovecote so you can rest. It will do you ever such a lot of good you'll see.'

When they were established there after she had conducted him as though he was an old man and he had sat himself down heavily he remarked,

'It come as a big shock to me my Albert leavin' the way he did.'

'But you knew he'd given in his notice love,' she objected.

'Of course I knew,' he replied querulous, 'but I never thought he meant to go, any more than Mrs Tennant took it that he did. As she told me.'

'I can't say I considered it was other than talk,' she agreed. 'To walk in just like that an' say look my month's up I must be off the way he did. I never guessed that bloodless abortion 'ad the guts,' he said with a return to his old manner.

'You never could abide him could you?' she remarked.

'That dam kid's attitude was what got my goat,' Mr Raunce explained. 'The high falutin' love he laid claim to, the suffering looks he darted, 'is faintin' snotty ways.'

Edith gave a single deep laugh.

'Yes go on and laugh,' Raunce said.

'No you made yourself awkward with that lad.'

'That's as may be,' he answered and seemed despondent. 'Yet there's only the one method to learn them kids a trade. It's no earthly good kissin' 'em as you did.'

'Me?' she cried. 'I never.'

'You did that and in front of the investigator johnny into the bargain.'

'Oh well,' she said.

'Have it your own way,' he replied. He relapsed into silence.

'What is it dear?' she asked.

'I'm worried,' he answered.

'What's worrying you then?'

'Nothing.'

'It's not about the old ring any more is it?' she enquired.

'Well Albert's goin' did set 'er mind on it once again. Seems that she'd told him she couldn't accept his notice while he was under suspicion, or so she made out to me. I thought we'd better make an end to that talk. "Look Madam," I said to her, "you can't deny you have the ring back so where's the evidence," I said. She says to me, "But it's what I suspect Raunce, that's where the shoe pinches," or some such phrase. "I can't guarantee it won't happen a second time Madam," I told her, "an' if anything should, then you report it to me Madam an' I'll see you don't have any more trouble. There's things I didn't know then that I know now," I says. "I see Raunce," she said. "Then you don't wish for me to do another thing and I can sleep quiet into the bargain?" "You silly old cow you can do just that," I said to her only I didn't.'

'Charley that's not very nice,' Edith objected.

'But we've 'ad about enough surely? There's more going on in the world these days than a little crazy bastard of a cook's nephew having the laugh on us. Secreted it right here too didn't he? I shouldn't mind if I never set eyes on these blasted white pigeons again,' he ended.

'Why,' she said, 'your pain you've got's upset you.'

'You're dead right it has,' he replied.

'You don't benefit by your night's rest,' she went on.

He appeared to warm to this description of his symptoms. 'That's exactly it,' he agreed. 'I sometimes just seem to do nothin' but turn over.'

'And d'you always think of me?' she asked taking tighter hold of the arm she had hung on to.

'You bet I do,' he answered. 'More'n you ever realize.'

'That's right,' she said, 'then you won't come by much harm.'

'I do love you Edie.'

'Do you?'

'D'you know I sometimes wonder if the air in these parts hadn't a lot to do with my stomach,' he began again. 'I couldn't say if it's too weak or too strong but there's something about these sea breezes might be harmful to a delicate constitution. What d'you say?' He was dead serious.

'No that's good for you.'

'Then what d'you reckon can be the matter with me Edie?'

It was plain she was not worried. 'D'you think Mrs Welch is slipping a pinch of something in your food?' she asked maliciously, hardly paying attention.

'I wouldn't put that past her,' he replied. 'But she's too set on keepin' young Albert over on this side of the water to start a game like it. Why if I had proof I'd choke the life out of 'er by pokin' a peacock down that great gullet she has.' Edith laughed. 'I would straight,' he assured her in a strong voice. 'And that's a death would be too good for the woman, the diabolical mason.'

'Women can't he masons. They aren't accepted.'

'Can't they,' he retorted. 'That's all you know then.'

'It takes all sorts to make a world,' she remarked.

'You're telling me,' he said. Holding one of her hands in his he shut his eyes and appeared to want to rest. 'I'd tear the 'eart right out of 'er,' he added in a weak voice.

'I had a look over that little house Charley,' she murmured soft after a moment.

'You what?'

'Where we're goin' to live when we're married,' she explained.

'So you did did you?' he said stirring in his seat.

'Why whatever's the matter now?' she asked. 'You wished me to surely?'

'I shouldn't wonder if my ideas hadn't changed,' he said cautious. 'About where we plan to find a home together,' he added.

'What's come over you Charley?' she enquired. She began at last to show signs of alarm.

'What experience I've had, and I've 'ad some mind, has gone to show that it's no manner of use hanging on in a place where you're not valued,' he said.

'But there are the little extras,' she cried. 'That two or three quid a week you speak about.'

'Oh well,' he answered, 'it's no more'n can he picked up in

any butler's job if you know the ropes. No, what's goin' on over in Britain is what bothers me. The way things are shapin' it wouldn't come as a surprise if places such as this weren't doomed to a natural death so to say.'

'Go on with you,' she replied. 'Why if Mrs Tennant loses all her dough there'll always be those that took it. Don't you tell me there isn't good pickings to he had in service long after our children have said thank you madam for the first bawlin' out over nothing at all that they'll receive.' She was beginning to speak like him.

'That's as may be girl,' he countered, 'but from all accounts there's some lovely money going in munitions.'

'Yes and then once this old war's over it's out on your ear with no work.'

'Yet you've just argued that there'll be jobs in service we can go back to,' he complained.

'Stay in what you know, that's what I always maintain,' Edith announced although she had never before expressed an opinion one way or the other.

'Well you may be right but it's this country gets me down.'

'You're fed up, Charley, on account of your stomach.'

'It's too bloody neutral this country is.'

'Too neutral?' she echoed.

'Well there's danger in being a neutral in this war,' he said, 'you've only to read the newspapers to appreciate that.'

'I thought you'd given up listenin' to such talk,' she complained.

'And then my lad going over to give 'imself up, to enlist.'

'What's that to do with you an' me?' she grumbled.

'I'm unsettled. There you are. This has unsettled me Edie.'

'Charley what's the matter? You tell. Nothing serious is it dear?'

'I received a letter this morning.'

'You've had bad news?'

'Not exactly,' he admitted.

'Then who was it from?' she asked.

'My mum wrote me.'

'Your old mother? Well what did she say?'

'She's not comin' over mate, that's what.'

192

'Not coming over?' she repeated in quite a loud voice. 'Why then we can have the little house all to ourselves dearest.'

'If we want to live there in the end,' he said.

'Whatever are you saying?' she cried really disturbed at last.

'I wrote to 'er see,' Raunce explained with some embarrassment, 'and what I said was I'd like to have her out of that awful air raid business. I know he's never been over Peterboro' yet but the way he's going it might be any minute now. I said she could do worse than come here and told 'er what you and I had thought of. It would be a weight off my mind I said and how you would look after 'er better than my sister Bell ever did.'

'Well what did she say?'

'I got the letter here,' he said. 'She writes she reckons that would be cowardly or something.'

'Can I see it?' she requested serious.

'No I won't show it to you,' he answered.

'Then there's matters disobligin' about me in it,' she cried.

'To tell you the truth there's no mention of you at all.'

'Well whoever's heard,' she exclaimed.

'I can't understand that part,' he went on. 'I said as clear as clear we were thinkin' of getting married but it's just as if she'd never bothered to read to the bottom.'

'Well I never,' Edith said cautious.

'It's that bit about being afraid that gets me,' he muttered.

'Afraid to marry me she means?'

'Not on your life. I told you she never mentioned you Edie. No she reckons we're 'iding ourselves away in this neutral country.'

'Here let me read it.'

'No mate I don't want you to get a wrong impression of the old lady, seeing that we're to be man and wife.'

'Your sister's put her up to it,' she said.

'My sister Bell?' he laughed. 'You wait till you meet.'

'You don't love me,' she wailed.

'Oh honey,' he said with a sigh, 'you'll never know how much I do.' But he made no move towards her. She had gone quite white. She chanced a quick look at him, noted that he seemed exhausted.

'Why dearest,' she exclaimed, 'd'you feel all right?'

'It's our plans,' he said. 'We'd just about got everything settled when this comes along.'

'But we could live here without your mother,' she pleaded. 'Oh you don't realize how I'll look after you,' she went on, 'and by this means I'll have twice the time to do it. Because I was never aiming to give up work at the Castle. Mrs Tennant can't get help. She'll be glad to have me over six days a week only the seventh I must keep for our washin'.'

He leant over to kiss her. She allowed it. Then she interrupted him.

'No Charley,' she said, 'we got to discuss this.'

'She's funny that way,' he remarked as though in a dream.

'What are you getting at?' she asked sharp.

'She's obstinate mother is. Always was. I remember when the old man wanted to chuck his job on the railway because 'e'd been made a good offer I can't exactly remember where now but I know it would've meant more money. Well she wouldn't 'ear of it, wouldn't even let it be mentioned twice. They had a rare argument at the time. I was only a kid but I can hear them now. But she got her way. He stayed where 'e was. And I couldn't say that he lost by so doing.'

'Yet she wishes us to throw this place up.'

'Yes Edie, but it's different this time.'

'I'm that bewildered,' she said.

'Now love,' he said in a voice that was weak with exhaustion, 'you're not to worry.'

'But we'd laid all our plans,' she objected and seemed to be fighting back the tears. Then she gave way. 'Oh our little 'ouse,' she sobbed. She turned to him like a child, and held out her arms. With a quick movement she got onto his knees. She merged into him and copiously wept.

'There sweet'eart there,' he comforted. She was crying noisily. He appeared to grope for words. 'Don't take on love,' he said. He shifted his legs as though the weight was beginning to tell. 'This would occur just when I'm not quite up to the mark,' he exclaimed. She gave no sign of having heard. 'There's other places,' he tried to appease her. 'We'll find you a lovely home,' he ended, and fell silent.

194

'Don't stop,' she sobbed into his ear.

'Why,' he said, 'I love you more than I thought I was capable. I'm surprised at myself, honest I am. If my old mother could see her Charley now she'd never recognize 'im,' he murmured.

She at once got off his knees. She started blowing her nose and cleaning up. He leant forward, gazed awkward into her face. 'I never seen anything like your eyes they're so 'uge not in all my experience,' he announced soft. 'Yet for eighteen months I didn't so much as notice them. Can you explain that?' Then, perhaps to distract her attention, he invited her to witness what he saw, the peacocks that had been attracted. For these most greedy of all birds had collected in twos about and behind the lilac trees, on the scrounge for tit-bits.

'Oh those,' she answered. 'It's wicked the way they spy on you.'

'They've been raised in a good school,' he remarked.

'There,' she said giving her face a last dab. She did not look at him. 'I'm sorry I did that. Well then Charley what's next?'

'You mustn't blame this on my old lady ducks,' he replied. 'She gets pig'eaded at times the way all old people do. But that's not to say she hasn't wounded me because she has and where a man feels it most, right in my pride in myself,' he explained. 'She knows I'm barely an age for this war, yet awhiles anyhow, yet she seems to think I'm not in it all I might be, d'you get me?'

Edith stayed silent.

'Oh this pain,' he suddenly groaned. 'It will nag a man.'

'I got some bicarbonate indoors will soon see to that,' she said.

'I was wonderin' if you could just nip over and fetch us some,' he suggested green in the face.

'We haven't finished,' she answered grim. 'There's a lot I want to get straight first.'

'What's that love?' he asked.

'What are we goin' to do then?' Edith continued. She spoke calm.

Raunce leant forward. In an effort to pull himself together perhaps, he squinted terribly.

'We got to get out of here,' he said.

'Leave this place?' she asked.

'There's nothing else for it sweetheart,' he replied.

'And go to the Agency in Dublin to find us another Charley?'

'No dear. We've just been in to all that. We'd best clear right out.'

'What and go to America somewhere Charley?'

'Not on your life,' he answered. 'It's back to the old country for you an' me my love.'

'And have me took up as I step from off the ship which brought us across by one of those women police waiting on the dockside to put me in the A.T.S.? 'Ave you gone out of your mind then?'

'Steady on Edie where did you get that from? They don't act in such a fashion, not yet they don't.'

'Out of your very lips and not so long since either. You sat at dinner and frightened my Kate out of her mind almost, so she shouldn't go.'

'Why it was only a tale,' he pleaded.

'How d'you know? You said so Charley.'

'You've got no diplomacy love, that's what's the matter. I didn't want you left with all her work or some dirty Irish judy brought in to help who you'd have to go round after all the time. Sure I pitched 'er a tale. Mind you they'll be forced to it in the end before this war's over, when the casualties start an' they get real short of labour. You mark my words we'll all be in uniform then. But just at present there's nothing of the sort I tell you.'

'And you're certain this ain't just your idea to get rid of me?' she asked tearfully once more.

He put an arm round her shoulders.

''Ere,' he said, 'what's up all of a sudden? It's not like you to have nightmares or see shadows followin' you round.'

'I'm that bewildered,' she explained again, settling her cheek against his.

'Now don't you fret,' he comforted. 'You leave all the brain

196

work to your old man. Lucky Charley they call him,' he said in a threadbare return to his usual manner. 'We want to get out of this country and when once we've made up our minds we want to get out fast.'

'Elope?' she cried delighted all of a sudden.

'Elope,' he agreed grave.

She gave him a big kiss. 'Why Charley,' she said, seemingly more and more delighted, 'that's romantic.'

'It's what we're going to do whatever the name you give it,' he replied.

'But don't you see that's a wonderful thing to do,' she went on.

'Maybe so,' he said soft into her ear, 'but it's what we're doing.'

'Oh I can love you for this,' she murmured. 'There I've said it now haven't I? You were always on at me to say. But go on.'

'That's all,' he announced. 'Only once I get hold of Michael we'd best get away out to-morrow.'

'Wait a minute,' she cried in a disappointed voice. 'And how about our month's notice?'

'We shan't hand it in mate that's all. We'll flit.'

'Oh but Charley that would be wrong,' she said in a low voice.

'Right or wrong it's what we'll do. We could get Kate to come along if you was to feel awkward.'

'Awkward?' she asked. 'How d'you mean?'

'Well,' he replied shyly. 'We can't get married before we've put the banns up a full three weeks on the other side. I was just askin' myself if you'd feel it was right our travelling without we were man and wife.'

She laughed. 'D'you reckon I can't protect myself from you after all this time?' she enquired gentle.

'I know you can right enough,' he replied, 'but I couldn't tell the way you'd see it.'

She did not answer this. She said, 'Kate would never come with us, not now.'

'How's that Edie?'

'On account of her Paddy.'

197

'Go on with that for a tale.'

'I thought you knew dear,' she said.

'Well I did in a manner of speaking but not to place any reliance on it.'

'It's true right enough. She says he needs 'er.'

'Then all I can say is that's disgusting, downright disgusting.'

'Dithtrething and dithtathteful?' she asked.

'No mate it's no joking matter. Why a big, grown girl like her an' that ape out of a Zoo.'

'There's the way things are Charley.'

'But how did this come about?'

'She was lonely,' Edith explained, 'an' she watched us.'

''Ere,' he said, 'don't go layin' Paddy at my door. Why it's unnatural.'

'Well she's made her bed an' she needs must lie on it.'

'All the more reason then for us to get quick out of here,' was his comment.

'And not say goodbye to a soul?' she now asked in an excited voice.

'Not to anyone,' he replied narrowly watching her.

'Oh I couldn't,' she cried as though all at once she had despaired. 'I must tell Miss Evelyn and Miss Moira.'

'That's been the cause of half the trouble in this place. Once they get hold of something it's taken right out of control.'

'But it wouldn't be right. Why they're innocent.'

''Ow d'you mean innocent?' he enquired. 'There's a lot we could lay to their door.'

'They're not grown up,' she explained. 'They've got their lives to live yet. They mightn't understand if I was to go off without a word.'

'They'll forget soon enough dearest,' he said.

'No Charley,' she insisted and appeared distressed, 'you don't know. It would be wicked that's all. D'you mean to say we've not got to say one word?'

'That's right mate.'

'But what about Miss Burch? How will she take it? Can you tell me? Or Miss Swift who's trusted me with the young ladies?'

He put his arms about her. He held her close.

'Look my own love,' he said, 'it's like this. Once we let it get about that we're goin' then they'll all of them begin to talk. Mrs Tennant will pay a call on Mrs Welch who will send for old Agatha out of her bed. Miss Swift'll 'ave 'ysterics an' the Captain will receive a phone call from Mrs Jack to stop you an' me on the boat. Michael will be threatened with the sack. They'll even tell the garage in Kinalty they mustn't hire to us.'

He could feel her trembling.

'But Charley dear,' she protested, 'this is a free country surely to goodness?'

'It's priest-ridden love,' he replied.

'But Mrs Tennant's got no right to stop someones, not if we give her a month's wages.'

'A month's wages my eye. That's a fine way to start bein' married, to throw good money down the drain.'

'All right then Charley. You know best I expect.'

'No,' he went on, 'it's on account of that ring. She's got her suspicions you see love. She let Albert find his way but with us she'd raise holy Cain, making out I was carryin' you off.'

'But that's what you are doin' surely dear,' Edith announced. She settled deeper in his arms.

'It's you cartin' me off body and soul more likely,' he answered. He fastened on to her mouth. His face was very white and green and grey.

When he lifted his lips from hers he asked,

'Then you will to-morrow, without a word said to any-one?'

'I expect so,' she replied.

'You don't sound very certain,' he remarked.

'Oh I will, I will,' she cried very loud and wildly kissed him.

'You could tell Kate if you wished,' he said when he had a chance.

'I'll not say a word to a soul,' she promised.

At this he began to flush. The colour spread until his face had become an alarming ugly purple.

'Why I do declare you're blushin',' she cried delightedly. 'You who never have.' Then as he leant himself back, obviously stretched and tested by what he experienced, she said nervous again,

'What's up with you? You're not goin' sick on me are you?'

'I'll be O.K.,' he said faint.

'Not just when we've got this great journey?' she added.

'It was only that I feared you'd never consent,' he explained in a weak voice, with closed eyes. 'If I know anything it's that they'll keep us here one way or the other if we let a word out. Oh sweet'eart darlin' I'd hardly liked to think you'd see it my way.' He closed his eyes. An arm was limp over her shoulders. 'We'll go straight to Peterboro' where my mum'll have a bed for you. Arthur Sanders the sergeant of police I was at school with will put me up at his place till we can have the ceremony. And we must find us a room for a start.'

'Yes,' she said. She kissed the inside of his hand.

'Why look who's here,' she exclaimed. He opened his eyes and found Badger wagging his tail so hard that he was screwed right round into a crescent. The dog seemed deeply ashamed of something.

'You go on out of it,' Raunce ordered. 'This no place for you when you're only after one of those pigeon to knock off.' The hound left, looking back twice as he went. And once be turned to stand with pricked ears, with a wild yearning look of grief.

'That dog's more trouble than he's worth,' Raunce muttered. He let his eyelids shut down over his eyes. 'He'd never catch a mouse that had lost all its legs not now he wouldn't,' he added in a voice of deep content.

'Well this is a fine elopement,' she remarked amused. 'I didn't gamble on you going to sleep on me I must say.'

'It's me dyspepsia,' he excused himself from behind shut eyes. 'That's a condition don't let up on you however you're placed.'

'You rest yourself dearest,' she answered then murmured happily to herself that in another minute she would have forgotten what they had come out for.

Accordingly she picked up the bag of scraps. She began to feed the peacocks. They came forward until they had her surrounded. Then a company of doves flew down on the seat to be fed. They settled all over her. And their fluttering disturbed Raunce who reopened his eyes. What he saw then he watched so that it could be guessed that he was in pain with his great delight. For what with the peacocks bowing at her purple skirts, the white doves nodding on her shoulders round her brilliant cheeks and her great eyes that blinked tears of happiness, it made a picture.

'Edie,' he appealed soft, probably not daring to move or speak too sharp for fear he might disturb it all. Yet he used exactly that tone Mr Eldon had employed at the last when calling his Ellen. 'Edie,' he moaned.

The next day Raunce and Edith left without a word of warning. Over in England they were married and lived happily ever after.